DEAD GIRL RUNNING

ANN M. NOSER

IMMORTAL WORKS
SALT LAKE CITY

Immortal Works LLC
1505 Glenrose Drive
Salt Lake City, Utah 84104
Tel: (385) 202-0116

Cover Art by Ashley Literski
http://strangedevotion.wixsite.com/strangedesigns

ISBN 978-1-953491-66-4 (Paperback)
ASIN B0CKPDDL35 (Kindle)

Dear Dad,
How can you be gone when we've got so much left to say?

THE NEW ORDER BRINGS PEACE
AND PROSPERITY TO ALL

Prejudice, greed, and an overemphasis on self-worth led early, unenlightened American Administrations to engage in Aggressive Warfare Tactics with other similarly misguided nations.

Without the ingenuity of the Great City Founders, World War III would have resulted in the complete Destruction of Life here in the Northern Americas.

The New Order rescued us from certain death and saved us from ourselves.

In their great wisdom, the Founders voted to provide All Citizens, by decree, the rights of Equality, Public Safety, and Provision of Basic Needs.

To fill these needs, a League of Representatives was appointed to oversee the fair and equal distribution of goods.

What The New Order has banded together, let no one put asunder.

HAPPY BIRTHDAY

I hate birthdays, especially when they're mine. The night I turned ten years old, Mom and I waited for Dad to come home after working late because his replacement didn't show up on time. Eight years later, the secret part of my heart still waits, but I've mostly accepted he will never come home again. Today I turn eighteen. Most kids would celebrate, but I wish it were any other day of the year.

Dragging myself out of bed, I'm relieved that I didn't let Mom talk me into requesting a Vacation Pass for today like we did last year. I just want to forget the whole thing and go help Gus prepare the chilled bodies in the hospital mortuary. I pull on teal scrubs and fumble for socks and shoes as a ray of early sunlight glints off my dad's picture hanging on the gray wall across the tiny room. Once again, his blue eyes capture mine as if he needs to tell me something important. I glance below the photo at a memory trunk full of how things used to be, pausing for a moment before averting my eyes. I won't open it today. I just can't.

Dishes clink in the kitchen. Mom calls out, "Hurry up, Silvia. I've got a surprise for you." She sounds happy, but I can't tell if it's real.

Since Dad's death, both of us have done a lot of pretending. So far this year we've been able to avoid Psychotherapy Services and Mandated Medications, but sometimes I wonder if I was sent down to Mortuary Sciences to push me over the edge. Fortunately, I find autopsies intriguing, not depressing. And since I never got to see Dad's body after the accident, caring for other people's dead soothes the empty ache inside. It also helps that my boss, Gus, is an excellent teacher and the closest thing I have to a best friend. He always knows what to say to me and what *not* to say.

Too bad Mom doesn't have a clue about that.

She glances up from her green tea as I enter the copper-colored, modular kitchen. "I planned a big surprise for your birthday."

I tense. "What is it?"

Mom slides over a bowl of organic oatmeal topped with raspberries, normally my favorite. "I got us Park and Art passes today."

"I'm not hungry." I shake my head. "And Gus is expecting me."

"No, he's not. He knows all about it. I told him weeks ago."

"Really?" I cross my arms, not sure if I believe her. "He must be good at keeping secrets. Gus didn't even mention my birthday yesterday."

Which proves he knows me better than Mom does.

She frowns. "At least eat the raspberries, even if you're not hungry. I had to barter for them. And if it makes you feel better, we can pretend it *isn't* your birthday. It's just some other special day instead."

I want to protest more, but there's a determined gleam in Mom's brown eyes—one that hasn't been there for a long time. And I don't want to be the one to snuff it out.

I half-heartedly take a few bites of breakfast, swallow my eight prescribed supplements, then return to my bedroom to change. All my clothes are soft and plain, without decoration. I grab jeans and a green, long-sleeved T-shirt made by hands like my father's. Except Dad proved himself to be Gifted, so he didn't make Basic Worker

Level clothes for long. Instead, he got promoted to Government Level clothing production—a promotion that cost him his life. I shake my head. I don't want to think about that today.

"Hurry up!" Mom calls from the front door of our small apartment.

We clamber down six flights of whitewashed cement steps, the stairwell so brightly lit with safety lights that one almost needs sunglasses. Once we arrive on the main floor, we push out into the swarms of people flooding the streets. Dashing across the busy bike path and two empty car lanes, we reach the closest walkway heading toward the park.

Traffic is orderly today. No bikers stray across the wide, white painted lines separating their lanes from ours. Men and women wearing blue scrubs of various shades hurry toward the hospitals and medical facilities. Those in green coveralls rush toward the monorail station to speed off to one of the numerous Plant and Protein Production Facilities.

I glance back at a beautiful, dark-skinned woman, trying not to feel envious of her green uniform. Usually, I don't mind my job. In fact, I feel more at home in Mortuary Sciences than anywhere else. But part of me still longs to spend all day surrounded by plants. Nothing can be done about it now. The Occupation Exam is over, and I've been placed where I'm most effective.

People whoosh past us on bikes as those on foot press forward. Only the car lanes remain vacant. Flapping flags in The New Order colors of red, white, and blue crack overhead. I shiver a little in the cool morning breeze.

We march past rows of tall silver-gray buildings—offices on the first two floors and apartments up above. We make good time until we hit the Citizen Family Planning and Reproductive Services Building. Traffic stalls. A tall man ahead of us shifts from side to side, waiting.

"What's going on?" Mom cranes her neck and rises on her toes. "Can you see?"

Indistinct voices argue up ahead. Strangers murmur but avoid making eye contact. After a long pause, the people in front of us begin to shuffle past the building. A few cast furtive glances over their shoulders. Everyone's in a hurry to get somewhere. Now I see who is causing the fuss—a red-haired girl about my age shoves an orderly away. The crowd behind us pushes forward. Tears stream down the girl's pale face. She backs away from the building and turns as if to run before doubling over. She cries out in pain and clutches her swollen belly, breathing hard.

In her moment of weakness, the Suits surround and restrain her.

"I won't do it! You can't make me!" the pregnant girl screams as they drag her away.

"Let's get out of here." Mom grabs my shoulder and tries to steer me onward.

"What's going on?" I refuse to move, staring as the bawling, red-haired girl disappears behind the Family Planning sliding glass doors. "What are they doing to her? It looked like they were hurting her!"

"Don't be ridiculous." Mom's eyes widen as the crowd spills around us. "And don't gawk."

An older woman grumbles, "Get out of the way. Get out of the way."

"Let's get out of here." Mom slips a slender arm around my shoulders and propels me ahead, whispering in my ear. "Don't let it ruin your birthday."

I pull back. I'm not the one who ruined my birthday.

She pushes harder. "Silvia, it's none of our business. She's probably having a bad day. Pregnant women get very emotional. I certainly did when I carried you."

Scowling, I step away, almost into the path of the first car we've seen all morning. A staccato of horn blasts chases me back into my proper lane of traffic. The long, black limo eases past as we hustle on our way. I peer into the dark-tinted windows but can't see a thing.

"Come *on!*" Mom grabs my arm, and we melt into the crowd.

"I just want to know who's in there."

She shakes her head. "You're always too curious for your own good. What difference does it make?"

"What's wrong with being curious?"

She winces. "Your father used to say that."

"Really?" My ears prickle. She never talks about him. "Tell me more. About Dad."

She takes a shaky breath. "Not today, honey." She pats my arm, a guarded smile on her face. "Try to be more careful, okay?"

We rush on in silence for the next three blocks until Mom pauses at Genetic Testing and Counseling.

"Why are we stopping?" I ask.

She averts her gaze. "You're eighteen now. You have to get tested."

"Today?" I can't believe this. "I thought we were going to the park."

"We are. But as a condition of both of us getting the day off, we need to stop here first." Her appeasing tone switches to don't-mess-with-me-now. "Don't give me that look. It won't take long. I promise."

"Fine. Let's get this over with. It's not like I'm afraid of blood or anything."

The overhead bell jingles softly as we enter the cool waiting room. Bamboo flooring muffles our footsteps as we approach the counter of nurses checking in patients. The bright blue banner over their head reads:

Genetic Testing: It's the right thing to do. Be proactive and informed about your health!

We are next in line. I cross my arms and tap my foot. This better not take too long. I don't want to waste any time we could spend at the park.

"Patient's name, age, and heritage?" a middle-aged nurse asks, clipboard in hand.

Mom nudges me forward.

I clear my dry throat. "Silvia Wood...eighteen years old, *exactly*." I turn so she can check the microchip embedded in my right upper arm, careful to keep my wrists covered with my long sleeves. "Half Japanese, half White European."

"Well, happy birthday to you." She smiles as she scans the microchip and records my Citizen Number. Her perfect teeth seem even whiter against her coffee-colored skin.

I tense, but her eyes are kind. She has no idea what this day means to me. "Thank you," I manage to choke out.

She leads me down a hallway. "We can take the first room on the right. Mrs. Wood, you're welcome to join us. We encourage family participation."

Once we reach the room, she flicks on the occupancy light over the door. "Please take a seat. My name is Lucinda Mayer." She smiles again. "It will only take a second to enter you into the computer, and then I'll ask you a series of questions."

"Okay." I sit on a wooden bench, surrounded by walls the same green as a leaf from a fig tree.

"No need to be nervous, young lady. I'm very good at drawing blood. It will only sting for a second."

"I'm not worried about that." Still unnerved by the crying girl a few blocks back, I try to sound braver than I feel. "I work in Mortuary Sciences. Blood doesn't bother me."

"Then there's nothing to be anxious about. Now let's get started."

Nurse Mayer fires off questions. Mom answers most of them before I can even open my mouth. I nod and grit my teeth, trying to hide my irritation.

Ever since my Occupation Exam, Mom keeps looking for opportunities for me to get ahead, to "stand out and shine" as she puts it. She is so disappointed I didn't test "exceptional" like she and Dad did. Instead I've been labeled "empathetic."

Empathetic? I'm not sure how they came up with that. I certainly don't feel very kindly toward my interfering mother at the moment.

"Are you currently sexually active?" Nurse Mayer asks.

Mom clamps her mouth shut and turns to me.

Nurse Mayer continues. "There's nothing to be ashamed of if you are, young lady. Just answer the question truthfully. It's important."

"No. I don't even like boys."

"Do you prefer girls? Because that alters which genetic tests we'll run. But either answer is perfectly acceptable."

"I know it is. But, no, I didn't mean that. I don't like anyone." I flush and stammer. "I mean, they don't like me. Most of my friends stopped talking to me when I started working in the Mortuary."

Mom throws me a warning look that says: *try not to look like a social pariah.*

"Not that I'm complaining. I like my job." I fake a smile to assure the nurse I'm perfectly normal.

The nurse raises her eyebrows. "You like your job?"

"Yes. It's interesting." I glance at Mom for support. "Aren't I supposed to like my job? Isn't that what the Occupational Exam is for? To make sure everyone likes what they do?"

Mom cringes. "Please just answer the questions, dear. Don't ask so many of your own."

Nurse Mayer chuckles. "My daughter is about your age. Just starting out too."

"What does she do?" I ask to be polite.

"She works in Food Growth and Management."

"That's part of Plant and Protein Production, isn't it?" I swallow my jealousy. "Does she like it?"

"Of course." The nurse types with lightning speed. "Okay, only one last series of questions regarding your general health."

"I'm ready."

"Have you ever used any tobacco products?"

Mom leans forward. "No, she hasn't. I check her clothes for traces every day."

"You do?" I don't know if she's telling the truth or covering for me for the one time I came home from work reeking of burnt hair. "I haven't used any of the Forbidden Drugs or Products. I wouldn't want to. I've seen first-hand what their use can do to the body."

Nurse Mayer glances at her computer screen. "Do you exercise the required thirty minutes a day?"

Mom interjects. "She insists on taking the stairs every time. She *never* lets me use the elevator, and our apartment is on the *sixth* floor."

Poor Mom. She so wants other people to be impressed with me.

I clear my throat. "I'm a member of 37th Street Health and Productivity Gym. You can check my account. I'm there every day after work from four until at least six. Even longer on my days off."

"Thank you. I'll include that information with the report. Now there's only one more question, but I'll check your vitals first," Nurse Mayer says.

"Why?" I ask.

Mom's face reads: *don't ask why.*

"Stress affects a person's blood pressure," the nurse explains. "Wouldn't want to submit an artificially elevated reading." She measures my height, weight, body fat with calipers, and blood pressure. "All your values are within normal ranges. Physically, you appear to be a very healthy young lady."

"I run at least an hour a day at an eight-minute-per-mile pace," I say and then cringe. Great. Now *I'm* the one trying to impress her.

"That's very good." Nurse Mayer laughs. "I could only do that if I was being chased."

"Who would chase you?"

"Hopefully that fine-looking actor in the latest James Bond movie, but then I would let him catch me." The nurse winks and sets aside the blood pressure monitor.

"I haven't seen that movie." Gus thinks I don't watch enough movies for a young woman my age. Maybe he's right.

"You should." She turns back to me, but now her face is somber rather than joking. "Are you ready for the last question?"

I nod.

"Okay." She takes my cold hands in her warm ones. "Now, Silvia, be honest. How many times have you attempted suicide since your father's death?"

2

WISH YOU WERE HERE

"What's the big deal?" I whisper as we exit the building, leaving the questions and blood collecting behind us.

Mom shakes her head. "How can you even ask that? Don't you know what you've put me through?"

How dare she say that! Doesn't she remember what she put *me* through? "But that was years ago. I'm better now. I've chosen therapeutic exercise as my treatment plan. It's much more effective than all those pills I was on."

She sighs. "I'll agree that running and yoga have helped. But this is *exactly* why I want to get you out of that Mortuary. I don't want you to spend your life surrounded by death and sadness."

"Stop complaining about my job. Working there doesn't depress me. How many times do I have to tell you that?"

We cross another crowded street and turn left at the tall streetlight. My gaze strays to the camera halfway up the light pole, constantly monitoring citizen activity. *Our vigilance keeps you safe,* or so The New Order claims.

The foot traffic thins as we near the Northwest Citizen Park. Most people head in the opposite direction. Past the endless rows of buildings, all at least a dozen stories tall, I can finally spot some trees in the distance. I can't wait to forget about today's miserable appointment and be surrounded by glorious colors: bright green leaves and flowers of every pink, red, and yellow imaginable.

"And what happened with all your so-called friends?" Mom asks. "Did you hear yourself in there? None of them call or come over since you started that horrible job."

"But I like working there. And you always told me that school friends didn't last forever, not that I ever had many good friends from my classes to begin with. Plus, you said I'd make better friends at my chosen profession when the day came. And that's what I've done."

She throws up her hands. "The only person you work with is a sixty-year old man!"

"Mom, Gus is the smartest person I've ever met. I'm learning so much from him. Why is his age such an issue for you?"

She frowns. "I just wish there were other kids your age working in Mortuary Sciences so you could make some new friends."

I shrug. "Gus says his interns don't usually last very long."

"Oh, hearing *that* really puts my mind at ease."

"I don't understand why everybody else leaves. I think the human body is fascinating."

She shudders. "Even when it's cold and dead?"

"Yes. A live body can hide so many secrets, but a dead body never lies. At least, that's what Gus says."

Mom shakes her head as we cross another street. "But how can you take seeing all the blood and broken limbs and everything, day after day? It must be so awful!"

I smile as the tall, black, metal garden gates come into view. "That's why you're the artist and I'm the clean-up crew. You're the sensitive type, and I'm hard as stone...or so I've been told."

"That's awful!" Her eyes widen. "Who said that?"

"My doctors. They all said I wasn't their typical suicidal patient." I smirk. "I took that as a compliment."

"I wish you wouldn't joke about it."

"What happened to 'laughter is the best medicine?' Besides, I only tried twice, and the last time was six years ago."

"On your birthday," Mom whispers.

"Don't you mean on the anniversary of Dad's death?" I tug on my sleeves, making sure the scars remain hidden.

Mom averts her eyes. "I want today to be special. Can we please focus on the future and forget about the past?"

"That would be a nice change, wouldn't it?"

We reach the front garden gate and hand our park passes to the attendant who scans our microchips. As soon as I step inside, the scent of fragrant lilacs hides the smell of the street. The lovely lavender and white blossoms make me forget, at least for the moment, how ugly everything else can be.

Mom grins. "See, I knew this would be the best present of all."

"You're right. I love it here." I can't help but smile. Whoever discovered how to use genetics to make lilacs bloom all summer is my personal hero. It's my favorite smell in the world.

"So, wouldn't you rather work here than down in that dark—"

I freeze. "Can we *please* stop arguing about this?"

She sighs. "Okay. Let's preorder lunch and then hike the paths." She checks her watch. "We've got an hour and a half before I have to... Well, let's just say I've got more than one big surprise today."

"Really?" I ask. Mom is usually much more predictable than this.

We peruse the simple menu then each select one fruit, one vegetable, and one grain-based carbohydrate from the available choices. We leave the short brown park buildings behind and follow the gravel paths into the lush gardens. The mulched flower beds overflow with plant life, the taller deciduous and fruit trees filtering the sun for the underlying hostas and ferns. So much green and so little brown. Each one labeled with its common name, scientific name, and how it helps support humanity. If a particular plant isn't used as food or medicine, it's described as an "air-purifier and oxygen producer."

We stroll past the human-made waterfall and across the bridge, so busy enjoying the lush displays that we don't speak. It's the best end to an argument we've had in some time. The warmth of the sun on my head and shoulders soothes away my irritation. I spend most days in the chilled basement of the hospital. Getting to work involves a walking commute through streets shadowed by tall buildings. The windows of our small apartment face north, so there's little direct sunlight in my life. I welcome today's rays with an upturned face and sleeves pushed up to the elbows. No one's looking at me anyway. They're here for the flowers.

Too soon, the hour and a half is over. With a secret smile, Mom points me in the right direction. After a few twists and turns, we approach the outdoor stage. The shiny silver acoustic shell projects high above us. Orchestra musicians adjust music stands, position chairs, and tune instruments. Colored lights twinkle above them in rainbow arcs.

"Wait a minute... Mom, isn't this your orchestra?" I pause. "I mean...the one you used to play for?"

She smiles. "This is the second big surprise. I'm playing again. This is my first concert. It's Morning Music in the Park."

I catch my breath. She hasn't performed since Dad died. And she never practices anymore, at least not at home. "Are you sure this is a good..."

"I've been working very hard, but I didn't want to tell you until I was positive I'd recovered from my...troubles. I'm not first chair yet, but I'll be there before the year ends. Trust me."

"Oh, Mom. That's so wonderful!" I hug her tight, almost light-headed with shock, and we stand still in time. Strangers pass by, but it's as if no one else exists. I don't know what to say. I'm so happy for her...and for me. Because this means maybe we can *live* again. If music has come back into her life, then maybe everything else long forgotten will come with it—happiness, laughter, and perhaps a bigger apartment? I'd love for the present to mean more than the past, but is that asking too much?

Finally, she breaks it off. "I've got to get ready." She dashes away.

Her face shines with excitement and happiness, just like it did in the old days. She's missed her music as much as I have.

The musicians warm up. The violinists pluck strings and tighten their bows. The conductor raises her baton, and the cymbals crash. Like a child, I'm enraptured by the waves of notes surrounding me, dashing back and forth, up and down. Fast and slow, proud then mournful, every instrument at once, then a single violin.

The solo violinist should be my mother. But Mom sits three seats down, watching the soloist nod his head as his bow sweeps out the poignant melody.

I flash back to a warm summer evening eight years ago—the concert I attended a week before Dad died. He looked so handsome in a suit he'd made for himself with leftovers from work. It wasn't considered a proper use of materials, but he said the risk was worth the pride in our eyes when he burst out of my parents' bedroom singing old show tunes, his red hair slicked back like a gangster from an old movie. Later at the concert, he stood by my side in this same park, watching my mother in first chair.

I rub my hands on my jeans, remembering the soft red fabric of the dress he'd made special for me out of somebody else's scraps. He told me he'd have to return the dress along with his suit the next day, so I should really enjoy it for that one special night. How I loved the feel of it, the swish against my legs, the surprised looks in other people's eyes that I was dressed like royalty when everyone around me was plain.

As the hour grew late, I leaned against Dad's side.

He put his arm around my shoulders and winked. "Don't fall asleep yet, hon, the next song is Mom's favorite. It's her big solo."

As stars sparkled overhead, Mom stood straight and proud, the overhead lights shining on her straight black hair, her face a study of concentration. With the graceful movements of her hand on the bow, she could make the listener feel the warmth of the sun on their face, make their heart soar in happiness, or make that same heart break like all hope was gone.

How I longed for Mom to play for me after Dad's death, but she refused, saying she didn't have it in her anymore. That she had nothing left to give to anyone once he was gone.

But now, she's playing again.

As the sweet melody ends, I glance next to me, half-expecting Dad to be there. The sharp pain in my chest reminds me he's still gone. In the applause that follows, I walk away from the mid-day crowd, away from the present, away from Mom in fourth chair.

If only I could have one more day of living in our old apartment, the one filled with sunlight, music, and beautiful plants—a mini version of this park. A home filled with happiness, love, and laughter.

Dad took all that when he left.

And, sometimes, I blame him for everything that happened afterward.

3

IT'S STILL ROCK AND ROLL TO ME

The next morning when I pull on my teal blue medical scrubs, I know they're on for keeps. Vacation Day is over. But I don't mind. Gus needs me. There's a lot of work to do, and I've got so much to learn. I fasten my smooth black hair in a twist then hurry into the kitchen for breakfast.

Mom's nowhere to be found. I scan the counter and find a lone Japanese teacup perched upside down on its saucer: Mom already left for the day, and when she returns, she won't bring any guests. It will be only her. Alone. Like every other day since Dad died.

I pick up the teacup and place it next to the others on the shelf. My family has never left notes for each other. Anything set out of place always means something. Together, we invented our own elaborate set of symbols. Dad had made it a game to make things interesting and save on paper. He also taught me to notice where cameras were in public places and how to remain just out of view.

I hate that we're always being watched.

At the old apartment, I'd hurry home after school and scour the front hallway for clues. Mom's shoe on the floor meant chocolate for dessert. Dad's shoe meant there was spaghetti for dinner—a real treat.

There used to be more glass trinkets and shiny stones. Each one had its own special meaning. But now, only three teacups remain. We lost so many things in the move. I don't even know how it happened. We had to pack in such a rush, I was taking meds, and I felt so tired all the time.

But I'm awake now.

One glance at the clock tells me to stop dilly-dallying. Soon, I'm out the door, speed-walking to the hospital. Two miles later, the Medical Facilities Northwest towers above me, all twenty-five floors casting long shadows over the shorter buildings surrounding it.

I slide my I.D. card through the scanner. The side door opens, and I slip inside. My feet hammer down the stairs, into the basement. The temperature drops with each step. With a low hiss, the heavy glass doors swish open. A guitar riff shakes my eardrums as I enter Mortuary & Autopsy Services, which takes up most of the bottom underground floor.

Gus glances up from an autopsy and yells over the beating drums. "You made it!"

I cup my hands around my mouth to be heard over the music. "Yes, sir. As my least favorite Psych Doc used to say, 'Silvia, you've survived another birthday.'"

Gus peers over his glasses. "You have such a charming way with words." Despite the option of free government dentistry, his two front teeth remain crooked, giving a rakish look to his grin. "No wonder you drive your lovely mother nuts."

I laugh, turn down the volume, and pull on gloves. "You wouldn't think she was so lovely if you knew she wanted me to get a different job."

"And what makes you think I'd miss you?" His blue eyes twinkle. "And turn Led Zeppelin back up. The dead don't mind. This kind of work requires a heavy dose of rock 'n' roll."

"If you insist." Drumbeats shake the metal gurneys. "Maybe you need hearing aids. Your music obsession is probably damaging my youthful eardrums."

"You're not twisting any of those little devices into my ears." He shakes his finger at me. "I can hear just fine. And I don't need anyone listening to my thoughts."

"They're called hearing aids, not mind readers, silly. And you're in the right age group."

He laughs. "How dare you throw my age up in my face, you young sprite." He waves a scalpel in the air over a dead body. "Now make yourself useful and get me another #10 blade. This one's deadly dull."

"Okay, Mr. Rock 'n' Roll." I grab it and change out the blade. "What're you doing?"

"This one died on those fancy docs upstairs, and now I'm supposed to tell them why."

Gus reminds me of Einstein with an attitude. He's got the crazy hair, he's brilliant, and he works best with classic rock blasting in the background. He collects old CDs like others accumulate china or figurines. No wonder I love it here.

Grabbing protective eyewear and a surgical mask, I lean in for a better view as Gus reaches into the abdomen. When he palpates the liver lobes, they immediately fall apart in his hands.

I gasp. "The liver's not supposed to do that!"

He nods, and his glasses slip down his nose. Since my gloves are still clean, I push them back up.

"No, it's not." He points across the room. "Get me some pathology jars. Let's send in a couple biopsy samples. I think this poor devil had lymphoma eating up his insides. His ultrasound was reported as inconclusive, so they would've had to take him to surgery to figure out more upstairs."

"I'll bet you're right." I grab the vials, remove the lids, and help Gus drop in the samples. "You always are."

"Of course I'm right. Except for the surgery part. I guess it wouldn't matter if they knew he had cancer since they wouldn't treat him anyway."

"Why wouldn't they treat him?"

"Check the chart."

After I label the samples, I grab the clipboard and read aloud. "Prisoner. Limited Diagnostics. Restricted Treatment. What did he do?"

"It doesn't say. Maybe he killed somebody. Maybe he stole something. Or maybe he just wouldn't play by the rules." Gus eyeballs me. "You wouldn't know anything about that, would you?"

"What are you talking about?"

He smirks. "You rejected the doctors' pills and therapies and chose yoga and running as treatment for your depression. Does any of this sound familiar?"

"Yes. And it worked. A lot better than anything else did."

"I know. But the docs upstairs don't like to be proven wrong. So you got labeled *uncooperative* and *unstable*."

"I did?" Damn those doctors.

"Yes. In bold letters across the resume they sent to me."

My stomach clenches. Why is he telling me this now, three years later? Did I do something wrong? "They told me I was labeled 'empathetic'."

"Oh, that was on there too. Along with your Occupational Test scores." He raises his bushy eyebrows. "And those three things aren't mutually exclusive, you know."

I shake my head. "I can never tell if what's coming out of your mouth is B.S. or the truth."

He grins. "It's all of the above."

"That's not helpful."

"It's not meant to be." Gus chuckles. "By the way, I got you a birthday present."

I place the pathology samples in the correct tray. "That's not funny. I told you not to—"

"Don't interrupt. And don't worry. I didn't get you a Barbie or new pink running shoes."

"Actually, I could use new run—"

"I told you not to interrupt!" He smiles, enjoying his little game.

"And anyway, this is *so* much better than that. It's something you've wanted for a long while."

I wait for his announcement, keeping my mouth shut this time. He hums a tune and closes the muscular abdominal wall using a continuous suture pattern without speaking another word.

I cut the ends of his sutures. "When are you gonna stop teasing me and tell me what's going on?"

He laughs. "I knew you wouldn't be able to keep quiet long. All right, Miss Impatient, I'll tell you... But first you need to take out the garbage."

I glare. "You're impossible."

"Okay, okay." He zips the bag up over the patient's head. "This has got to be the best birthday present anyone's ever given you, Miss Silvia Wood. I'm taking you on a little field trip."

"Where are we going?" My eyes widen. This is awesome. I never go anywhere.

He drops his voice to a side-whisper. "You get to help me with the next body disposal."

"Really?" I ask, breathless. "I've never even been to the edge of the city before. I've only seen pictures of it. It's part of the reason why —" I press my lips together. I don't want to offend him or hurt his feelings.

"Yeah, I know Mortuary Science wasn't the job you've always dreamed of. But you fit in so perfectly here. In fact, maybe sometime we'll drive by Green Food Production when they're in the middle of Natural Fertilization so you'll believe me that it smells worse there than it does in here."

I grin at his pride. "Thanks, Gus."

"You're welcome. Think of it as a little vacation. You, me, three dozen dead bodies, and the Incinerator."

"I can't wait." Funny thing is, I mean it.

4

ROAD TO NOWHERE

My head buzzes with questions on my way to the Gym after work. What will I learn at the Incinerator? What will I get to do? And the biggest, most wonderful questions of all: What does the edge of the city look like? Will I finally get to see what's beyond the fences?

I've wondered about the Dark Woods ever since I can remember. I've heard tales of endless forests filled with life-giving trees and life-taking monsters. My grade school Health and Safety book contained pictures of wolves feasting on human flesh, their teeth ripping and tearing muscle tissue right off the bone.

Wait a minute. Human Disposal always happens at night, so everything will be dark. I won't be able to see anything anyway. Shoot. That sucks.

I step into the shade of the 37th Northwest Street Gym. After swiping my I.D. card through the scanner, I enter and hustle up the stairs. The third floor is packed like never before. I pass by a crowd of people gawking at the electronic bulletin boards. There must be a new class or something, but I'm not interested. I've reserved a treadmill for an hour, and I intend to use it. In the locker room, I approach the uniform counter to place my order.

"Running shorts and tank top, please," I tell the skinny, ponytailed attendant.

"Are you in training?" she asks.

"For what?"

"The Race for Citizen Glory. Didn't you see the notice up on the boards? Everybody's doing it because of all the awards."

I shake my head. "I'm not interested in any race. I just run for me."

"Okay, then." She hands over a worn pair of black and white shorts and a faded pink tank top.

On my left, a young woman pushes her way to the counter. "I need running clothes. If I'm going to compete in that big race, I'd better get in shape. It's only two months away."

The same attendant hands her a brand new pair of shorts and a bright green T-shirt sporting the slogan: *In Training for Citizen Glory.* The young woman struts off. Her legs don't have any muscle tone. I could *so* beat her.

I turn to the attendant. "Did she get nicer shorts than me just because she's training for that race?"

"Of course. It's a big deal. Why aren't you doing it? You're here all the time anyway."

"I don't know. Maybe I'll think about it," I tell her, but that's a lie. I run for myself and no one else.

I wander into the changing area and switch into my government-issue workout clothes. I check my watch. There's fifteen minutes left before my treadmill reservation, so I march up to the electronic bulletin board. Words flash across the screen during the muted video announcements. The reel starts over every few minutes, showing old footage of runners, all in the same uniform, racing the streets of Panopticus. Two lanes have been blocked off for the race. Yellow words slide across the bottom of the screen:

Accept the Citizen Challenge to run 13.1 miles. Win prizes and improve your fitness profile. Receive increased food and equipment allowances. Don't miss out on this great opportunity. After the last Race for Citizen Glory, three of the top ten finishers were Chosen for Highest Level Citizen Employment.

Although I've been running a few years now, I've never raced—except for secretly battling the people on either side of me in the long row of treadmills. In fact, I've never run anywhere except in this very room, because it's not allowed. The streets are too dangerous.

I glance at my watch again. It's time to get started. Using the provided spray bottle and towel, I wipe down my machine then climb on and set my pace. Visions of runners racing through the city streets flash through my brain. My legs go faster and faster. The room disappears as I imagine I'm leading the race.

"Hey. It's busy in here today, isn't it?" A deep voice on my right disrupts my dreams of glory.

"What?" I hate when people try to talk to me at the gym. My mind wanders when I run, and I don't like my fanciful imaginings to be interrupted. It makes me feel like someone else can see inside my head. I don't like that. We're watched enough as it is.

I sigh and turn to the guy on the treadmill next to mine. He's blond. Fit. And gorgeous. His chin held at a jaunty, confident angle. Like half the other jocks at the gym, he's so full of himself there's no room for anything else. And, apparently, he won't stop talking to me.

"Everybody here thinks they're going to win that race." He smiles like he knows the overhead lights will glisten off his pearly whites. "But they're wrong. *I am.*" Naturally, he's sporting new shorts and an *In Training for Citizen Glory* T-shirt.

"Oh, are you?" I ramp up my settings. "How can you be so sure?"

"I'm the best." He chuckles.

I remember that his name is Liam. At least, that's what the girls clamoring for his attention every night at the gym call him. I roll my eyes and catch him staring at my shorts. My cheeks flush, and not just from my pace. "Were you checking out my butt?"

"Of course I was." He laughs, not even embarrassed.

I cover my backside with my hands. "Well, stop it."

He shakes his head. "Most girls like that."

"I don't." My nostrils flare.

"Don't get so huffy. I'm not even hitting on you."

My cheeks burn even hotter. "I didn't say you were."

"Okay then." He turns back to his machine. "Because you'd know if I were interested."

"Just so we're clear: I'm only here to run." I reset the treadmill controls. This conversation is over.

He clears his throat. "I'm simply wondering why you aren't training for the race."

I sigh. He's taking over my hour of peace. "I never race."

"Why not? You're the fastest girl here. I see you running all the time. Your legs fly. You could probably place. You might even get Chosen."

Chosen. The greatest honor bestowed on any member of the city. Mom would be so proud of me. So happy. And, finally, she'd be satisfied.

I turn to glance at Liam, the golden boy. He's conceited. He's full of himself.

And he also happens to be right. About the race at least.

"Maybe." This could be exactly what I need. Or at least what Mom needs.

Liam grins. "That's the spirit!"

"How about this? I *will* enter. And I'm going to beat you." There. Take that.

"I accept that challenge." He reaches over and shakes my sweaty hand. "Hey, what's your name?"

"It's Silvia." His vigorous handshake catches me off guard, and I try not to fall off the treadmill.

AN HOUR later I approach the front desk. Liam stands beside me, egging me on. My hand shakes as I scan my I.D. card, officially signing up for the Race for Citizen Glory. This could all be a big mistake. Heck, I've never even run on a road before.

The athletic trainer behind the table hands me a cloth bag. "Here's your race packet. The New Order congratulates you on making the commitment to better health."

"All right! You did it." Liam slaps me a high five. "I'm glad you're on my team."

"What team?" My eyes narrow. "You never mentioned a team."

He shrugs. "That's because I just decided right now. We should train together. That way, we'll win together, you know, running as a pack."

"What if I don't want to train with you?" I ask as we move away from the front desk.

"Why wouldn't you?" He follows me toward the girls' locker room then leans on the wall outside the door, blocking my way. "I'll push you hard, and you'll do the same for me."

"I guess you're right." I hear myself agreeing with his plan as two girls approach. Their matching ponytails swing in unison. Both girls sport a perfect glow of after-workout sheen. The brunette throws a longing glance at Liam. The blonde raises a questioning eyebrow at me. Liam moves so they can enter the locker room.

"Get used to it." He grins. "I'm always right."

"I doubt that." I shake my head. "Listen, I've got to get home to make supper for my mom. It's her late night at the orchestra hall."

"That's cool." Liam eases his way down the hallway. "See you tomorrow. Be ready to run outside."

"Outside? But that's not allowed. What if we get in trouble?"

He laughs as he reaches the corner. "Don't worry. There are approved training runs in your packet. You'll see."

I glance at my race bag. Just by signing up for this stupid race I get more freedom? It's worth it already. I reach into the bag, pulling out running socks and sports bandages, both meant to prevent blisters, and a green *In Training* T-shirt.

Still digging in the bag as I enter the girls' locker room, I bump into someone.

"Hey, watch where you're going," a voice snaps.

"Oh, sorry." I start to turn away, but she's not done with me. Neither is her friend. The two of them, dressed in identical race shorts and shirts, glare at me.

"I don't know why Liam wants to train with *you*," the brunette says.

"Yeah." The blonde makes a show of sniffing the air. "You smell like dead people." They cackle and congratulate each other on how cool they are. I remember them from grade school. They were snots then too. I guess some people don't improve with age.

"Maybe he's tired of desperate girls like you who can't keep up with him," I say.

"So you think you're better than us?" The brunette plants a hand on her hip.

I smirk. "I'm faster than you. And that's all that counts in a race."

The blonde narrows her eyes. "At least I don't smell."

"Actually, you do." I sniff her as I pass by. Two can play at this game. "You stink like a sweaty avocado." Actually, she doesn't. I just know she works in a deli.

"Oh, my gosh... Do you really?" her bitchy friend asks.

The blonde's face flushes, and she bends down to sniff her shirt.

I walk away, victorious.

⚘

"How was your day?" Mom asks as she breezes into the kitchen, grabs the soymilk out of the mini-fridge, and pulls a chair up to the metal kitchen bar. "Mine *dragged*. I'm so glad to be home."

"My day was good." I clear my throat. "I signed up for the Race for Citizen Glory. I even have a training partner."

"You do?" Mom pours herself a glass. "Someone I know?"

"Nope. You've never met him."

She pauses before taking a sip, the glass hanging in mid-air below her lips. "A boy?"

I nod.

"Even better."

"Yeah, I think it'll be fun." I hand her a plate of pesto noodles.

She smiles. "Running isn't fun, in my opinion, but I know you love it."

"And I have even better news." I grin, barely able to control my excitement. "Gus is taking me to the Human Disposal Facility."

She grimaces, setting the forkful of noodles she was about to eat back down on her plate. "Why on earth would you want to do that?"

"Come on, Mom. Don't deflate my happy balloon. This is a good thing for me. It means I'm being given more responsibility. It means they trust me."

"You mean Gus trusts you. As far as anyone else..." Mom's eyes dart around as if searching for someone to jump out at her. "Well, you never know what The New Order thinks. Let's talk about something else." She grabs the remote and turns on the news.

A perky anchorwoman flashes onto the screen. "Earlier today, the Representatives paid tribute to the twenty-fifth anniversary of the WWIII ceasefire with compelling and, at times, fiery speeches. Their important words remind us of all we have to be grateful for here in Panopticus, the Green City of Peace, Unity, and Equality."

Mom mutes the reporter. "Just look at Representative Waters-Royce! She's practically full term, and she looks like she's gained ten pounds, max. Probably hasn't even gone up a size. How do famous people manage to look so good pregnant? It's not fair. But, I suppose, after all the miscarriages she's reported to have had, she deserves her chance at happiness." She unmutes the program as the red-haired Representative Waters-Royce shakes her fist in the air.

"The Citizens of Panopticus are fortunate to be living in the year 2065," Waters-Royce continues. "Because of The New Order, no one is homeless. Because of The New Order, unemployment is at zero percent. Because of The New Order, there is no more war. Rape and domestic violence have been eliminated. Unplanned pregnancies no longer occur—"

"How long do you think she'll keep talking?" I ask.

"Silvia, don't be so impatient," Mom scolds. "Oh look, is this what you were talking about?"

Now on the screen is the same race footage I'd seen earlier that day at the gym.

"Yes, that's it!" I point. "That's the race I'm gonna run—or win, if Liam has anything to do with it."

She swallows, eyeing me closely. "So, his name is Liam, is it?"

I tense. Crap. Why'd I have to tell her his name? Now her nosiness will go into overdrive. "Don't get too excited. He's just a friend. Well, sort of. I mean, I've seen him around, but I've never talked to him before."

"Maybe he likes you."

I shake my head. "I think he just wants to win."

"You *are* getting to the age where—"

I cut her off. "Mom, do you think I smell like dead people?"

She frowns. "Did he tell you that? Because, if so, don't bother with him."

"No. Some mean girls in the locker room said that to me."

Mom sets down her fork. "Well, what did Liam say?"

"He told me I was the fastest girl in the place. He thinks I could win."

Mom raises her eyebrows. "Really? I'd stick with him. He sounds like he's worth your time. Ignore those worthless girls."

I nod. I don't tell her what else Liam had said. I don't want to get her hopes up.

Because I'm pretty sure I'll never be Chosen.

5

STAY UP LATE

The next day at work, I double-check the bodies intended for disposal. All the corpses are lined up on metal tables. I move from one to the other. Has the microchip I.D. been extracted from the upper right arm? Check. Has the birth control capsule been removed from the left? Check. As usual, we haven't missed one. On each body, the fleshy tissue has been incised two inches below the top of the shoulder, parallel to the long humerus bone. The microchips are collected for recycling of the electronic components. The hormone-infused capsules are removed to avoid contamination of the food and water since the ash from the burned bodies is used as fertilizer. Not every crop benefits. It all depends on the pH but, as with everything else in Panopticus, nothing is wasted.

Gus says there used to be large open spaces where the dead were buried called "cemeteries." That wasted too much land, so a new system had to be implemented. Any remaining cemeteries were reclaimed as public property after the last war. He showed me a few pictures of old cemeteries that have long since been destroyed. The whole idea seems so odd to me—that families would want to stand above their loved one's decomposing body. If everyone's so grossed out by my job, then why did people, years ago, want to visit the grass covering a bunch of rotting corpses?

After checking the last prepared body, I close the final biodegradable body bag. I glance at the clock. "Gus, I'm all done. What do you want me to do until we leave for the Incinerator?"

He's perched at his computer, filling out disposal forms. "Go home, nap, and eat, or whatever. Be back before dusk."

I peel off my gloves. "Sure you don't need me?"

His eyes remain on the computer screen. "No, I'm fine. Get some rest. We'll be working late."

I grab my gym bag. "Actually, I'm supposed to go running outside today." My feet feel light, as if on springs.

He cocks his head. "Outside?"

"Yeah. I signed up for that Race for Citizen Glory. Now I'm allowed to run outdoors on select routes. I even have a special training uniform." Okay, I'm not so psyched about the uniform. But running *outside*? That's going to be so different from what I'm used to with the treadmill. I'll actually *go* somewhere for once, not just run in place.

"They're doing that again, already? Well, take it easy. Don't forget you'll be up all night, helping me."

I grin. "How could I forget?"

Gus turns back to his computer. "I'll bring snacks."

I head out the door. My heart races before I even reach the gym. I can't wait to run outdoors. Not that most of the approved routes are exciting or anything. I'll mostly be running in between tall, glass buildings. The only scenic part is in the Park, but I'd use any excuse to spend more time amongst the plants and trees and flowers.

I jog up the stairs of the Gym, slide my card and push my way inside. I hurry past the front desk when a voice interrupts my thoughts.

"Silvia Wood? I have a message for you." The female attendant reads from a hand-held screen. "From Liam Harmon... 'Sorry, I can't make it in today. But I should be there tomorrow. Run fast. Pretend

I'm chasing you.'" The girl smiles as she slides over the monitor. "That Liam is so cute. Here—I need your electronic signature that you received this message."

I sign, my shoulders slumping. Now what do I do? Run outside on my own today or wait until tomorrow for Liam? He's basically a stranger to me, so I've no idea how reliable he is. Waiting for him might be a bad idea. I drag my feet to the locker room, undecided. I don't know Liam enough to miss him, but I do miss the sun on my face. What a letdown. After getting dressed and leaving the locker room, I stare out the window for a moment. I consider going out on the government-endorsed routes on my own. In or out? What should I do?

After changing my mind ten times, I turn away from the glass-filtered sunlight and enter the workout room. Several of the treadmills are vacant, probably because so many people are taking advantage of the outdoor opportunities. I type in my code and settings and let the world melt away as my legs come to life.

⚞

FULLY RELAXED from my post-run yoga class, I go back to work, eating a nutrition bar on the way. There's still at least an hour before dusk, so I can probably nap before we leave. I descend into the chill of Mortuary Sciences and glance around. Gus is nowhere to be seen. He must've gone out to get something to eat. All the prep tables are empty except for one. I drop my bag and move closer.

Jars of colored powder, bags of hemp-tipped applicators, and wrinkly sheets of some strange material I've never seen before cover the table. After some hesitation, I pick up one of the sheets. It's lighter than a piece of paper—more like a tissue.

Gus enters the large room with fabric lunch sacks hanging off each arm. "As you can see, I also had some free time today."

I carefully set the sheet back on the table. "Sorry. I didn't mean to pry."

"Don't worry. I don't mind. I think I've already told you this, but before I spent ten years in medical school, I used to work in theater and costume design."

"Yeah. I vaguely remember that."

He rearranges the table, sorting the pieces by size. "Do you have any idea what this is?"

I shake my head.

Gus grins. "It's magic. Here, I'll show you." He sets his arm on the table, dips an applicator in adhesive, and then brushes it across his skin. He picks up one of the smaller sheets and smooths it onto his arm.

"And now, the final touches." Gus grabs another applicator, mixes pink, red, and purple powders, then dabs them in an expanding pattern on his skin. "Viola! A birthmark."

I touch his arm. "But it looks so *real.*"

"Of course it does. I used to be quite good at this. Naturally, you have to modify your technique for something up close versus from the stage."

"I'm impressed. What else can you do?" Gus is amazing. So many hidden talents.

"I could make you look ten or sixty. I could make you black, white, or any shade in between. I never got too good with reshaping noses, but—"

"How about burns? Can you do burns?" The question bursts out before I can think about it.

Gus flinches.

"Come on. I've been here three years now. You never let me see the burn victims. You don't have to keep protecting me like that. I want to know what it looks like." I need to see it for myself, since that's what happened to Dad. That would make his death more real because I need to believe he's gone. A tiny part of me keeps hoping that someday, he'll come back. It doesn't make any sense, but sometimes I feel like, instead of The New Order, it's *him* who's watching me.

Gus pauses. "That's a bit more difficult. Give me your hand."

I pull up my sleeve and rest my arm on the cool metal table. I don't mind if Gus sees my scars. He already knows my story. I watch Gus work, amazed at the process of transformation. After applying adhesive, he layers three sheets over my hand and wrist, scrunching them in spots and stretching them in others. He dips into the colors over and over again. Sweat beads on his brow as he labors. Twenty minutes later, he sets down the last applicator.

"Well, Silvia, what do you think?" he asks.

I flex and extend my fingers. "It looks *awful!*" My skin appears raw, the fingers blackened and charred, the flesh pulling away from the bone. "This is amazing. It doesn't look like makeup at all. It looks real. At least to me. Not that I've ever seen a burn victim up close before."

"Unfortunately, this is precisely what a burn victim looks like." He sighs. "Now you know why I don't let you see them. Because that ten-year-old girl who lost her father is still alive inside you."

I hold up my hand, in awe as flashes of my dad's face and the layers of char on my flesh melt together in my mind. I move my fingers and images flicker in my head of all the workers who burned to death in the fiery explosion. After the accident, the news focused on the story for days, posting pictures of the victims smiling with their families. The whole city mourned their demise while my eyes remained dry. Painfully so. I couldn't grieve, because I couldn't believe Dad was really gone. It took the therapists a long time to convince me of the truth.

My shoulders slump. "I get your point."

The back door of Mortuary Sciences slams open. A Handler in full black uniform marches two steps into the room and halts. "The bodies have all been loaded. We're ready to go."

"We'll be there in five minutes," Gus replies.

The Handler exits by the same door. Gus tosses his makeup supplies into a side drawer.

"How do I get this off?" I ask, still staring at my deformed hand.

He gestures toward the sink. "It washes off, but you'll have to use the industrial soap."

As I scrub in the sink, Gus rolls out a tall tool chest, double-checks the contents of the drawers, then turns to me. "When you're done, grab those lunch sacks. And bring an extra sweater. The refrigerated car gets a bit frosty."

The back door of Mortuary Sciences leads to an underground loading dock just big enough for the transport truck to pick up the bodies. We step into the dimly-lit area. Two Handlers wait on either side of the truck. We climb into the back, and the door locks shut as we take our seats. Gus flips on the travel lights. It's us and the bagged bodies. Everyone who died in the last month in the Northwest District rests on the rolling double stretchers before us, awaiting their group cremation. Each black bag is strapped down to a silver bed, one above and one below, like bunk beds for the dead.

Gus hands me a sandwich. "The scenery isn't great, but I guarantee the eats are good. Made them myself."

The metal floor shakes beneath our feet as the truck roars to life.

"How long does it take to get there?" I ask before taking my first bite.

"Oh, about an hour. Not bad. But I'm afraid you won't get to see much of your Plant Production facilities riding in back with me where there are no windows. You might get a glimpse of it once we get there. It will be dark out, of course, but it's pretty lit up even at night."

"That's all right. I'm actually more interested in what's *inside* the Plant Production buildings, although I suppose I'll never get to see that."

Gus gives me a sympathetic smile. "Your mom's okay with me keeping you out so late?"

I laugh. "As long as I don't talk to her about working Human Disposal, especially while she's trying to eat, she's okay with it. She doesn't find it a very appetizing topic of dinner conversation."

Gus chuckles. "I bet."

"I feel bad she's eating alone tonight."

"Doesn't she have anyone else?" His question hangs in the air.

I pause before answering. "No. Just me. People try to set her up all the time, but she refuses."

"Yeah, I can understand that. Sometimes trying to find someone new is ten times more lonely than accepting the fact that it's over and you're on your own now."

"So, there's been no one since Ben?" I ask, hoping I'm not getting too personal.

He clears his throat. "No. No one."

"Then I have an idea. Why don't you come over to our place for dinner sometime?" I would love this. Mom could get to know Gus better, and maybe, if he impressed her, she'd stop bugging me about my job. Plus, I'd like to give Mom something to do. She never invites anyone over anymore, and this might liven things up.

He raises his eyebrows. "Are you sure your mother would approve? We might talk shop."

I laugh. "Yes, I think so. I'll ask her first, of course. You've never seen our apartment, you know."

"Too bad I can't see your old place. The way you describe it, it sounds heavenly, almost like an indoor arboretum with all those plants in there. No wonder you wanted to go into Botany Sciences."

"Yeah." I pick at my sandwich, not because it isn't good but because he's hit on a touchy subject. "Our last place got way more sunlight. Once we moved, the plants started dying, one by one."

Gus nods. "I know it's standard policy, but sometimes it seems like pouring salt into a wound to make a family move after their loved one dies."

"Did you have to move, too, when Ben died?"

He nods. "Everyone does. I guess it makes sense, conserving resources and all. And, in fact, it might have been for the best. Ben died at home, and I cared for him at the end, so staying there might have been too hard."

"What about your things? Did you get to take all of it when you moved?"

"Yes, of course." He cocks his head to the side, watching me. "Even my La-Z-Boy. Man, that thing is ancient. I've re-covered it twice. It was my father's. But why do you ask?"

"I don't know." My memory of the day we moved is still so fuzzy. "It's just...some of our belongings went missing when we moved. Mom swears she packed them. She thinks it's my fault, that I misplaced the boxes or something. We still fight about it sometimes, but I swear I was as careful as she was and didn't throw anything away. I wouldn't."

Gus glances around as if someone besides the dead bodies can hear us in this noisy, bouncy truck. "What went missing?"

"Mostly my dad's stuff. So, it shouldn't matter, but I'd like to have it to remember him by."

"I bet you miss your dad quite a bit."

"I think about him every day."

Gus frowns. "I'm sorry about that."

"Isn't it weird how everybody says they're sorry? It's not like they had anything to do with it. It's not their fault. They've nothing to be sorry for."

He pats me on the back. "Well, I'm sorry just the same."

I stare at my hands. "My therapists told me Dad's death made me grow up faster."

"You kids grow up too fast already. Full time jobs by fifteen—or highly specialized schooling." He pauses. "That's where you should be, you know."

"Where?"

"Medical school. They need more students who are 'empathetic.' Plus, you're whip-smart. You remember everything I tell you. I never have to explain things twice."

I frown, thinking of the real reason I'm not in medical school or at the Plant Production facility. The Suits and the therapists would never let me. Tears sting my eyes. "You're the only one who says nice things like this to me...besides my mom, I mean. But she has to. I'm her daughter."

"Well, you deserve it." His voice is kind. "And everything I said is true."

I shake my head. "My therapists didn't think so. That's why I turned to running and yoga to fix myself because they make me feel better. Therapy only ever made me feel worse. All my therapists told me I was too emotionally unstable for higher learning and that no one would bother teaching me."

Gus shakes his head. "They're wrong. I'd be happy to teach you anything I know. And, as you well know, I *am* a genius."

I smile weakly. "I've learned a lot from you already, more than my mom would probably like." I rub the scars on my wrists. They itch every time I think about my first suicide attempt.

A shadow crosses Gus's face.

"You know, when I tried to kill myself, sometimes I think the only reason I didn't succeed was because I didn't know how to." I trace a line down my veins. "Now I do."

6

GREAT BALLS OF FIRE

Gus covers my scarred wrists with his two large hands. "Silvia, have you talked to your mother about this?"

"Argued is more like it."

He clears his throat. "What I mean is: did you tell her what the therapists said to you?"

I turn away as if to examine the metal racks housing the dead. "No, I didn't. She had enough troubles, anyway, with work and dealing with her own grief, but things should get better now that she's playing again."

Gus is still watching me when I turn back. "It will look good for your family to have her perform again. People loved to hear her play. You might have been too young to know this, but Yoshe Wood was a famous name in performance music in her day."

"Once, when I was alone in the apartment, I found an old recording of one of her concerts in The Archives. You should've seen her face when she got home. She looked so sad and begged me to turn it off, but maybe now that she's back in the orchestra, things will be different."

"If I'm cooking something special, I always play one of those government-sponsored programs in the background." Gus grins. "Makes me feel real high class. When The New Order rebuilt after the last war, they put a heavy emphasis on the arts."

"Why? It seems like they'd have so many more important things to do."

He shrugs. "That's a valid point. The New Order initially formed to feed, house, and protect all the war survivors. Rebuilding was endless after all the destruction—windmills, solar panels, and greenhouses all over the place. It was a remarkable time."

"What was it like? Living through The War, I mean."

Gus's shoulders slump. "Be thankful we have peace now. You have no idea what it was like, always being at war—and with so many countries at once. Everyone throwing bombs at everyone else. After the nuclear fallout, everyone rushed to the nearest radiation treatment center. My family came here, but everyone died except for me."

"I'm so sorry, Gus." I shudder, imagining what war would look like, remembering the pictures I'd seen in school. Flattened homes. Burned bodies. "Did you get sick too?"

"No, but remember, that was many years ago. I was a robust young man back then. One of the doctors did say that Ben's cancer might have come on due to after effects. We'll never know for sure, of course. People got cancer before the war too."

"How many people died, really?" I want to know if what Gus says jives with what I learned in school.

"Before World War III, I'd guess America had a population of about four-hundred million. And now, it's a tenth of that. Millions died instantly in the direct nuclear attack. Millions more died shortly thereafter with horrible, incurable ailments. So many people dying with no way to treat them. No way to stop their pain."

I shiver, imagining a long hallway crowded with stretchers and dying patients crying out in agony. "Were you in medical school then?"

"No, I was still studying theater. But there was a real shortage of medical workers. After I watched my three sisters fade away, one after the other, I switched from theater to medicine and never looked back."

I bite my lip. "Gus, I'm so sorry about your sisters. That would be awful to watch someone you love die."

"Thanks, but everyone lost people they loved. Back before The War, everyone worried about population control. Now, it's the opposite problem. There's so much infertility. The miscarriage rate is three out of every four pregnancies when it used to be one out of three."

I nod. "Mom used to light candles for her miscarriages when we celebrated my birthday."

Gus releases a long breath. "No wonder you hate your birthday."

"She doesn't do that anymore. My first therapist made her stop."

He raises his bushy eyebrows. "At least *one* good thing came of your therapy."

I smile. "I actually liked that therapist. She was nice. But after a month, they replaced her with some jerk. All he ever wanted to do was talk about my father—which is ironic, really, since I was supposed to be moving on, you know? Not constantly dwelling on the past."

Gus stares at me, an unreadable expression on his face. "What did that therapist ask, exactly?"

"Everything. What my dad ate for breakfast, what his childhood was like, who were his friends. It was stupid." How I hated that man. My hands clench as I remember the way he'd lean in close, asking his questions louder and louder when I'd refuse to answer.

Gus shakes his head. "I don't know much about psychotherapy, so this isn't what you would call an educated opinion, but that doesn't seem very helpful to me."

I shake off the uncomfortable memory and pat Gus on the shoulder. "Pretty much everything you say is an 'educated opinion.' Admit it: you've probably read tons on the subject already."

"It's possible." He smirks. "Would you like some grapes?"

"Yes, please." Time to focus on the present.

He hands them over. "I'm glad you're better now. I'd like to congratulate myself on being part of the reason, but I pretty much think you did all the hard work yourself."

The armored truck jerks up and down, and I almost drop my fruit.

Gus glances at the ceiling where the overhead light flickers. "We must be getting close. These roads near the periphery get a bit bumpy." He reaches into a cooler-bag. "Care for some milk? I've got both soy and rice. Which would you like?"

"Rice."

He passes the bottle. "You know what I miss from before The War? Besides my family, of course? I miss cows. You know, you never got a chance to eat real ice cream, Silvia, and that's a shame. Tastes a whole lot different now."

"I still like it. Not that we eat it often."

"That's because you don't know any better. You've never even seen a cow, except maybe in a picture, which is ironic since you were born here in the Midwest—in what used to be known as dairy country."

I take a sip of milk. "What else do you miss? Besides cows, I mean?"

He gazes off into the distance. "I miss a lot of things: hiking in state parks, real hamburgers—also made from cows—and phones."

"We still have phones."

"Public phones, yes. But no personal lines. No portable cell phones like the one I used to carry around in my pocket. Everyone had them before the bombs destroyed all the communication towers."

The truck hits a pothole that almost launches me from my seat. "No wonder you have to strap down the bodies so well." I grip the bench below me with both hands to keep from falling off.

"Less than five straps per body results in quite the mess." Gus pushes his falling glasses back up. "I forgot to inform you that our field trip included a free loosening of your teeth. But don't worry—we should be there shortly."

The vehicle squeals to a stop. Incoherent voices yell to each other outside. I stand up for a second then fall back onto the seat as the truck turns around and backs up. Soon, the lock slides with a sharp clank and the doors swing open. The truck fills with blinding light.

"We're here at last." Gus jumps up. He's very limber for a sixty-year-old man. "You stay here for a minute while I talk to the Overseer. I'll be right back."

He hops to the ground and disappears from view. At first, my legs feel shaky as I stand and gingerly move about. I peer out the opening. The truck backed up to a black metal ramp. That should make it easy to move the racks of bodies into the building. I crane my neck to view the sandy grounds surrounding the Incinerator. The lot is vast and empty.

Gus hops into the truck again, rubbing his hands together. "We're all set. They've got the records. We'll move the bodies, starting with these two."

We roll the first double stretcher up the ramp.

"Okay." Gus pants. "The rest of the way is flat, so breathe easy."

"How have you done this by yourself all these years?" I ask, working up a sweat as we push uphill.

"I used to ask the Handlers for help, but you're a better conversationalist. Plus, I got the impression they thought this was beneath them. Needless to say, I'm glad you're here."

Two by two, we transport all the bodies to a great room, unfasten the straps holding them to the stretchers, and carefully place them on the wide conveyor belt. We roll in Gus's storage unit full of supplies. He double-checks all the bodies again and collects their toe tags. After we finish, thirty-six bodies lie waiting to be consumed by fire. I glance ahead at the opening to the Incinerator. The air is heavy. We've only been here a little over an hour, and my skin already feels as if it is covered in ash.

"Creepy, isn't it?" Gus follows my line of vision.

I nod. The gaping cavity is built of a reddish-black metal, resembling an open mouth. I wonder if this is on purpose, someone's sick sense of humor. The room is blasted hot, and I'm sweating so much from the labor and the heat that I feel like I'm being slowly cooked both inside and out.

"Now what?" I ask.

Gus hands me a water bottle. "Here, drink this. Looks like you need it."

I gulp down half the bottle before pausing for breath. "I don't know how you've done this all these years."

He takes a small sip of water. "This isn't the easiest part of the job, but it has to be done. And I like it to be done right." He gestures to the bodies awaiting cremation. "These people deserve respect. That's why I'm here."

The Overseer, dressed in what appears to be a fireproof yellow uniform, steps forward. "All set?" he asks.

"Yes." Gus taps the toe tags bulging in his pockets. "All thirty-six bodies accounted for."

"You're staying to watch, as usual?" the Overseer asks.

"Of course," says Gus.

"Her too?" The Overseer points to me.

Gus doesn't look for my approval before he answers. "Yes. She's staying too."

After the Overseer leaves, a moment of panic sets in. What if watching this brings back the nightmares of my father burning to death? I don't want to go back there, to wake up in cold sweats, gasping for air, gagging on my fear. Just as I decide to tell Gus I can't stay, the fires begin.

A whooshing sound fills the air, clogging my ears.

My heart stutters as I stare at the gaping hole. A great ball of fire flickers to life deep within the open mouth. Blue flames turn to orange.

My mouth dries out.

With a hum, the flames climb the walls.

The heat hits me, toasting my face. I force my shoulders to relax. I must watch this. I have to. I can't pretend Dad's accident didn't happen.

The bodies move forward on the humming belt, each one dropping into the mouth with a dragging noise, then a hungry crinkle sounds as the flames lick up the sides of the body bag. One after another, the corpses disappear forever. My jaw relaxes. The air smells like the one time Mom left a pan on the burner too long.

I turn to Gus. "Thanks for taking me here."

"And thank you for the help."

I place a hand on his arm. "No, I really mean it."

Gus presses his lips together, looking uncertain.

I rush to reassure him. "I feel like I finally got to say goodbye to my dad. He would've been brought here. And someone like you would've taken care of him, respectfully, like we did with all the bodies today. I'm glad I finally got to see what happened."

He opens his mouth, but I interrupt.

"Because now I finally know the truth."

7

PLEASE DON'T LEAVE ME

As bodies feed the Incinerator, Gus and I close the fasteners on the empty stretchers. With the pull of each strap, I feel a rip inside my chest saying goodbye to my father. The Handlers come and go, collecting the double-decker stretchers and rolling them back to the truck.

As flames devour the final body bag, Gus turns to pack the supply cart. He stuffs a wad of identification tags into a drawer and slams it shut with a clang. The tools snap into place in the top drawer. Gus's key clicks to lock the cart. The Handlers grab the last stretcher and hurry off.

"Time to go," Gus announces. "Help me push."

The supply cart bounces across the rugged floor. Metal tools clink inside as we roll alongside the conveyor belt. Halfway to the end of the belt, the whole cart jerks to a stop. I run smack into it.

Gus yanks on the handle to no avail. "It won't move. It must be caught on something. Have a look, will you?"

I peer underneath the cart. "The front wheel's stuck in some sort of grate."

Gus squeezes past me, jimmies the wheel, and pops it back out of the groove. "That should fix it. Let's go."

He steps back around as I peer between the metal slats. It's pitch black down there. I can't see a thing.

"What's the grate for?" I ask.

"It's a drain in case they have to turn on the emergency sprinklers." He points overhead at extensive plumbing.

A Handler calls in from the exit. "We're fully loaded."

Gus waves. "We're coming."

We reach the transport truck where the Handlers load the supply cart for us.

Gus elbows me then gestures toward lights in the distance. "There's the start of the Plant Production facilities."

Glowing greenhouses stand in parallel rows, stretching far into the dark night. I envision myself working inside one, wearing a shiny, white laboratory jacket over green scrubs, watching as seedlings grow into fruit trees in fast motion. A lost dream. But with every loss there is a gain. There would be no Gus for me in Plant Production Sciences. I would be one worker out of a hundred, probably nobody special or important.

I clear my throat. "How many greenhouses are there?"

"I don't know. Must be hundreds of them. Maybe more."

"They seem to go on forever." I sigh. "I'd love to see inside one of them."

A Handler slaps the side of the truck. "Get in. It's time to go."

Gus gestures for me to step into the vehicle first. We both sit, the door locks, and the truck rumbles off.

"I've been in there." Gus nods in the direction of the Plant Production facilities.

"Really?" This is the first I've heard of this.

"Sure, lots of times. Ben worked there until he died nine years ago. Things have probably changed a lot since then."

"What did he do?" How I wish I could've met him. Gus doesn't talk much about his relationship with Ben. I never push the issue because I know how painful it is to think about someone you love when they're gone and never coming back.

"Ben worked in research. He developed a lot of their most productive food lines." Gus pauses to rub a hand over his tired face then mumbles. "Still it wasn't enough for them."

I suddenly feel like I don't know Gus at all. "What are you talking about?"

His eyes flicker toward mine then away. "This is a very touchy subject for me."

Before I can stop myself, my gaze scans the back of the truck for hidden surveillance.

Gus chuckles. "Don't worry. No one bothers listening to what the dead have to say. Nobody can hear us in here."

I raise my eyebrows, not sure I believe this.

"I've checked this truck over a million times. Never found a thing. 'Course you're usually not with me, and nobody's interested in listening to an old man talk to himself. That's one benefit of getting old and never retiring. I've been doing this job for too long for anyone to care about me."

My eyes widen. "You don't want to be watched, either? I thought you liked The New Order." Gus has never talked this way to me before. Of course, we've never met anywhere else other than work—where cameras monitor our every movement.

"I can appreciate what they've accomplished: clean energy, the end of war, equality independent of gender, race, or orientation." Gus examines his hands. "But..."

"But what?" I lean closer.

Gus chokes out his next words. "They wouldn't allocate Ben any more pain meds. At the end, when his suffering was the worst, he'd used up his Lifetime Medical Allowance. And mine as well. Which is why I can never get sick." He turns to me, smiling weakly. That's Gus for you, still making jokes when his heart is breaking.

"He died of pancreatic cancer, right? That's really painful, isn't it?"

His eyes well with unshed tears. "I'd taken him home by then to save on hospital beds. It wasn't fair to the others, they said…but he preferred to die at home, anyway, looking out the window."

"How did he manage without pain meds?"

Gus pauses. "He didn't. I found another way—the Underground Market."

"Did you really?" I whisper. "You could've gotten into so much trouble."

His eyes turn cold. "You'd do the same for someone you love."

Now it's my turn to pause. "Yeah. You're right. I would."

He smiles only a little. "I know you would."

I lean against the wall of the truck, fiery images of the Incinerator flashing through my mind. After ten minutes pass by, I yawn.

"Poor little Silvia. You've been up too long. If you lean into the bench like so"—he demonstrates the position—"you can sleep without much chance of falling off." Within minutes, Gus's soft snore adds to the metallic lullaby of the rattling tool cart and double-decker stretchers.

But I can't sleep. My mind races. Gus sounded just like Dad tonight. I wonder if he goes to "meetings" too? My heart clenches. I'd never survive if I lost him too.

8

THE STRANGER

The transport vehicle stops with a jolt, flinging me to the floor. I grit my teeth and brush the debris off my hands then rub my banged up knees.

"Are you hurt?" Gus stands and offers me a hand.

"Just my pride." I stand as the locks pop, and the back door swings open. The double stretchers clank down the ramp and across the floor as the Handlers unload them in a rush.

"You look exhausted." Gus puts an arm around me, leading me into Mortuary Sciences.

Half-asleep, I lean against his shoulder, grateful to have someone taking care of me for once. He escorts me into his tiny office tucked between the main prep area and storage. The room is barely big enough for his desk, computer chair, couch, and bookshelves. Large windows look out into the prep room.

He smiles kindly. "Why don't you catch a few more hours of shut eye then work a short day before heading home? You can start your day off a half day early."

"But where are you going to sleep? Don't you want the couch?"

Gus shakes his head and hands me a thin blanket. "No, I'm perfectly happy with my chair."

I drop down and stretch out on the sofa, glancing around at the familiar surroundings. Maps, thumbtacked into floor-to-ceiling bulletin boards, cover the walls. Gus is as crazy about maps as he is about rock 'n' roll. Some of his maps are of real places, such as the Museum of Fine Arts. My favorites are the story worlds like Narnia and Florin. There are even maps of places that used to exist, like old state forests and wildlife areas. Arrows and lines are drawn across each map, leading me to nowhere and everywhere all at once. My sleepy gaze follows these imaginary paths until I fall asleep.

THE NEXT MORNING, I slog through the motions of prepping the most recently delivered bodies.

"Hang in there," Gus cautions after I drop the same clipboard twice in a row. "Are you sure you want to go running today?"

"Don't worry." I yawn. "It'll wake me up."

He snorts. "Or do you in."

After every corpse is tagged and bagged, he releases me from duty. "You better go get that run over with before you fall asleep standing on your feet."

I grab my bag. Just hiking up the staircase takes twice as much effort as usual. Maybe I *am* too tired to run today. But then I think about actually running outside, and the stubborn part of me won't give up this opportunity.

AFTER I CHANGE in the locker room, I find Liam waiting for me near the front steps of the gym.

"You look terrible," he says with a grin. "What did you do? Forget to sleep for a week?"

"No." Why does he have to say that? I don't need an extra reminder of how tired I am. "I worked all night, delivering bodies to the Incinerator."

That shuts him up for a second.

I do some lunges to stretch out my hip flexors while Liam fiddles with his watch.

"Aren't you even going to stretch beforehand?" I ask.

"Nah, I don't need to." He taps the huge square screen on his wrist. "Darn it. I can't get this to work right."

"What is that, and why are you wearing it?"

"If I can ever get this to work, you're gonna be so jealous and want one of your own. It's so awesome. It shows your pace, heart rate, calories burned, and has a built in GPS."

"I don't really care about all that. Let's see how this goes today, okay? I've never run outside before. I'm kind of nervous about it, actually."

"How much different can it be?"

As soon as we start, my legs feel disconnected with my body. I keep glancing around, distracted by all the voices and people. Even though I've been running for a long time on a treadmill, it's like I'm running again for the very first time. This is so awkward with my feet slapping heavily on the ground. Why do my footsteps sound so loud out here? I never noticed them inside. I force my shoulders to relax. It doesn't matter how much noise I make.

As soon as we reach the park, I inhale the heavenly scent of lilacs. I'm finally getting the hang of this running outside business by the time we reach the mulched trails. But the uneven terrain causes my ankles to bend and pitch out to the sides.

"Why is this so hard for me?" I ask. "I swear my ankles are tired. I've never felt that before."

He slows the pace but only a little. "You'll get used to it. I've heard it takes weeks to build up ankle and calf strength on a different terrain."

"This feels so strange. And why can't I focus? I keep looking around instead of just ahead."

"Then it's a good thing we're practicing, right?" He grins. "Let's repeat this loop one more time and call it a day."

"Okay."

At the end of the loop, we stop, panting. I lean over to catch my breath and stretch my hamstrings.

Overhead, a deep voice drawls. "Hey, Liam, I thought you said you were in shape. Both your little sisters could beat you, and they're only nine and eleven."

I glance up, sweat dripping down my hairline, and brace my hands on my knees to support my ragged breathing. A tall man shakes his head at Liam. He narrows his impatient, dark hazel eyes, like a troubled prince in a fairy tale.

"I thought you wanted to meet for coffee, that you had something important to tell me," He quickly checks over his bike then leans it against his hip.

"I do." Liam wipes sweat off his brow.

"Okay." The stranger glances at me then looks away as if already bored. "Then why'd you bring *her*?"

Liam chuckles. "She's not a spy, you idiot. She's helping me."

"Oh, I get it," the tall man scoffs. "She's just another one of your stupid girlfriends."

"I am not!" I stand, hands balled on hips.

The instant our eyes meet, I notice everything about him: how one cheek has a slight dimple; how the sunlight catches on the green and gold flecks in his eyes; how his clothes are rather unusual for Panopticus. Where did he get them? Black combat boots, cargo shorts, and... No, it can't be—a green scrub top under an unbuttoned faded jean jacket.

He works in Plant Production.

"Oh, really?" The stranger examines me again, this time showing interest. "Then who *are* you?"

"I'm not even his friend. I'm his running partner," I stammer.

"He roped me into training for this race together..." My voice trails off. Why do I care what this guy thinks, anyway?

"What race?" he asks, his pretty eyes narrowing again.

I don't answer, going on attack instead. "How do you get away with wearing *that* if you work in Plant Production?" I motion to his ironically attractive outfit, my gaze catching on the well-defined musculature of his legs. My cheeks flush. Look at that gastrocnemius. What kind of workout does he do to get muscular calves like that?

He laughs. "You've got a problem with the way I dress?"

"No..." I pause, my thoughts muddled. "But I thought everyone who worked there had to dress the same."

He steps toward me to whisper, "If you make yourself a valuable enough player in the game, you can wear whatever you want."

He smells slightly sweet, like the foamy, rich soil Dad used for planting. My mind flickers back to helping him out on the Community Deck, dividing and repotting his giant fern.

Liam clears his throat, and I return to present day, backing up a step and struggling to get my heart rate under control.

"You weirdo." Liam punches the guy's shoulder. "Silvia doesn't want to hear all your stupid theories on life. Quit being rude."

He shrugs. "It's not rude to tell the truth."

"With you, dude, *everything* is rude." Liam laughs. "Ignore him, Silvia. That's what I do."

The stranger adjusts a setting on his bike. "So why did you force me to meet you here if you're just going to ignore me?"

"I need you to help me convince Mom about this race," Liam wheedles.

He groans. "What race? I don't know what you're even talking about."

"Are you two brothers or something?" I ask, interrupting what sounds like the beginning of a lifelong argument.

"No. Franco's just my cousin," replies Liam. "He's not cool enough to be my brother, and those two little sisters waiting at home to attack me are more than enough, let me tell you."

I crack a smile, imagining them pestering Liam, shadowing him from room to room. "I hope they give you as much trouble as you give me."

Franco raises a hand to cover a smirk. "Okay, I believe you now." His eyes catch mine as he jabs a thumb toward his cousin. "You're much too clever to be one of his girlfriends."

"Thanks a lot," mutters Liam.

"Do you work at Plant Production too?" Franco watches me closely as if puzzled. "You look familiar."

"Quit hitting on my running partner," grumbles Liam.

Hitting on me? Is he really doing that? I flush, suddenly worried that I might smell bad after our run. "No. Mortuary Sciences."

Franco raises his brows. "Then I was right. You must be smart. Are your parents doctors or something?"

For once someone is impressed by my job. That's a first. "No. My father's dead, and my mom plays the violin."

"Oh." The look of puzzlement returns to his face. "Is she any good?"

"Of course she is. She's Yoshe Wood."

His handsome jaw drops. "Then you're..."

Liam helps him out. "Oh, sorry, I never introduced you. Silvia, this is my cousin, Franco Harmon. Franco, this is—"

"Silvia Wood." Franco covers his eyes for a moment, his tone hollow. "Of course. I should've known."

"Why should you have known?" I ask.

"Let's go, then." Franco sets off at a fast pace, walking alongside his bike. "If you've got something important to say to me, Liam, I prefer we talk on the move."

Liam falls into step with his cousin. I lag behind, my tired legs as heavy as a thick wooden chair, wondering why he didn't answer my question but too tired to do much about it. Their conversation floats back to me on the early summer breeze.

"Why didn't you tell me?" Franco growls.

Liam shrugs. "What does it matter who she is?"

My steps pause. Why would Franco be so upset about who my mother is?

"Why do you want to be Chosen, anyway?" Franco snaps. "It's crazy. You want something without even knowing what it is that you want."

"To be Chosen is the greatest honor—"

Franco grabs Liam by both arms. "But what happens to the Chosen? Their families never see them again. Is that what you want to do to your mom and your sisters?"

I hurry to catch up but hang far enough back to stay out of Franco's way. He seems to get easily pissed about everything.

"But think about the possibilities." Liam grins, his face rapt. "The Chosen go to another Great City and get a good job."

"Why do they have to go to another city?" Franco asks. "Aren't there any decent jobs left in this one?"

Liam throws his arms in the air. "You're so paranoid, it's ridiculous."

Franco turns to confront me. "Why are you helping him with this...this joke of a race? I suppose you want to be Chosen too."

I take a deep breath, his intense gaze disarming me, making me tell the truth. "Well, my mom would like it. She wants me to be special." I blush at how infantile I sound, but something about Franco doesn't allow me to be any other way but honest.

"What's wrong with the way you are right now?" he asks.

I self-consciously cover my wrists. How could he possibly hit on the same question I often ask myself? Franco's dark eyes pierce right into mine, making me wish I could say something—anything—that would make him smile again. Why do I care if he's happy?

I clear my throat. "That's what I ask my mom, but ever since I tested into Mortuary Sciences instead of Plant Production, she's been on a mission to 'better my life,' as she puts it."

"Gotcha." He frowns for a second. "Family's important. The most important thing, really."

Avoiding his intense stare, my gaze descends to the collarbones peeking out of his scrub top. What lovely clavicles. I almost reach out and touch them.

What is *wrong* with me? I must be so tired from our run that I'm losing my mind.

"Okay," Franco says. "Fine. I'll take you."

"What?" I'm lost in his beautiful anatomy. "Take me where?" *What's he talking about?*

"Isn't it obvious?" His eyes widen. "I'll take you for a tour of Plant Production."

I struggle to focus. "Why?" Did I miss part of the conversation?

He cocks his head. "Don't you *want* to see it?"

"Yes, but—" I feel like a bouncing ball, trying to catch up to his next emotion. Friendly, angry, distressed—what's next?

"Then it's settled. You'll come tomorrow on my short day." Franco turns his attention back to Liam.

I stand in a daze. The outside world fades away. I get to see inside the greenhouses. I really get to see them. But why is Franco taking me? He's obviously not doing it just to be nice. *Nice* isn't really the right word for him.

"Silvia! Did you fall asleep?" Liam calls.

The guys are far ahead of me on the path. I hurry to catch up.

Franco elbows Liam as I approach. "Maybe she found out that you still play with dollies and is trying to ditch you."

Liam laughs. "More likely she doesn't want to hang out with you, the mad scientist, always thinking everybody is after your Top Secret super fruits and mega-vitamin vegetables."

"I've got more secrets than you'll ever dream of," Franco warns then turns to me. "But if you don't want to see my section of Plant Production, you don't have to. I just thought you might find it interesting."

"Yeah, I want to go." My eyes catch on the way his muscular shoulders (deltoids, trapezius) fill out his jacket. *Oh, do I ever.*

"That is, if it's okay with your mom." Franco pats his pockets, searching for something.

"It's my day off tomorrow, so she'll be fine with it." I don't have to ask her permission. I'm old enough to make up my own mind, thank you very much, even if *he* doesn't think so.

"Franco, you should work in Business Management like me," interjects Liam. "Don't you ever get sick of digging in the dirt?"

He shakes his head. "I've been there over ten years now, and it only gets better."

"Ten years?" I ask. That would make him at least twenty-five.

"Yeah." Franco reaches in a pocket and pulls out a small book. "I interned with the best. Now I'm—"

"The best?" Liam smirks. "You see, Silvia, my cousin holds a very high opinion of himself. Always has. Always will."

"Please shut up, Liam." Franco glares good-naturedly at his cousin. "What I was going to say is: now I teach my own interns." He turns back to me and places a small book in my hands. "Here, take this."

I glance down, hiding the blush that flares in both cheeks as his gentle touch sends a thrill up my bare arm. *Good grief—what is wrong with me?* The cover is hand-drawn, flowers spiraling along the border. I flip it open and scan the contents.

1. *Edible plants.*
2. *Poisonous plants.*
3. *Medicinal plants.*
4. *Plants to produce or dye clothing.*
5. *Plant proteins.*

"Is this my homework?" I ask.

Franco raises one eyebrow. "I didn't realize you were averse to learning."

"I'm not!" I flush even hotter. Now he thinks I'm lazy. "That's not what I meant at all. I *want* to read it." I hug the book close, struggling with embarrassment as we exit the park.

"It's a copy I made of the original. But I'd appreciate it if you took good care of it. I'll see you tomorrow."

"Where? When?" I flinch, hoping he doesn't notice the desperate tone in my voice.

He stops to think. "You belong to the 37th Street Gym, right?"

I nod.

"Then I'll meet you there at eight." Franco's gaze lingers on a group of people gathered together at the far end of the street. How I wish he thought I was that interesting. "Bring your bike."

"Um...I don't have a bike. I'm within walking distance of work, so—"

Franco frowns slightly. "You do know how to ride one, right?"

"Yes." Of course I do. Everyone gets taught in grade school. But I haven't ridden anything except a stationary bike for years now.

"Good. Because the monorail only goes so far. My station is ten miles past the last stop."

My heart sinks. Oh, no. This is going to be like treadmill versus road running. I am going to look like an idiot. And I might die, riding a bike that far.

Not sure which is worse.

"Okay. I'll meet you in front of the gym tomorrow at eight." I stretch my tired arms over my head, still clutching the plant book in my sweaty hand. "It's going to feel so good to sleep in my own bed tonight. I haven't been home in two days."

Liam snickers.

I flinch. "Wait—that sounded bad. I wasn't—"

Franco lifts up his hands in mock surrender. "Listen, it's really none of our business."

"Actually," Liam interjects, "I wouldn't mind hearing about fancy Silvia's nighttime activities."

Franco shakes his head at his cousin.

I'm blushing so hard; it's giving me a hot flash. "It's nothing like that. Seriously, you two, I was *working*. And Liam, don't act so suspicious. I already told you that I helped Gus bring the bodies to the Incinerator last night."

"Really?" Franco pauses. "I work in the Plant Production building right next door."

My stomach sinks. *That's* where we're biking to? "The roads out there are crummy."

"Does this mean you're backing out?" Franco asks.

I cross my arms. "No. I can do it."

"Don't worry, cuz." Liam smirks. "She'll probably kick your butt."

I seriously doubt this. Biking out there is not going to be easy. The only ass getting kicked will be mine.

9

I WILL REMEMBER YOU

I leave the guys, clean up, and hurry home. At the apartment, my mouth waters at the smell of lasagna coming from the kitchen. Mom must've really missed me.

"I'm home!" I drop my gym bag near the front door and head for the kitchen counter.

"Good." Mom hands me a plate.

I suddenly detect a faint scent of something unpleasant. My nose crinkles as I poke the lasagna with a fork.

"Oh, don't give me that face," Mom says. "You can't even taste them in there. I swear you can't."

"I knew it!" My fork stabs a pink gelatinous protein cube. It jiggles as I hold it in the air. I sigh and shake my head. "Such a disappointment. It's an insult to tomato sauce and cheese to hide these in there."

"You're too fussy for your own good. They're perfectly nutritious. And you need your protein if you're going to train for that race."

"They're perfectly disgusting." I remove the blobs and shove them to the side of my plate.

"Well, you can't blame a mother for trying." She takes a seat and starts eating without complaint.

"I'm sorry, Mom. I can't stand the feel of them. They're squishy and sticky. It's like eating glue. So gross." After my systematic dissection, I take my first bite of supper. "But otherwise, this is really good. Thanks."

She sighs, and I feel bad for a moment. It's not her fault, but swallowing down those plant protein cubes always makes me gag. She's tried everything. She's fried them, breaded them, and hidden them in hot dishes like this one. But it's no good. I can always find them.

"You know"—Mom holds a flier of race info, the bag open and perched at the feet of her chair—"it says in here that if you log enough miles on one of their running watches, you'll earn extra protein rations."

"What kind of protein?" I point my fork at the limp pink globules. "I don't want any more of this crap."

"It says *alternative* sources of protein." She shrugs. "Whatever that means."

"You've been through that whole race bag, haven't you?"

"Of course. You didn't tell me anything."

"That's 'cause I haven't had a chance to read half that stuff yet."

"Well, it was quiet here without you last night, so I had some time on my hands." Mom brushes imaginary crumbs off her lap. "Want to go shopping with me tomorrow morning? The cupboards are bare. I slapped this dinner together with scraps."

"I can't..." I pause, not sure she'll be happy or upset about my news. "I'm getting a tour of Plant Production tomorrow."

"Really?" Mom smiles, and I realize at once that she's gotten the wrong idea. "Are they considering you for a job?"

"No." I shake my head. "That's not it. I met someone today who works there."

"Are they an intern like you?"

"No, he's older." I avoid her penetrating gaze. "He's a relative of Liam's."

"Is Liam going too?"

"No." The thought makes me smile. "He's not interested in plants or dirt. He likes business."

Mom dabs her mouth with a cloth napkin. "Are you taking a tour with Liam's uncle, then? That's nice of him to take the time to do this."

"No. Franco's his cousin."

Mom raises her eyebrows. I should've known I couldn't con her.

"How old is he?" she asks.

I clear my throat. "Maybe twenty-five." Give or take a few years.

"Behave yourself, then. Maybe you can make a good impression. It would be good for you to get out of—"

"Don't say it. You know I like my job. Stop worrying about me so much."

She frowns. "I'll worry about you if I want to. You like that creepy job more than you should."

"It's not creepy. It's *interesting*. There's a big difference." I stuff lasagna into my mouth to stop myself from arguing the point any further. I'm tired of fighting about my job.

THAT NIGHT I can't sleep. Even exploring Franco's book on plants doesn't calm my mind. All I can do is think about the strange way he dresses and the odd things he said. My stomach flips topsy-turvy at the thought of spending time with him—alone—tomorrow. I really should get some rest. I'm running on empty after half my normal sleep last night, and that outdoor run today really took a lot out of me.

But it's no use. I roll to my side and fret some more. If I don't sleep, that bike ride is *really* going to kill me. I shake my head. Positive thoughts. I need some positive thoughts, here.

Nope. Not coming up with any.

My tired gaze lands on my father's photo across the room. The moonlight hides his expression, and if I didn't have the picture memorized, I couldn't tell if he was happy or sad. The memory trunk below his face is shrouded in dark shadows, but it calls to me just the same.

If I can't sleep, I might as well do something.

I throw off the sheets, flick on a light, then go sit cross-legged beside the trunk. With a creak, the lid opens. I line the items across the floor, one after the other. First to come out is Dad's old sweater, then his favorite childhood books, and a picture of his parents. Sometimes, I think I have to check everything to make sure something else hasn't gotten lost—or taken away, perhaps.

With a longing sigh, I hold up the red dress I so loved as a child. Dad never got a chance to return it. He died a week after that summer concert. When the Suits went through our belongings, asking me and my mother a million questions, they found the dress. Dad had forgotten to give it back, which was strange. He was usually more careful than that.

When one of the Suits tried to confiscate it, Mom went ballistic, screaming and hitting him. "Leave her alone! You can't take all her memories! How could you be so heartless?"

My eyes water as her tearful cries echo in my ears. I hold the dress close to my heart, wishing it still smelled like summer, popcorn, and my father. But only the recollection of a scent remains. Sometimes, it feels like Mom and I are still living in the past and half-asleep in the present. I'd like for today to be more important than yesterday. Not that I want to forget my father, I'd just like someone—or something—else to make me as happy as he did.

It's time for some new memories to be made.

Starting tomorrow.

10

I WANT TO RIDE MY BICYCLE

The red dress guides my dreams and cushions my sleep. The next morning, I wake on the floor, clutching the soft, luxurious fabric. Before Mom discovers I've been dwelling in the past, I tuck everything back into the memory trunk, pausing to gently fold the dress in half before hiding it away.

I rush my morning preparations, leaving the apartment before Mom wakes up. I speed-walk toward the 37th Northwest Street Gym. Thank goodness it's my day off. I can't wait to see Plant Production... and Franco. When I reach the last block before the gym, I slow my pace, hoping the sweat across my back dissipates before he arrives. I'm not sure what I'm more curious about: the tour of the Plant Production facilities or the tour guide himself.

Franco's nowhere to be seen when I reach the steps in front of the gym. I scan the walking and bike paths but can't find him. Disappointment pinches my gut. Did he forget about me? Or simply change his mind?

Five minutes later, he strolls around the corner with his bike, and my shoulders relax. He's wearing the same jean jacket and boots as yesterday, along with what must be his typical green scrub top and cargo shorts. My stomach flip-flops. I hope I don't embarrass myself too much today.

"You're on time," Franco notes. "Good."

He's so calm and collected, the complete opposite of me. My heart's racing, my palms are sweating, and he's acting like he's conducting a field trip for little kids.

Oh crap, that "little kid" is me!

I dart over to his side. "I still need to check out a bike." Why didn't I do that already? Why did I just stand around like an idiot?

Because part of me thought maybe Franco wouldn't show up, and I'd be left standing alone, waiting in vain.

"Okay," he says. "But hurry so we can catch the next monorail."

I rush inside the gym, check out a bike, then speed-walk back to Franco.

"Let's go. I think we can still make it." He hops on his bike.

I take a deep breath and push off on the pedals. As I follow in Franco's path, I wobble at first then straighten up after a block or two. At the end of the short trip to the monorail station, I'm pretty confident I can handle this biking thing.

Even though it's a Saturday, the station is busy. We weave through the travelers heading toward the last few cars. We crowd into the train, standing close to each other and holding onto the bikes.

As the train pulls away from the station, Franco turns to me. "Did you look through that book?"

"Yes. Where'd you get that, anyway?"

"I copied it, taking bits from lots of old books and putting them together. Back before the war, people hiked and camped for fun. All sorts of pocket-sized plant guides were written to help identify plants, what was safe or poisonous to eat. There were other books, too, on birds and such. Apparently, staring at birds was a big hobby for some people."

The train swerves, and Franco's arm bumps mine. I'm so distracted by the heat rushing to my face that I can't think of a reply.

We both remain silent for what seems like the longest pause in conversation in history.

Eventually, my mind clears enough to say, "Gus, my boss in Mortuary Sciences, has lots of state park maps on the wall of his office. I guess he'd be interested in this type of thing too."

Franco glances out the window. "Yeah. Maybe."

"So...what exactly are you in charge of at Plant Production?"

He smirks. "Are you worried I'm going to bore you?"

Heck, no. Furthest thought from my mind. I flush. "No. I was just curious."

"I'm in charge of a very exciting project at the moment: the hyper-production of fruits, vegetables, and alternative protein sources."

Oh no. It can't be. "Alternative protein sources? What does that mean, exactly?" I cringe. "You're not the one who developed those gelatinous protein cubes, are you?"

"No way." Franco chuckles. "I hate those things."

I breathe a sigh of relief. "For a second there, I worried they'd be your pet project and then I'd have to pretend to like them."

"No worries." He smiles. "I have nothing to do with them. And I won't make you eat anything unusual, either. I'm not that cruel."

All too soon, the monorail slows at the last stop. The robotic female voice announces overhead, "Last stop of the line. All Citizens must exit on the left side."

The brakes squeal, I pitch forward, and the train comes to a stop. We wheel our bikes into the warm sunshine. There's no Citizen Housing out this far. Only large, windowless buildings covered with large solar panels and construction sites as far as the eyes can see.

"What are all these buildings?" I ask Franco, but he's already jumped on his bike and taken off down the road.

"Ten more miles to go," he calls out over his shoulder. His wheels spin at high speed, leaving me in the dust.

You wanted to see the edge of the city, lady, I remind myself. *So suck it up and go for it.*

I pedal as hard as I can. Ten minutes in, my thighs are on fire, but I still haven't caught up with Franco. Plus, I'm so busy dodging potholes that I can't work up any real speed. Although this doesn't appear to be an issue for Franco. He fades away into a small dot far down the road ahead of me. I guess this explains his well-developed gastrocnemius muscles, biking twenty miles each workday. I start to worry that I'll lose track of him on this bumpy road. But he eventually glances back to discover what a bike-wimp I am and hits the brakes. I pretend to be focused on the potholes as he approaches. He slows as he reaches my side then turns around, so we're both facing the same direction.

"I guess cross-training isn't your thing?" he asks with an unexpected grin.

I return the smile, suddenly worried what my hair looks like. "Not really. And I haven't ridden anything but a stationary bike in at least five years, so I'm not very good at this."

"No need for *you* to apologize. I'm sorry I lapsed into autopilot back there. I don't usually have company on this part of the route, but we've got time; don't worry. Look, there's the start of Plant Production."

We pass row after row of greenhouses. I can't believe how many there are. Thousands of people must work in Plant Production. It can't be that difficult to get in—except for me, that is. As we finally near the end of road, the Incinerator unloading dock comes into view.

"Where do we park our bikes?" I ask, relieved to be done with the ride. My butt has fallen asleep.

"Why don't you hang out here, by the entrance in the fence? We'll walk our bikes down to my greenhouse in a minute." Franco frowns. "I need to talk to these guys first."

Grateful for a break, I stop the bike and lean it against the barrier, halfway between the Incinerator and the last green house. Feeling a bit stiff, I do a few stretches as Franco crosses the dusty lot and approaches the Incinerator workers.

"You again?" One of the workers raises his gloved hands. "What's wrong now?"

"I've told you a million times: your filters aren't good enough," Franco yells. "You're polluting the air over my crops. I can prove it. You're lowering my yield on corn and blueberries and—"

"Yeah, yeah. Take it up with The New Order." A worker waves him away. "Don't complain to us. We're not the ones who installed the equipment. We just run it."

"Have you no respect for the Citizens of Panopticus?" Franco gestures toward the smoke trailing out of the Incinerator tower. "Don't you care about the health of your family? Everyone eats what I grow. Do you want to give them cancer?"

The Incinerator workers walk away, shaking their heads and ignoring him.

I back into the fence, worried Franco's going to scream at me next for helping incinerate the bodies with Gus. But I told him that yesterday, and he didn't say a thing. Why is he giving these guys such a hard time, then?

Franco continues to rant. "Do you want your wife, your sister, or your daughter to get sick from the chemicals you're spreading through the air?"

When the workers continue to ignore him, he swings back toward the greenhouses, covers the dirt lot in a few steps, and greets me with a warm smile. "Ready for your tour?"

I fight the urge to jump back on the bike and pedal away. "Okay." I follow after him, wondering when Franco will turn into Mr. Hyde again. Is it possible he's even crazier than me?

Franco leads me to his office, which is just a table piled with both old and new books. He gestures toward a few hooks on the closest wall. "You can hang up your stuff over there." He takes down a long white lab coat and hangs his jean jacket on one of the hooks. On the collar of his jacket, someone has scrawled: *Property of Franco Harmon.*

Talk about multiple personalities. Now he's a third grader, and his mom put that label on his clothes. Or else he's afraid someone will take it. What a weirdo.

I hang up my windbreaker and trail after Franco into the bright lights of the green house. The walls are made of a light green, glassy material, and the air smells sweet and earthy, like flowers mixed with soil. Like home—or at least how home *used* to be. The ceiling is formed of clear pale green glass rectangles connected with metal brackets. Ceiling fans hang down every few feet, twirling lazily in the humid air. A million different plants surround me, and my spirits soar. I can't even identify most of them. My dad would've loved to see this.

The humidity hits me, and I push up my sleeves, but when Franco glances back at me, I force them back down. I don't want him to see my scars.

He leads me to a table surrounded by interns. In front of each intern is a tray of biodegradable planting pots, organic soil mixed with worm compost, and seedlings.

Franco turns to me with a question in his eyes. "Have at it."

No need to ask me twice. Dad taught me everything I needed to know about writing, reading, and repotting plants. I slip on gloves and dig in, putting just the right amount of each soil product in each pot, gently transplanting the seedlings, and then watering to encourage growth.

Someone whispers, "Isn't she going to wait for instructions?"

Franco watches me with arms crossed. "I don't think she needs them."

I don't look up until after I've finished the entire tray. My eyes widen when I realize none of the other students have even started. They all stare at me. Except for one. A skinny girl at the far end struggles to straighten a freshly potted seedling. With one wrong move, her whole tray goes crashing to the ground.

I flinch, expecting Franco to scream at her. Instead, he gently pats her shoulder as her eyes glisten with tears of humiliation.

"I'm so s-sorry..." she wails.

"There's no need to cry." Franco helps her clean up. "You'll get the hang of it in time."

A gangly guy next to me stifles a laugh as I puzzle over how Franco can be screaming one second and gentle the next.

"And for the rest of you," Franco's voice carries over the table, "ask Silvia what to do. She appears to have the exercise down pat."

I clear my throat then begin to teach the others. As we finish, I feel Franco watching me again. When I glance up, our eyes lock. He's studying me, but I can't figure out why. His gaze travels down my arms and pauses on my partially exposed wrists. I cover my scars and back away from the table.

He comes to my side. "They'll be busy for a while. Let me show you around."

Again, I play follow-the-leader with Franco, trailing along the tables heavy with growing foodstuffs. Raspberries hang on vines that climb on metal racks to the ceiling, see-through glass tanks reveal carrots and potatoes pushing through the dirt, and proud sunflowers tower as tall as the greenhouse.

"How did you know how to do that?" He gestures at the other students.

"We used to have a really sunny apartment...back when Dad was still alive. He taught me all about plants. Ever since I was four or five, he'd drag me to any government sponsored event that handed out cuttings. He showed me how to sprout them, what size pot to use, how much to water...everything."

"I used to work those events." Franco fusses with a blueberry bush, his eyes averted. "I might have seen you there."

"Really? Well, I guess I wouldn't remember you anyway. That was a long time ago...before Dad died. And now all the windows in our apartment face north, so we don't get much sun. All of Dad's plants died, so they ended up in the community compost pile. It broke my heart to dump them, but what else could I do?"

"I don't understand why you're not here," he says, turning to me.

"You're so talented. Why are you in Mortuary Science when you should be here?"

"That's funny. Gus says I should be in Medical School instead of Mortuary Science. You say I should be here. I guess the Occupation Exams aren't all they're cracked up to be."

He nods, his lips pressed tightly together like he's holding back words. A few stray hairs fall into my face, and I swipe them away. Franco stares at my suddenly exposed wrist. I yank down my shirtsleeve, but it's too late. He steps closer and takes my hand, then traces my scar with his finger.

I yank my arm away, heart racing. "Don't touch me!" It's bad enough The New Order thinks I'm crazy. That Mom is embarrassed by me. I don't need Franco judging me too.

"Why'd you do it?" Franco stares at me so intensely that I can't look away.

Again he wrenches the truth from me better than any Psychiatrist. "Because I didn't want to be here anymore, all right? I wanted to be with my dad instead."

My words hang in the air. I glance around as if the sky is about to fall. I just admitted out loud one of my most guarded secrets. Why didn't I keep my mouth shut like I usually do? I brace for Franco's response.

"What about your mom?" His voice is even-toned, but his jaw is clenched, and I can't tell if it's due to concern or pity. "Didn't you care what happened to her?"

My breath catches. It's like I'm back in Psychotherapy, except this time someone's actually asking all the right questions. I clench my hands, forcing myself to calm down. "Of course I care about my mom. And she and I have talked about this. We were both being selfish at the time, only thinking about ourselves and not being there for each other. Everything is better when one lives not only for oneself."

"You're quite the philosopher. Or did you read that on a propaganda pamphlet?"

My head spins. Is he being sarcastic or kind? "You ask too many questions."

His face relaxes into a smile. "So I've been told."

I cross my arms, careful to turn my inner wrists to the inside. "How about you let me ask the questions for a change?"

"Okay."

"Why'd you offer to show me around Plant Production? Did you owe Liam a favor or something?" Oh man, where did that question come from? Franco never should've mentioned my scars. That always sets me on edge.

He shrugs. "That's a fair question, and I've been too nosy. I asked you along because of your dad."

My eyes narrow. "Why do *you* care about my dad?"

Franco's smile falls. He pulls me deeper into the greenhouse toward the end of a row of sunflowers. We stand alone, separated from all other human ears.

He takes a deep breath. "My uncle worked with your father. He was killed in the same explosion."

11

HOT FOR TEACHER

Back at work again the following morning, I hum the haunting melody Mom practiced on her violin last night. We'd barely spoken after I got home, which wasn't all that unusual. Her tense face warned me to be quiet and give her the space she needed to focus on her music. Plus, I needed the time to process everything Franco had told me about his connection to the accident that changed my life. His uncle had died alongside my father. He knew what my family had been through. Franco was a genius. He'd described all of his many projects to me in detail. He was as smart as Gus. Almost.

Mid-morning, Gus clears his throat. "Silvia, is there a reason you keep repeating the same five bars of music over and over again? Or is this an evil plot to make me lose my mind?"

"I met someone." And I can't stop smiling, even though our main topic on the way home last night was my father's death. It should depress me, but it doesn't. Instead, I feel like I've finally got something in common with someone. And that someone is Franco. All I want is to see him again. Soon.

"I knew this would happen to you eventually." Gus sighs dramatically, reminding me of his past days in the theater. "I suppose this means it's all downhill from here. You'll float around in a daze, get sloppy in your work, and ruin my high opinion of you."

I laugh. "I promise I won't let it affect my job."

"Glad to hear it." He turns back to his autopsy. "Hand me a new scalpel. This one's dull already. They sure don't make things like they used to."

I scurry across the room, unwrap the foil protecting the blade, and hand it over.

"What's this lucky guy's name?" Gus waggles his unruly eyebrows.

"Nobody you know," I assure him.

"Maybe I should meet him. Make sure he's good enough for you."

I chuckle. "One of the things I always liked about you, Gus, was that you weren't nosy. So much for that, I guess."

"Since I don't have any children, I've got to be protective of somebody. You're always hanging around here, so it might as well be you."

"Okay, I'll tell you." I take a deep breath. "His name is Franco Harmon...but don't say anything to anyone because—"

The fresh blade clatters to the floor.

"What's wrong? Are you feeling okay?" I swoop down to gather the instrument then glance up at his pale face.

"Sorry about that. You have no—it's just—I'm sorry." Gus wipes his brow with the back of a bloody glove and takes a deep breath. "I haven't heard that name in a very long time."

"You know him?" I stand and set the scalpel holder on the tray.

"For a short time he was Ben's student. His prize intern, in fact."

My heart sinks. Poor Gus. I hate reminding him of his sad past. "He said he studied under the best," I murmur.

Gus smiles weakly. "Ben expected big things out of that boy. But that was many years ago. He must be..." His eyes widen.

"Yeah...a few years older than me." I shrug. "Please don't say anything to anybody. It's really just a stupid crush of mine. He did give me a tour of his greenhouse yesterday, though."

Gus raises his eyebrows. "And how did you like it?"

"Honestly, the interns there are only doing baby steps. I feel like I'm doing much harder work here. I think this job is *much* more challenging. And I like to challenge myself. I don't want to be bored all the time."

"Good. And you're right. Most of Plant Production is very menial work. Of course, I'm sure your not-so-young Franco has moved up in the ranks."

"Yes. He's in charge of quite a few projects."

Gus makes a silly face. "He sounds so *dreamy*."

I laugh. "That. And a bit mad. His mood changes 'faster than the weather' as my mom likes to say."

Gus focuses his gaze on the autopsy on the table. "I'm not following you."

"Well...the greenhouse he works in is located right next to the Incinerator. When we got there, he shouted at the workers about some pollution thing then turned around, all polite-like, and took me for a tour of the green house. One second he was flailing his arms and screaming, and the next, he was cracking jokes."

"How peculiar. Better get a new boyfriend."

"And I thought he'd be mad at me, as well, for bringing bodies to the Incinerator, but he didn't seem to care one bit."

"A little uneven personality, I'd say. You could do better."

"Then when one of his students spilled something, I braced myself, expecting the worst, but he was so kind to her."

Gus smirks. "Was she pretty?"

"Very funny." I shake my head. "I just don't get him."

"He sounds like a mad scientist. You'd better stay away."

I narrow my gaze at Gus. He almost sounds...serious. Why is he acting like this? Does it have something to do with Ben? I force Gus to look me in the eye. "Why do you say that? Is there something about him you're not telling me?"

He smiles serenely, an innocent look on his face. "No. Nothing comes to mind. Like I said, I haven't heard his name in years."

I shake my finger. "You promised to never sugar-coat anything and to always tell me the truth."

"In general, that is true. But keep in mind: it's impossible to keep every promise you make."

"Seriously, Gus, I trust you. Is there a real reason you don't want me to be friends with Franco?" I ask, hoping he doesn't have any actual objections.

"Not really." He sighs. "I just think he's too old for you. And maybe...too associated with the past. You need to move into the future, not dwell any more on what might have been."

"I agree about the future. And, as far as age goes, my mom thinks you're too old to be my friend too."

"Ha!" Gus laughs. "Good thing for me you never listen to your mother. But, truth be told, if you were my daughter I'd probably say the same thing."

"Don't worry. I'm not dwelling on the past. But I can't talk to Mom about the accident. Whenever I try she goes dark for days. I hate doing that to her. So it's nice to finally have someone to talk to whose life was turned upside down that day too."

Gus turns away from me. "Believe me, Silvia, you weren't the only one whose life changed that day."

12

(HE) BLINDED ME WITH SCIENCE

After work, I hurry to the gym to meet Liam for another run. I'm breathless with the possibility that Franco might be hanging out with him. I take the gym stairs two at a time, scan my card, and rush inside. Right away, I spot Liam loitering near the front doors, surrounded by pony-tailed girls and no Franco in sight. I sigh and swing my gym bag to my other shoulder.

Liam excuses himself from the crowd. "You ready to run?"

I snort. "Sure you want to leave your fan club?"

He laughs. "You bet. I've been waiting all day for this. So hurry up."

I change fast then meet him back at the front glass doors. Trying not to be obvious, I scan the room one final time in the fading hope that I'll find a too-old-for-me, split personality, handsome botanical genius. No such luck.

"Should we do the same route as the other day?" Liam adjusts his watch. "Get used to it before we go further?"

"Hey, wait." I point at his watch. "I want one of those too."

He grins. "So, you've finally seen the light."

I shake my head. "I'm simply interested in the extra protein rations. Where do I sign up?"

"See? There are benefits with cooperating with The New Order."

Liam leads me to the front desk where I rush through the paperwork as fast as I can, slap the GPS watch on my wrist, and head outside. Despite the long bike ride yesterday, my legs feel fresh today instead of tired. Now that we know the route, we run as one, moving in unison until we reach the park. Surrounded by the heady smell of lilacs, I glance over my shoulder, sensing someone is near. A dozen faces stare back, none of them familiar.

"Your head's spinning like a top," Liam pants. "What are you looking for?"

"Do you ever feel like you're being watched?" I whisper.

He shakes his head. "I should've known that you spending time with Franco was a bad idea."

My ears perk up at the mere mention of his name. I try to sound nonchalant. "Why is that?"

"Franco's a great guy. Don't get me wrong. I mean, he's related to *me*, how could he be anything but awesome? But, seriously, the guy is hyper-paranoid, conspiracy-theory, brainiac-scientist kind of crazy."

"Really? I didn't notice." Oh, yes I did. And Liam forgot to mention Franco's split personality.

Liam chuckles. "He always thinks someone's hurting his precious plants or after his top-secret scientific experiments or that the environment isn't clean enough to sustain human life."

I play Devil's Advocate. "And what do you think?"

"I think he worries too much. Life is meant to be enjoyed. That's why I'm training as hard as I can—with your help, of course—to win this race so my work ethic and athleticism are noticed by those who matter."

"You really think you'll get Chosen just by winning this race? That is, assuming you can win it. What if somebody's faster than you?"

We turn another corner and run under the cover of some shade trees.

"Nobody wants this more than I do," Liam says. "I've *got* to see what else is out there. Travel to all the Great Cities. See what life's like at the top. Don't you want more than you have now?"

I shrug.

He smirks. "Then what is it that Silvia Wood wants from life? Why are you training for this race with me?"

We pass by the open-air pavilion. A young girl watches us run by, her arm raised up to hold hands with her father. Her mother stands across from them, a camera in hand, and says, "Mila, look at me. Now smile!"

My breath catches in my throat.

That's what I want. My childhood. All over again—up until it abruptly ended eight years ago.

Liam interrupts my thoughts. "Hey, look who's here!"

I shake my head, my vision fuzzy for a moment, and I see *him*. Franco leans on the back of the refreshment stand, flipping through what I presume is one of his many treasured books. We turn in his direction and slow our steps. I'm immediately concerned that I may not have put on enough deodorant today.

Liam waves as we approach. "Hey, Franco. We were just talking about you."

Franco looks right at me. "Yeah, I bet you were."

My stomach performs a double flip. His gaze sets my face on fire. Yep, I definitely don't have enough deodorant on for this.

"You should join us tomorrow, man." Liam punches Franco on the shoulder. "You bike while we run."

Franco frowns at his cousin. "That sounds sort of lame."

"Come on," Liam wheedles. "We need a timer to tell us when to run up-tempo. I can't figure out how to set this watch alarm to ten-minute increments, and I'll lose focus if I have to keep checking the time."

"Yeah. We need you," I agree, jumping on board with Liam's

plans. Even if I have to be all sweaty and gross, I'll grab any opportunity to spend more time with my super-scientist crush.

"Fine." Franco sighs. "But we can't do this here in the Arboretum. It's way too crowded."

Liam glances at the crisscrossing walkers. "I suppose you're right. But where, then?"

I instantly devise a plan. "How about the road out to your greenhouse? It's ten miles long, and there's hardly any traffic."

"That's not a bad idea," Franco agrees. "But you'll have to get permission, of course."

"What kind of running surface is it?" Liam shifts from side to side to keep up his heart rate.

I have Franco's presence to do that for me.

"Gravel...with a lot of potholes," I explain.

"Okay." Liam wipes his brow. "That should be challenging enough. I'll put in a request at the gym."

"Just let me know when and where to meet you." Franco straddles his bike.

I tighten my ponytail, my mind racing in search of something to say to keep him around.

"What is *that?*" Franco grabs my wrist, looking at my watch.

Again, an electric shock jolts up my arm, but apparently I'm the only one who feels it.

"I thought you weren't going to wear one of these." He scowls.

Liam shakes his head. "Don't harass her. She's doing it for the extra protein rations. And she'll need them with all the miles we'll be logging."

Franco drops my arm like it's coated with poison. "I guess everyone has their price."

I flinch, trying to hide how much his words sting.

"How long will it take for you to get permission?" Franco asks Liam.

"Not sure." Liam scratches his head. "I'll ask as soon as we get back, so hopefully tomorrow."

"Let me know." Franco sets a foot on the pedal. "You know I'll always help you...even if I don't approve of what you're doing."

Frowning, I watch him leave, the back of his jean jacket shrinking in the distance. "Why is he so mad about this contest?"

Liam sighs. "Ever since my dad died, Franco's never trusted anybody outside our family. He can be overbearing sometimes, but he means well."

I bite my lip. "About your dad... I meant to bring this up earlier today, but it's not like it's a happy subject. Franco told me that your dad died in that big fire in the Wardrobe District eight years ago."

For a moment, Liam's eyes don't glow with their usual brightness. "Yeah."

I hesitate a moment before speaking. "Did you know I lost my dad in that same accident?"

Liam's mouth falls open. "No. I don't usually talk about what happened because then it seems like I'm just looking for sympathy. But I never knew—I mean, I never expected. Of course, so many people died—"

"Fifty-three." I hate that number.

He nods. "I've met a couple other people whose relatives died, but..." His eyes fall on my scarred wrists, but for once I don't flinch. I don't care that he sees them. He raises his gaze, his eyes questioning mine.

"Yes. I did it because I missed my dad. Don't you?"

Liam shrugs. "Lucky for me, after Dad died, I had Franco."

"You did?" This I've got to hear. I lean in closer.

"Franco saved our family. He gave us his rations. He'd already been working at Plant Production for a few years. He even lived with us for a while, so we didn't have to move into a smaller apartment. We were lucky to have him. He made sure I would be okay. And so I am. I've never felt deprived or"—he glances at my wrists again—"depressed or anything."

I flush. Too bad Franco doesn't want to be my knight in shining armor—or a shiny white lab coat. I could so handle that. Instead he makes me feel dirty for wanting more food.

"And I have two sisters, so we had each other," Liam continues. "You're an only child, right?"

I nod. "Maybe that makes a difference."

"Maybe. Plus my mom was really strong through it all. How'd yours cope?"

I blink back tears as painful images flood my mind. Every night, after Mom thought I was sleeping, she'd sob into her pillow, my father's picture in her hand. She never realized I could see through the crack in her bedroom door. I'd wait there in the hallway until she fell asleep then creep back into my own bed and shiver under the covers.

I straighten my shoulders. "Mom fell apart. I'm the one who had to put us back together."

"You?" Liam can't help but glance again at my wrists.

"Yeah. Me. That's why it took so long."

13

STOP MAKING SENSE

After logging a few more miles then cooling down with yoga, I shower at the gym and head for home. Our apartment is filled with the heady scent of tomatoes and melted soy cheese. Ever since Mom rejoined the Orchestra, she's been cooking up a storm. I take this as a good sign.

"Mom, I'm home," I call out.

"I'm in the kitchen." Pots bang and plates clank. She's really going all out tonight.

I let the gym bag slide to the floor and head in for supper. Mom's humming and smiling to herself. For a moment, I wonder if she's met someone new. Can people her age get crushes too? Why not? I guess. I want her to be happy, but part of me doesn't want her to forget about Dad. But then again, if Mom never moves on, she'll always be sad.

She pulls out two cloth napkins. "How many miles did you run today?"

"Nine. Trail running mostly, but some on the road."

"That's nine more miles than I'll ever run." She dishes up a spaghetti-style hot dish. "Dig in. Don't worry—there's no protein cubes. I used nuts this time."

"Franco says everyone will have fish soon. He's so smart about everything. He's even helping out on a huge hydroponics project."

"Oh, that's right. You had a Plant Production tour yesterday. How did that go? Do you think you could transfer there?"

I shake my head. "I don't think I belong there."

Mom pauses mid-step, holding a pot in the air. "Why do you say that? It's what you've always wanted, ever since you were a little girl. You and Daniel used to..." Her words stumble over Dad's name.

"I'm not saying I don't like plants. And the greenhouses were like a dream. Dad would've loved them, for sure. Beans trailing down from the ceilings next to sunflowers stretching two stories tall. It's remarkable."

"Then why don't you want to work there anymore?"

"I don't know." I shrug. "Honestly, I don't. I *should* want to work there."

Mom frowns. "I don't understand you."

"Maybe this won't make any sense to you, but it hit me while I was there that I didn't belong with all those shuffling white coats quietly working in the humid, hot air. It didn't feel like home to me. I belong in the cold basement of the hospital. With loud classic rock in the background. With Gus."

Mom snorts.

"Gus needs me. Besides, as marvelous as all of Franco's experiments are, the human body is the biggest miracle of all. I love everything about it. I mean, isn't it amazing how we're put together? How every organ has a job—the kidneys, the liver, the lungs? And most of the time they work in perfect unison."

Mom shakes her head. "But all the bodies you work with have already failed. Don't you find that depressing?"

"No. I don't find anything depressing anymore."

Mom picks up her fork. "Well, I'm glad to hear you say that."

I smile and dig in. All this running makes me ravenous.

Mom clears her throat. "And now I'd like to hear more about this Franco person. Is he giving Liam some competition for your attention?"

I try my best to avoid her pointed gaze. "He's been working at Plant Production for quite a while now. He's in charge of a lot of projects. He's really smart."

"He must be if you keep saying so." Mom raises her eyebrows. "What I'm more curious about is whether or not you think he's cute."

I clear my throat. "Very much so, I'm afraid."

She laughs. "You know, before I met your father, I had a crush on my Orchestra Conductor. And he was quite a bit older than I was."

"Not that ancient guy who's there now, I hope." I shudder, remembering how he used to glare at me as a child.

"Not at all! This was a different conductor. But then I met your father..." She sighs. "But enough about me and my foolishness. Let's focus on you. Tell me more about this Franco. He's not married, is he?"

"No. At least, Liam didn't mention it." The thought makes my heart sink. But surely it would've come up in conversation by now. Right?

"Then Liam knows Franco? Does he know him well?"

"Yes. They're cousins. In fact, it sounds like Franco took care of Liam's family after the accident."

"What accident?"

I cringe, realizing my mistake. Mom and I never talk about my tenth birthday, for good reason, and now I've brought it up without thinking.

I clear my throat. "*The* accident, Mom."

Her face pales. "What's Liam's last name?" she whispers.

"Harmon. Do you remember them?"

She stands up, pushing her plate and chair away. "I can't believe you're friends with *them*. Harmon was Dad's replacement. The whole reason your father died is because that man didn't show up for his shift."

My eyes widen. I don't remember any of this. "Are you sure that was the name of Dad's replacement?"

She glares. "It's not something I'd likely forget, is it?"

I scramble for the TV remote. "I'll bet there's a history file on the Memorial Service. It was sponsored by the government, after all." I click on the search function, punch in the date, and wait for the programs to load.

"Are you sure you want to see that?" Mom wrings her hands, hovering a few feet behind me.

I answer her question by clicking on the Memorial Service program option. Yellow words flash across a black screen.

In the worst factory accident of modern times, fifty-three people burned to death in the Wardrobe Production District. The New Order investigation found faulty wiring to be the cause. Due to this horrific incident, new regulations on the use of electric heat and lighting have been implemented. This will never happen again.

Mom exhales. "That's what they always say. So many empty promises."

Footage of the families follows. I remember the long line of mourners, every one of them wearing the traditional black scarf of mourning around their necks. A long row of sympathizers passes by, shaking everyone's hands, perhaps giving a quick hug. It's so odd to watch myself staring at the ground, shunning any gesture of comfort. That day, all my senses were muffled. I could barely hear my mother's voice or see her face. Everything was fuzzy. Even her hand, pulling me from place to place, felt fake.

But this time as I watch the footage, I'm fully awake. I search for one face in particular, to prove he's telling me the truth. First I see Liam, a young light-blond boy with a face smeared with tears. My heart reaches out to him. After the long line finishes, I see him walk slowly, hand-in-hand with one of his younger sisters who was just a toddler. They walk past me, my ten-year-old self. Liam pauses for a moment, his sister breaking away to move on ahead without him, then a younger Franco crosses the screen, puts his hands on Liam's shoulders, and steers him away.

I point. "That's him. That's Franco. And Liam is the blond boy in front of him."

Mom doesn't say a word. I feel bad for making her relive the worst day of her life. The names of the fallen roll across the scene. *Daniel Wood* and *Jack Harmon* jump out at me.

Mom's voice sounds hollow. "When your father called that night and said he'd be late, it was because Jack called in sick. Why would you call in sick and then show up afterward? And why didn't Daniel come home when his replacement arrived? Why were they both killed? None of this makes any sense to me. It never has."

14

HURTS SO GOOD

The next morning, Mortuary Sciences is swamped because we've taken on another hospital's deceased as well as our own. The other facility is having "technical difficulties," whatever that means. I'm actually grateful for the extra load. There are a million questions racing around my mind, but there's only one person I want to discuss them with—Franco. And I've no idea when I'll see him again.

Gus throws concerned glances my way all day, but I pretend not to notice. I'm thorough in my work, concise in my answers to his questions, and perform the clean-up routine with perhaps more vigor than usual. I feel slightly dirty, or tainted, and I don't know why. But I mean to find out.

On the way to the gym, I try to convince myself that it's silly to hope to see Franco today. After all, he can't bike with us until Liam gets permission, and who knows how long that will take? I idly wonder what would happen if we went out there and ran *without* permission. Would helicopters fly down at us from the sky like I saw in one of Gus's old movies once? Would the Suits haul us away like they did with that poor, pregnant red-haired girl?

Maybe I don't want to know what would happen.

Squelching one last silent plea for Franco to make an unexpected appearance, I reach the 37th Northwest Street Gym and race up the steps to the glass doors. Again, Liam is waiting for me, a sheepish look on his face.

He grimaces. "You're not really going to make me take this yoga class, are you?"

"You promised you wouldn't weenie out on me. Come on. We need to strengthen our core muscles just as much as we need to log miles."

He groans.

"Plus, it decreases our chances of getting injured." I start to bluff. "And last night I read an article about someone who won this race once, and she did yoga three times a week."

Liam's eyes widen. "Really?"

"Um. No. Actually, the woman came in mid-pack, but—"

Liam puts his palms together to beg. "Please don't make me do this. It's all girls in there."

"Yeah, girls wearing tight tank tops and clingy shorts." I put my hand on my hip. "But I thought you'd like that."

Liam grins. "Okay, you've convinced me. Now I'm looking forward to it."

"Promise you won't embarrass me in there."

He winks, and I hurry off to the locker room then pick up two yoga mats before hunting for him in the hallway. After passing the classroom twice, I duck my head in to find him chatting up the lithe, petite instructor. I roll my eyes, but at least it should be easier to get him in here next time.

Liam knows nothing about yoga, and this is a moderately advanced strength class. He teeters in tree stance. He wobbles in warrior. He falls down doing a backbend, causing a smattering of stifled giggles across the classroom. The instructor smiles and gives encouragement. She circles the room, assisting everyone, but pays particular attention to Liam, the golden-boy.

By the end of the class, Liam shows his exhaustion. He remains in Savasana—the corpse pose—long after most students have left the room. A slow, grinding noise emits from his throat.

"Are you actually snoring?" I poke him. "I can't believe you! How could you fall asleep in a room full of people?"

He doesn't move. But he opens one blue eye and moans. "You failed to mention how hard this was going to be."

I laugh. "You wouldn't have believed me if I told you."

"That's probably true." He slowly sits up. "And you profess to find this a relaxing stress-reliever?"

I smile. "Yes, I do."

"That's because nobody laughs at you."

"It was your first time." I hide a smirk. "Cut yourself some slack. Besides, it's so obvious all those females thought you were adorable."

He grins. "Told you I'm irresistible."

"Okay, Mr. Popular. Now all you have to do is win this race, and you'll have a ton more fans."

"And what about you?" He stands and rolls up his yoga mat.

I do the same. "I just want to make my mom happy. Plus I love running outside. I don't know what I'll do once we're stuck back on the treadmills."

"That will suck," Liam agrees. "Let's see if our permission to run out in the boonies came through yet."

We approach a perky woman working the front desk.

"Liam, I've been looking for you," she says. "Here's your permission slip. It says that since those roads are mainly commuter tracks anyway, your training team can use them between the hours of four and seven p.m. each day."

"That's excellent news." Liam flashes a winning smile. "Thank you."

"When can we start?" My heart races. Despite my growling stomach, I'm ready to go right now if it means I can see Franco.

"Tomorrow," Liam answers. "I'll meet you out front here. We'll take the monorail out, and Franco can bike back to meet us. Okay?"

"I can't wait." And, boy, do I mean that.

When I get home there's no warm meal waiting for me. Just leftover spaghetti dish—not a good sign. A crack of light shines around Mom's bedroom door. I peek through to watch her tuning her violin. When she starts to play, the mournful melody that pours from her soul through the strings stabs my heart.

This is probably my fault.

I back away from the door, careful not to make any noise. If I'm going to dig more into the past, I'll keep it a secret. She's been hurt enough as it is.

AT WORK the next day I barrel through a mountain of paperwork. Gus is too busy and distracted to send any more questioning looks my way, which is a relief. My limbs overflow with nervous energy. Every single part of me, starting with my brain, wants to see Franco. I need to get him alone to explain what happened with his uncle. I don't want to do this in front of Liam. I don't want to hurt him like I hurt my mother.

Work can't end fast enough. I rush to the gym, change, then use the steps outside the front door to help stretch out my calves.

"Why are you so hyper today?" Liam approaches from the street, squinting into the sunshine.

"I've just got energy to burn."

"Well, the workout I've planned should take care of that. I've already discussed it with Franco. He'll time us with his watch. We'll warm up for twenty minutes running easy then do ten minutes on, ten minutes off up-tempo run. That sound okay?"

I'm barely listening. "Fine. I'll run whatever you want."

We catch the next monorail out. It's standing room only, which is okay, but it makes it a little hard to stretch my quads and hamstrings. The car empties with each passing stop. Once we reach the end, the overhead robotic female voice announces: "Last stop of the line. All citizens must exit on the left side." We exit the train car. I do a few lunges, but Liam's eager to dash off.

"Didn't that yoga class teach you anything?" I tease.

"The earlier we start running, the sooner we get to Franco, and the faster we can get started on the pick-ups."

"Let's go." With the mention of his cousin, my interest in active stretching wanes.

We start slow to warm up. I glance over at Liam. "What does your family think about you doing this race—besides Franco, I mean?"

Liam smiles. "They're into it. My sisters are making race day posters. They've plotted out points in town where they're going to cheer me on."

"That's sweet." It occurs to me that I haven't even asked my mom if she's going to watch the race or not.

"How about your mom?" he asks.

"She's pleased I'm getting involved in activities, but I think she'd be happiest if I didn't work in Mortuary Sciences." I tighten my slipping ponytail. "How about your mom?"

"She's been cooking up a storm. And even though Franco doesn't approve, he's pitching in his rations again, so he's eating over most nights, and the dude never misses a chance to tell me I'm crazy for signing up for this race." Liam points at a speck far down the road. "Speak of the devil, I think that's him. That dot out there."

It's him all right. My heart rate climbs much higher than it should for the easy warm-up we're doing.

Franco reaches us and stops his bike. "Greetings, running freaks."

No jean jacket in all this heat. Just a T-shirt. *The better to see your muscles, my dear.* I flush at my own thoughts.

"Let me set my watch and we'll get started," Franco continues. "And, thanks to Liam's instructions, I now look like a weirdo with *four* water bottles taped to my bike."

Liam jogs in place. "We're ready for the first up-tempo."

"I'm game if you are," I profess, but my heart's racing way too fast as it is.

"Okay, give me a minute to get situated here." Franco starts biking alongside us. "And it's five, four, three, two, one—go!"

Liam takes off, and after a moment of confusion, I race after him. Heart hammering in my chest, I pull up alongside. We huff and puff, throwing glances at each other as we dash down the street. After a while, I wonder why we didn't start with five minute pick-ups instead of ten, but I don't give up. I match Liam, pace for pace, until Franco calls out, "Okay, stop!"

We slow to a crawl, breathing hard, and run easy for another ten as Franco hands us each a water bottle. Now we're passing greenhouses on the left. The sun warms my hair, and I tighten my ponytail, which loosened again during the run. The air smells different out here. Despite the greenhouses, it doesn't smell like plants. More like...ash. Something that burned a long time ago. Must be the Incinerator. No wonder Franco doesn't like it.

Long before I'm fully rested, I hand back the water, and it's on for ten again. I barely have a chance to throw longing glances at Franco, but the thought of him kissing me makes me push my legs a little bit harder. Can't think about that right now. Got to focus on these potholes so I don't wipe out and hurt myself. During the next ten minute slow down I peek at Franco, wondering what he'll say about his uncle. But then we're on again. And all my questions are thrown to the wind.

On. Off. On. Off. Exhausting and exhilarating at the same time. Halfway through, we turn around and head back toward the monorail station. Then it's on and off again for another five sets.

"That's the last one." Franco pedals alongside us. "It's time for a cool down."

Liam puffs. "I want to keep going." He pulls ahead.

Franco turns to me, narrowly missing a pothole. "How about you?"

"Not me. I'm good right here." I need to get him alone. I've got so many questions.

"I'm sticking with Silvia!" Franco calls out.

Liam waves back.

Franco hands me a water bottle. "What do you want to do?"

"Run a slow ten to fifteen minutes. And then walk the rest of the cool down."

"Okay, gotcha." Franco eases his pace.

"Thanks." I take a deep breath. It's now or never. "Actually, I'm glad I have you alone."

"You are?" He smirks, and the way he raises one eyebrow tugs at my heart.

"I want to ask more about your uncle," I explain. "And I didn't want to do it in front of Liam."

Franco averts his eyes. "Okay, then. Shoot."

"My mom says that your uncle was Dad's replacement that night." Despite the slow pace, my heart races while my voice remains even. "That the reason Dad didn't come home on time for my birthday was that your uncle called in sick. But then he was there after all. How could he be out sick *and* there at the same time? It doesn't make sense."

Franco clenches his hands. "That's a fair question."

"And?"

"He wasn't sick. I was there that night at Uncle Jack's apartment, so I know what happened."

My gut clenches. "Then why did he call in?"

Franco sighs. "Jack and Linda—that's Liam's mom—were fighting about the kids, or cleaning, or something stupid like that. Linda didn't want him to go in to work, so he made up an excuse. Then he felt bad and went in after all."

"That's it?" What a simple answer to a complicated question.

He nods. "That's it."

I frown. I want to say, "My Dad would be alive if Jack had gone in on time like he was supposed to." But that's too harsh to speak out loud. It's not like I'm the only one who suffered. Franco lost his uncle and Liam his father.

"Poor Linda," I say, finally. "I'll bet she wishes she'd kept fighting. Then maybe Jack would be alive."

We carry on in silence for a while. Franco opens and shuts his mouth a few times, but he never says a thing. I don't trust what I'd say out loud at this point, so I concentrate on my cool down. Eventually, I can't take the emptiness between us, and I grasp for a safe topic.

"Liam took his first yoga class yesterday."

Franco laughs so hard he has to stop biking.

I run in place, turning to face him. "Is it really that funny? It's a good thing to do."

"Okay. I'll try to control myself." He wipes his eyes. "I'm sorry to tell you this, but you've just given me hours of enjoyment. I'm going to torture him forever. You'll have to forgive me."

"Yoga isn't just for girls." I frown. For a grown man, sometimes he acts awfully immature. Is that normal?

"Of course not. But Liam swore to me, years ago, he wouldn't be caught dead doing any of those girly classes at the gym. This is priceless, really."

"I don't think I understand the relationship between you two."

"It's simple. We bug each other to death." Franco glances first at his watch and then down the road ahead of us. "It's already been ten minutes. Here comes Liam." He catches my gaze, suddenly serious. "And if I could ask you a favor, please don't talk about Jack around him, okay?"

"I won't," I promise.

Franco raises his voice as Liam approaches. "And over there's the hydroponics project. I'll have to bring you there someday. We didn't get a chance to go through it last time."

"Why's it so far away from your other projects?" I ask, playing along. "Isn't that inconvenient?"

He shrugs. "It was the only greenhouse available when we

started. It's only a hassle during the winter months when travel sucks."

Liam stops in front of us. "Don't tell me I'm going to have to listen to all this scientific crap every time the two of you are together."

Franco tosses me a secret smile, then dismounts from his bike. "Man, my muscles feel tight. And I wasn't even running. Hey, Silvia, since you're the yoga expert, what are some good stretches for biking?"

"It depends. Where are you stiff?" *Oh no. Please tell me I didn't just say that out loud.*

THE SECOND we get back on the monorail, Liam collapses on the nearest open seat. The car is mostly vacant since rush hour is over. Franco stands nearby, steadying his bike with one hand. I lean against a support pole and stretch my quads.

"Oh, man. I've never been more tired in my life." Liam moans and closes his eyes.

Franco smirks. "I told you running this race was a stupid idea—on so many levels."

After checking that the seats behind me are empty, I lunge forward to stretch my hip flexors. Upon rising, I find Franco's eyes upon me.

"So, yoga goddess, what's that pose called?" he asks.

My cheeks blaze. "Dragon."

"Dragon, huh?" Franco keeps watching me. "Show me another one."

Feeling like an idiot, I draw up my foot to my inner thigh then raise my arms in the air, hoping the train doesn't make a sudden sharp turn and topple me over.

"That one must be called music box dancer," guesses Franco.

"Nope. Tree." I put my foot back on the ground.

"You don't look much like a tree, and I should know. I work in Plant Production." Franco kicks at Liam's foot. "What do you think, Mr. Yoga? I heard you took a class yesterday."

Liam opens one eye to glare at me. "Traitor."

"There's nothing wrong with yoga," I argue.

"Unless you're a boy," interjects Franco.

"Don't be so closed minded. Saying things like that will only make it harder to convince Liam to go with me."

"I'll make you a deal: if you've ever been to a yoga class with more male than female students present, I'll take it back. Now, tell the truth. Has that ever happened?"

I pause to think. "Okay, you're right. It's never happened. There's only a few guys present, if any."

Franco nods. "I told you."

I narrow my eyes and point at him. "But just to play Devil's Advocate, did you know that there are now twice as many women as men working in Plant Production?"

A slow smile crawls across his face. "Yes, I did notice that."

Liam smirks. "So how come you still can't get a girlfriend?"

Franco glares at his cousin.

I'm very glad to hear this but keep talking to hide my joy. "So, by your reasoning, if yoga is just for girls, due to female to male ratio, then so are the Botanical Sciences."

"I stand corrected." Franco mock-bows. "But let me assure you that you'll never get me into any yoga classes."

"You're missing out. And speaking of that, Liam, you should be stretching right now." I bend over to loosen my hamstrings then keep readjusting my stance because I feel self-conscious about shoving my butt in the air. Before I can really get a good stretch in, I stand to avoid the whole issue altogether. "You're going to cramp up from the lactic acid, plopping down like that after a hard workout."

"I'm curious about something, Silvia." Franco smirks. "How do you seem to know so much about running? Poor Liam here knows absolutely nothing."

I put a hand to my hip and lean to the side, trying to stretch my IT bands as inconspicuously as possible with Franco's gaze still on me. "Whenever we're slow at work, Gus lets me surf the Archives Files. I found a lot of info in there when I first started running."

"I haven't been down in Mortuary Sciences in years." Franco runs a hand through his hair. Part of me wishes I could do the same.

Wait a minute.

My eyes widen. "You mean you've been there?"

"Sure. Sometimes I'd ride back into town with Ben after work. When he first got sick, Gus secretly asked me not to let him bike back to the monorail alone. Gus was worried Ben might take ill. Of course, I never let on that I was babysitting him because he would've gotten grumpy about it."

"What was Ben like? I'm kind of sad I never got to meet him."

Franco smiles. "Quiet. Soft-spoken. A complete genius."

Liam scoffs. "Idol worship. Don't get him started. When Franco first got that internship, Ben was all he talked about."

I chuckle. "Mom complains I talk about Gus too much too."

"Maybe you just like your job," says Franco.

"She also thinks I should make more friends my own age. She says Gus is too old for me." I cringe. Why on earth did I say that? No need to remind Franco of our age difference.

"Hey, I'm your age, and I'm your friend," says Liam. "You should introduce me to your mother. That should get her off your back. I tend to make a good impression on people."

Franco laughs. "Or so you think, Romeo."

"It's true, and you know it. Everybody's mom loves me." Liam stands as we near our stop then cries out, grabbing at his right calf. "Holy crap! I can barely walk."

"Silvia warned you to stretch out your gastrocs," Franco mocks him. "This is your own fault, buddy." He winks at me.

My stomach does a backflip. How adorable. He just called the gastrocnemius muscle the "gastrocs."

"Seriously, Silvia," Liam pleads. "Tell me what stretch to do and I'll do it."

"Too late." Franco heads for the door. "This is where we get off. Let's go."

I help Liam limp off the monorail. Once we get outside, he stops and leans against a railing, breathing hard, his face pale.

Franco waits with his bike.

I step next to him to whisper in his ear. As I lean in, the smell of plants and earth added to something musky and male almost overwhelms me. I take a shaky breath. "I think Liam's really hurting. I don't know how much farther he can walk."

Franco sighs. "Fine. Let's take him up to my place, then. I only live a few blocks away."

"You lead the way. I'll help him." I scurry over to Liam's side before Franco can change his mind. Good timing for Liam to cramp up. Now I get to see where Franco lives.

Liam limps the five blocks from the train station to the apartment, leaning heavily on my shoulder the whole way.

Franco strolls alongside, rolling his bike down the walkway. "Liam, you big wuss. The only way you'll ever win that race is if Silvia carries your sorry ass across the finish line."

"Oh, shut up and leave me alone." Liam groans as he gimps up the three steps into the lobby. "Thank goodness we're here. Please tell me the elevator is working today. I can't climb any more stairs."

Franco chuckles as he locks his bike onto the first floor bike rack. "Sure thing, wimpazoid."

He pushes the "up" button by the single elevator.

The doors slide open and we squeeze inside.

Liam groans. "Careful. Careful."

"You're pathetic." Franco shakes his head. "Silvia, could you hit floor eight, please?"

"Sure." I press the button. Eight just became my new favorite number.

Franco digs out his keys as the elevator slowly slides upwards.

"Floor eight. Doors open," a robotic female voice instructs from overhead.

"Hang a right," Franco says.

Liam and I lumber after him down the hallway. The floors are dark laminate, the walls whitewashed, and the trim as dark as the floors. Very sterile-looking. The smells of spicy food and old handkerchiefs linger in the air. Franco's already at the far end of the hallway, unlocking his door. I've never been so excited to see where someone lives. The wooden door swings open, and I peek inside.

"It smells like the greenhouse in here," I exclaim.

I wander in, shove the whimpering Liam in a chair, and marvel. The room is crowded with plants. African violets perch on every available surface. Flowers of pink, purple, and white peek out between lush, green leaves. Long chains of Pothos plants trail along bookshelves, over picture frames, and around the arch of a second window on the same side.

"This looks like my old apartment from when I was a little girl. It's not shaped the same or anything, but you have such wonderful light." I'd love to live here.

"Yes, I love the light in here. In a few hours, you can watch the sunset out that window." Franco points past the micro-kitchen tucked into a corner on the left.

Brushing up against the cupboards is a huge Ficus tree filtering bright sunlight from a large, square window through its green, diamond-shaped leaves. It shades a round table covered with piles of papers.

Liam moans as he massages out the knots in his calves. "This running business is hard work. My legs are killing me, and now I'm starving. You got anything to eat around here?"

"I'll see what I have left." Franco heads to the kitchen cupboards.

"I'll clear a space for you to eat," I say.

Using any excuse to snoop, I stack the papers that are strewn across the table into a pile to make space. There are dozens of elaborate botanical illustrations done in pencil.

I hold up a gorgeous drawing of bee balm. "Franco, the detail here is amazing. How did you learn to draw like this?"

"Wait a minute!" Franco hurries over and grabs the sketches.

I catch a fleeting glimpse of the image of a girl, but it's gone before I can tell who she is. All I see is her ponytail before he whisks the drawings away to another room.

15

WHO'S THAT GIRL

The brief glimpse of the girl's ponytail haunts me. Who is she? An old girlfriend? Or, even worse, a current one Liam doesn't know about? I need to find out more about this mystery girl. I scope out the apartment, starting with the long row of hooks near the entrance. A sweatshirt and Franco's trademark jean jacket hang from the wall. No sign of a female presence there. A walkway between the round table and a couch leads to a curtained-off area where Franco stashed the pictures. Presumably, his bathroom and bedroom are back there.

Not wanting to be obvious, I wait to ask permission to use the bathroom. Plus, Liam is miserable and needs babying.

Franco gestures toward his whimpering cousin. "Silvia, he's driving me nuts. Can you fix him please?"

"He needs yoga and salt." I frown. "But I don't know how long it will take for the cramping to go away. Liam, come here. You need to stretch your legs out and move around a bit."

I spot a large, heavy book on the floor. "Franco, can I use this?"

"Use whatever you need," he says, digging in a cupboard. "Just get him to stop whining."

"Take off your shoes, Liam," I instruct. "And put your toes on this book. Here. I'll show you." Standing tip-toe on the huge text, I lower my heels to the floor, leaning with one hand on the table for support. "That will help stretch out your calves. Now you try it. But go slow, 'cause it might hurt."

Liam moans as he does the same thing, his legs shaking. "Man, this sucks."

Franco sets out soy peanut butter, a few crackers, and orange juice. "I can't believe you're sweating all over my best Plants of the World book."

Liam shrugs. "It was either that or use it as a doorstop."

Franco scoffs. "You certainly would never read it. And after you're done dripping on it, it will smell too bad for anyone else to, either."

Liam stops stretching and sits down to eat.

I tap him on the shoulder. "You should stand."

"Seriously?" Liam asks. "I'm exhausted."

"Don't you think you should listen to her?" Franco sniffs his book then tucks it away on a tall bookshelf near the curtain on the far end of the room. "You both did the same workout. You're dying of pain, and Silvia's fine. She obviously knows what she's doing."

"Fine. You win." Liam stands and leans on the table, stretching from side to side in between bites.

Franco slides the crackers toward me. "Silvia, are you hungry? Help yourself."

"Yes." Liam chuckles, a few crumbs collecting on his lips. "These stale crackers are *awesome*. You wouldn't want to miss out."

Franco fake-punches Liam's shoulder. "Whiny-baby beggars can't be choosers. Besides, all my good rations are at your house now."

"Quit punching me," Liam grumbles. "You're such a loser."

"I'm not the one crying like a baby."

The two of them begin to swing and duck, mock fighting like idiots. I don't understand the male species. At all.

I back away from them, glancing back at the curtain. "Thanks for the offer, but I don't need any crackers. But I might need to...um...use the facilities before I head home."

"Go ahead." Franco points toward the curtain. "It's through there. Down the hall on the left side. You can't get lost. I guarantee it."

Like a detective in an old movie, I narrow my eyes as I pass through the curtain. Back here, the air smells of soap and old paper. Stacks of books line the dimly-lit hallway. A closed door is on the right. Probably his bedroom. The bathroom door is cracked open.

I go inside and pull on the overhead light. A quick sweep of the room reveals that the pictures aren't in here, which is to be expected, I guess. It's a Spartan bathroom, just a white pedestal sink and toilet on the right with a shower tub at the far end. A small window, high up on the left wall, lets in light. A medicine cabinet hangs over the sink. I turn on the water to cover the noise of my snooping and open the cabinet.

Toothpaste. A hairbrush. Floss. A comb. I examine every shelf. No tampons or other sanitary products. That's a good sign. I remember Chrissy Chang, one of Mom's work friends, who gave me dating advice back when I was probably fourteen or so. Chrissy had broken up with her longtime boyfriend and showed up at our apartment, seeking a sympathetic ear.

While Mom gathered blankets and a pillow, I perched next to Chrissy on the couch, handing her tissues.

"Silvia, listen to me," she advised between sniffles. "If you're ever interested in a guy, make sure to keep your eyes open. Check the shelves in their cabinets. Check their drawers. They're probably hiding something. Don't assume that things are as they appear on the surface."

Then she burst into tears, wailing something about the bedroom. At that point, Mom sent me to my room with strict orders not to come out until she gave me permission. So, it's Chrissy's fault I'm snooping. I'll blame her.

I shut the medicine cabinet, and that's when I see them: four toothbrushes hanging from the rack on the wall. One of them is pink. Another one is purple. The other two are different shades of blue.

BANG. BANG. BANG.

The door shakes, and I jump back a foot, about all the space I have without hitting the wall.

"Are you done in there?" Liam calls from the hallway.

"Almost!" I turn off the sink and open the door, making a big show of wiping my hands on a towel.

"Okay. You might want to leave...now." Liam pushes me out and slams the door shut. "And *don't* come back."

I grimace. Yep, I really don't get boys. They don't even try to hide how gross they are.

Back in the hallway, I notice that the door to Franco's room is now open. I step further into the hallway, trying to peer into the bedroom. Just as I get a good look into the room, Franco appears in the doorway. I stop short. Busted! Oh, crap.

"Hey, Silvia, come here." He waves me into the room. "I want to show you something."

"You do?" Seriously? He's *inviting* me into his bedroom?

He digs in the top drawer of an old dresser. "Yeah, but I gotta find it first." He yanks out a clean T-shirt and changes right in front of me.

Pectorals. Biceps. External obliques. Muscles flexing and stretching all over the place. My eyes widen at the beautiful anatomy lesson. As his shirt drops down to cover his perfection, Franco turns away to shuffle through various stacks of papers and books on yet another bookshelf across the room. I try to slow my breathing and calm my over-stimulated heart.

After a few minutes, Franco hands me a glossy piece of paper. "Here it is. I was beginning to think I threw it away."

My hand shakes slightly as I take the flier.

"It's all about the Citizen Race for Glory," Franco explains. "For some reason, The New Order makes a huge fuss over this stupid thing. There's a big awards festival after with a dinner and dancing.

And over at the library, some kids built a huge model of the race out of recycled materials."

My heart chills. "The library?"

"Yeah. Wanna go see it? It's supposed to be pretty neat. Plus, it might help you strategize for the race—you know, picture it in your head."

"I..." My hands clench the flier, which, all of a sudden, feels like a weapon. "I haven't been to the library in years."

Franco raises his eyebrows. "Really? You seem like the type who likes to read."

"I do. In fact, I used to spend a lot of time there. But..." Since it's summer, I no longer have sleeves to pull down and hide my scars, so I cover my wrists with my hands.

Somehow, Franco understands. "That's where it happened?" His hands cover my futile attempt to hide the past. He gives my damaged wrists a gentle squeeze.

I nod, tears threatening to form. "On my birthday. When I was eleven."

He exhales. "Do you want to talk about it? I don't mean to force you, but I'm willing to listen if you want."

Again, I feel the need to tell him everything. With everyone else, I always feel the opposite. But he's different. And so I begin...

16

UNTIL I FALL AWAY

"I used to love the library." I envision the endless shelves of books, the colorful paintings of famous fairy tale characters in the children's corner. "After Dad died, I spent every weekend there. It was safe."

Franco tenses. "Safe? From what?"

"The Suits." I tremble at the memory.

Franco eases me onto the corner of the bed. "Just sit down. It will be okay."

My legs collapse beneath me. "You know who I mean, right? Solid black suits. Crisp white shirts. Short hair, practically down to the scalp. And glasses, always with black glasses. They can't all have bad vision and light sensitivity, right? It's about intimidation."

"Yeah, I know who you mean." His eyes flash, and I detect hatred in their depths. Then he blinks, and it goes away.

"Then you know about the questions."

Franco takes a deep breath. "What did they ask you?"

"About Dad. Over and over again. They asked about meetings, and names, and papers."

"What did you tell them?"

I narrow my eyes. "I told them to go to hell."

"You told them...to go to hell? Weren't you just a kid?" Franco releases his grip on my wrists. "I mean, I realize you're still a kid, but—"

I stand, brushing him away. "I'm not a kid."

Franco holds up a hand in supplication. "I'm sorry. I didn't mean it like that, but...that's so *bold*. Weren't you scared of them? I mean, how old were you back then?"

"Ten." I put my hands on my hips. "Because I'm eighteen now. Got it? I have a full-time job, and I'm *not* a child."

"I said I was sorry." Franco pats the bed beside him. "It's just that I don't understand. You tell the members of The New Order to...well, basically, to go screw themselves—which is amazing. But if you had such courage, then why did you..."

I shudder, my eyes filling with unwelcome tears. "Because they kept coming back." I sit down, my legs weak again. "I thought they were done with me, that they'd leave us alone after everything that happened. But they came back and ruined the one place I felt safe."

Franco hands me a tissue and leans against my arm. He feels warm. "Why don't you start there?"

"On my birthday? A year later...when I was eleven?"

"Yes." He runs a hand through his hair. "Tell me everything."

Franco's room fades away. I see my apartment, the cramped one we've been forced into. Plants with limp, yellow leaves languish on the counters, dying for light. It's my eleventh birthday. I get my own breakfast like I've done every day since Dad's death. Mom only picks at the food I place in front of her as an afterthought. Eats only enough to stay alive. After I finish, I shuffle over to my mother in stocking feet. She's only bitten off the corner of a single slice of toast. She didn't even get as far as the jam.

"Mom?" I shift my feet.

"Hmm." She stares out the window like she does every day since Dad died. She's stopped working. Her violin gathers dust in the corner. She ignores everything—and everyone—including me.

I do the laundry, the dishes, and make each meal the best I can. All she'll do is sit there.

"Mom, it's my birthday."

"Hmm." Her hand floats back to pat my arm, but she never even looks at me. "I know. Happy birthday, dear."

Of course, my birthday also means the one-year anniversary of my father's death, but for days, even weeks now, I've been hoping she's planned something. A cake, a trip, something special. So we can set everything behind us and just be happy, even if only for a day.

"What are we going to do for my birthday?" I ask.

She sighs, her face still turned away. "What do you want to do?"

Disappointment pierces my chest. She hasn't planned anything. She really doesn't care about me anymore. This day will be like any other. I say nothing because I know that, if I speak, the tears will start falling. If I cry, Mom will walk away, go in her room, and shut the door. Then I'll be even more alone.

"Why don't you go to the library?" she offers. "You like it there. You could spend the whole day reading books. It would be fun."

"Are you coming with me?" I wipe away a stubborn tear.

"Why would I come? It's a children's library. There's nothing there for me."

I pack a sandwich in my backpack and leave her sitting in the window seat, knowing she'll still be there when I return. I walk the few blocks to the library alone, say hello to the librarians who know me by name, then run my fingers down the aisles of book titles, searching for something I've never read before. After I find a small stack, I choose a quiet corner, set the pile beside me, and get lost in another world. Some place better than mine. I stay in that same spot all morning, eat my lunch, and have started on a new book when I feel a hard tap on my shoulder.

I glance up.

It takes a moment to focus in on the dark glasses. There are three Suits this time. They form a semi-circle, hemming me in. The librarians whisper in the background, hovering together, staring as the Suits shatter the quiet comfort of the library. One of the Suits steps forward and leans down, his black glasses filling my line of vision.

"Silvia Wood?" He growls in a heavy, almost inhuman voice. His breath smells like metal and mint.

I don't want to answer, but I have to. "Yes, that's me."

"Come with us," he orders.

The other two grab my arms and lift me onto my feet. Books drop to the floor. They drag me across the room, my toes barely touching the ground.

At first I assume they're taking me to the elevator, but they step just to the side, insert a metal key, and unlock an almost-hidden door. It's so smooth you can barely detect the outline. I've never noticed it before. They yank me inside.

It's another White Room. Like all the others.

White ceiling. White floor. Mirrors on all sides. Blinding light.

A chair in the middle, which they shove me into.

"Do you know what day this is?" the head guy demands.

"Yes. It's my birthday."

CRACK!

My cheek stings after he smacks me across the face. But I smirk at them instead of crying. My hate is greater than my pain.

"Show some respect," he growls. "It's the one-year anniversary of the accident claiming fifty-three lives—all lost because of your father."

It takes a moment for his words to hit me. "What did you say?"

"Our investigation revealed that *your father* caused the explosion. He was a rebel, working against The New Order. He was responsible. He caused the deaths of fifty-three people and the endless suffering of their families. It was only due to his own stupidity that he died during the explosion. He planned it so that he'd be gone while the others suffered at his handiwork, but he didn't leave in time."

The room spins. These damning words hurt worse than any slap to my cheek. I turn inward, blocking everything out. Even as they scream in my ears, the Suits fade away.

Instead, I see my birthday cake, left uneaten. Mom dancing with me, singing "Happy Birthday," interrupted by Dad's phone call telling us he'd be late. Waiting for hours for his return. The loud knocking at the door just before the Suits barged in, yelling questions, going through our things—throwing them around, breaking many of them. Mom leaning against the wall, almost comatose. Me running around our disheveled apartment, hollering at the Suits to go away.

Then they pulled out my red dress.

Mom flew across the room, ripped it out of their hands, and screamed in a strange, high-pitched voice. "Leave her alone! You can't take all of her memories! How could you be so heartless? It's all she has left!"

And that was the last time she'd shown any interest in me.

Everything has been gray from that point on. The sky is gray. The light in the apartment is gray. And Mom's face, once so lovely, is drawn and gray.

And this is how it will always be.

It will never get better.

And it's all my father's fault, or so they say.

It's hard to know what's true or false.

The Suits surround me on every side. My head swims. I can't stay here in this horrible white room. I need to escape from their scowling faces, their accusations, and their lies.

I struggle to my feet. "I have to use the bathroom."

They shove me back into the chair, skidding it halfway across the room. "That's all you have to say? Tell us about your father. Tell us everything you know. We know you're covering for him. We'll beat it out of you if we have to."

"All you'll get is pee all over your clean floor if you don't let me use the bathroom," I warn.

The Suits argue. One gestures at another. "Take her, then. And hurry."

"Thank you." I smile, knowing I'm not coming back.

I walk calmly to the bathroom, lock the door, and hunt for an escape. All I find is my face in the mirror. I grab the metal chair in the corner of the room and smash it against my reflection.

My face shatters.

Voices yell in the hallway.

The doorknob rattles but holds.

Shards of glass scatter across the floor.

I grab one and plunge it into my flesh. The pain will rescue me.

They aren't going to get me. I'll fly away. Any way I can. Even if it kills me.

Warm blood spurts over my hands.

I slide to the floor.

The room turns so cold.

I tremble.

It's not like Mom will even notice I'm gone.

17

(MY) LIPS ARE SEALED

"And then I woke up in the hospital."

Back in the real world of Franco's apartment, I take a deep breath and focus on the books on the shelves, a lone sock stuck in a corner, and my clenched hands. Franco remains wordless, his face a mask of guarded inexpression. I avert my eyes, fidget with the bedspread, and a stuffed toy shaped like an elephant falls onto the floor.

That's strange.

I turn to ask, "You sleep with stuffed animals?"

His face relaxes. "No. That's not mine. Sometimes the girls stay over if Linda works the night shift. I don't think you've met them yet, have you?"

"No, I haven't. But why don't they stay home with Liam? I mean...not that it's any of my business or anything."

He shrugs. "Sometimes he's busy. And they like it here." He waves to his room. "I let them stay in here together, and I take the couch."

I stare at him. He really did save Liam's family. He does a lot for them.

"So, you believe me about the toy, right?" Franco smiles.

"Yes." I smile back. Thank goodness I haven't forgotten how, even after reliving my eleventh birthday. "Of course."

He chuckles. "Well, for a moment there, you didn't look so sure."

All of a sudden, I realize how close we are sitting together, and this renders me silent.

Franco clears his throat. "If you don't mind me asking, what happened next? I mean, once you got to the hospital."

I frown. "They put me in 'intensive treatment for depression,' or so they said. But since then, I've read several Psychology texts, thanks to Gus, and I don't think those doctors were the real thing. I think they were still the Suits, dressed up like psychiatrists instead."

Franco's eyes narrow. "Why do you think that?"

"Because they asked all the wrong questions, like: 'Why can't you accept that your father did this?' and 'Could you have done anything to prevent this from happening?' or 'Why won't you answer our questions? We're trying to help you.'"

I stand and pace the room. "I mean, why would they ask stupid crap like that? Once in a while they'd ask 'and how does this make you feel' questions, but, even then, it was always about my dad. Never about me and my mom—which was the real problem."

Franco rubs the five-o-clock shadow on his face. "How did your mom react when you tried to kill yourself?"

"Well, she finally woke up, which was good. But then she went into hyper-drive, always worried about everything. At the hospital, she thought they were feeding me too much broth. Once I got home, she would go into a total panic before each appointment that we were going to be late or something else as equally stupid."

Franco watches me pace without interruption.

"And she got so mad when I told her I hated the sessions. She called me ungrateful and uncooperative. But I'm sure that's what the psychiatrists told her to say. It's not like she attended any of the sessions."

"Do you think it would've helped if she was there?"

I put my hands on my hips. "I think it would've helped if we were at a *real* psychiatrist's office. We had a lot of issues, but, I guess, maybe it didn't matter because they weren't the reason I did it." I fiddle with my wrists. "I did it because they kept coming after me, saying stuff about my dad." I pause, trying to calm my racing heart. "And the second time—"

Franco's eyes widen. "Wait a minute—there was a *second* time?"

"Well, sort of. My mom says so, anyway, but I don't think it should count." I drop back down on the bed, keeping a small space between us that I wish he'd close.

"Tell me," he prods gently.

"They came after me again, a year later, those sick bastards. They always played the card that my birthday was on the same day Dad died. When I arrived at my so-called appointment with the fake psychiatrist that day, the Suits were there in the room along with her."

"Go on," Franco murmurs.

"With the Suits standing behind her, the psychiatrist told me that my sessions had been a failure because I never accepted 'the truth' about my father. So I was going to have to be hospitalized and begin further treatment, shock therapy and such."

"What did your mom say about all this?"

"She wasn't in the room. She didn't know." I cross my arms. "But I wasn't going to let them take me."

His eyes widen. "What did you do?"

I take a deep breath. "I raced out of the room, knocked over an umbrella stand in the lobby, and then broke off a piece of this really ugly metal artwork hanging on the wall. It had sharp edges, and I used it to smash open a window. Then I climbed onto the desk nearest the window and threatened to jump."

Franco pales. "How high up were you?"

"Eight stories, but I didn't jump."

He shudders. "Well, thank goodness they stopped you in time."

I scoff. "No, I stopped myself. That's the funny thing. They could've easily overpowered me. I was only twelve, remember? But I think they *wanted* me to kill myself. They were sick of me. I wouldn't help them, and they were tired of trying to break me."

"But didn't threatening to jump just put you right back in the hospital?"

I shake my head. "No. Of course Mom was totally freaking out, but I swore to her that if she let me quit therapy I'd never hurt myself again, but if she let them hospitalize me I'd find a way to finish the job."

Franco takes a deep breath. "And did she believe you?"

"Yes, all of a sudden, she did. She told them, 'My daughter's never lied to me. Not even once. I believe her, and we're going home.' And we walked out of there together and never went back."

He shook his head. "I don't understand why they let you go like that."

"I told you; they were done with me. But what I can't understand is this: did you ever hear on the news reports that my father was to blame?"

Franco averts his eyes. "No."

"If their investigation really led them to believe my father did it, that news would've been all over the place. Don't politicians love a scapegoat? At least, that's what Dad used to say. But the only person the psychiatrists and the Suits told was me. Not my mother, just me."

Franco remains silent, staring far across the room.

"When I got home, I told Mom they said Dad caused the accident. I hadn't before because I was scared—scared she'd say the stories were true. She was horrified. She said Dad would never do such a thing. He'd never hurt people like that."

I hold back angry tears. "But instead of being mad at the government, she's spent the last six years trying to make them like me again, or at least that's what it feels like. She's convinced that they sent me down to Mortuary Services as punishment. And she'd do anything to fix that. I'm sure that's why she's playing the violin again."

Franco continues to avoid my gaze. I wonder what he thinks of me now. And why do I always want to tell him everything?

Well...*almost* everything.

Some things I keep to myself.

I'll never tell anyone that Dad went to "meetings."

I won't tell Franco.

And I won't tell Mom.

Because she's wrong.

I *have* lied to her.

I've lied to everybody.

And I'll never, ever tell the Suits the truth about my father.

18

DR. FEELGOOD

Liam pokes his head into the room. "What's going on in here? Meeting of the minds?"

"Yeah." Franco throws a pillow at him. "That's why you're not invited."

Liam catches the pillow and chucks it back in his cousin's face. "Hey, man, how do you get that window open in your bathroom?"

Franco raises his eyebrows. "Is that where you've been all this time? Never mind. I'll get it, although I'm slightly afraid of going in there after you."

His cousin laughs and plops down next to me on the bed.

Now it's really getting crowded in here.

Liam elbows me. "You ready to go? I can walk you home."

Franco scoffs. "Better watch out, Silvia. He might get another cramp and you'll end up carrying him home."

Liam stands with a scowl. "I'd like to see you try running as far as we did. You'd never make it."

"I'd never be foolish enough to try." Franco also moves off the bed, which bounces up. "But I don't hear Silvia complaining."

"That's cause she's amazing." Liam gestures for me to leave the room first.

I exit like a self-conscious engine leading a little train down the short hallway and into the main living area.

"Are you coming over for dinner?" Liam asks Franco.

"No, I'll stay home tonight. I've got some stuff to do."

"Suit yourself, but you don't have anything here worth eating," Liam says as we head out of the apartment.

Franco stands in the open doorway as we walk down the corridor. Every time I glance back, he's still there, watching me, an unreadable expression on his face. I might have ruined something between us by telling him my secrets tonight. What if he acts strange the next time he's around me?

As Liam and I near the elevator, I turn back for one last glimpse of Franco to find he's shut the door. My chest aches as I imagine him avoiding all eye contact and making sure he's never alone with me again.

"I can't believe you're totally fine after that workout." Liam studies me as we begin to descend. "I'm completely exhausted right now, I'm going to be super sore tomorrow, and you look like you could run another six miles if you wanted to."

"Actually, it's been a long day," I admit.

"You know, Franco thinks we're crazy for doing this."

"Yeah, I noticed." No kidding.

Liam shakes his head. "He doesn't understand why this is so important to me. But you get it, right?"

I shrug. "I'd just like to make my mom proud of me, for once. I'd like to see her happy again."

"I'm doing this for my mom too. I mean, maybe we can get a better apartment if I do well. I'll never accomplish that with my dead-end job in Human Relations. Winning this race is the only way I can distinguish myself to The New Order. You know, really stand out and make them notice me."

"Yeah…" I think back to my parents' old beautiful apartment

filled with sunlight. "I'd absolutely *love* getting a better place to live, but I don't think running this race is going to change anything for me. Maybe it's just a whim, after all."

He frowns.

I release a pent up sigh. "Let's be honest here. I know I can't make my mom happy. Only she can do that."

MOM POPS her head into my room early the next morning. "Genetic Testing and Counseling called. You've got an appointment before work today."

"What for?" I scowl. What a crappy start to the day. "Do they need to run more tests?"

"No. They said you passed. But they want you to go to Family Planning right away for your birth control implant."

Unconsciously, my hand travels up to touch my upper left arm. "What's the rush?"

Mom raises an eyebrow. "Maybe you should tell *me*."

My cheeks burn. "I don't know, Mom. I haven't even had sex yet."

"Well, you *have* been spending a lot of time with those Harmon boys."

I narrow my eyes at her. "What are you saying?"

She sighs. "Nothing, Sylvia. Don't get so upset every time I open my mouth. I was just teasing. Now hurry up. We don't have much time."

I pull on my teal scrubs and my shoes then rush into our tiny kitchen. Mom snatches two protein bars from the cupboard by the fridge, hands me one, and we head out for my Citizen Family Planning appointment.

On the walk over, I can't shake the feeling that the skin on my left upper arm buzzes in protest. Even my flesh knows I don't want another implant. My hands itch to tear out the identification microchip that lives just under the skin of my right arm. But like a good girl, I march through the front doors, along with my mother, and approach the front desk.

"Silvia Wood, here for my post-genetic screening appointment," I announce, my legs jittering. I don't want this. I want them to leave me alone.

The receptionist scans my microchip and records my Citizen Number. She gestures to the seating area. "Grab a chair and we'll be with you shortly."

Soon, a curvaceous nurse with long red hair and a bright smile approaches. "Silvia Wood? Please come with me."

I read her white name tag: *Jen Pringle.*

As Mom and I follow her down the hall, my mind jumps back and forth between her flowing red hair and that of the pregnant, sobbing teenager I saw outside this building a few weeks ago. How had that girl managed to get pregnant? The New Order always brags about their low unplanned pregnancy rate. How come she didn't receive the implant?

I shudder and enter the cool exam room.

Nurse Pringle hands me a clear plastic cup. "We need to make sure you're not pregnant before we administer the implant."

I try to hand the empty cup back. "I'm not pregnant. Guaranteed."

She refuses to take it back. "We have to be sure. Sorry."

"Just pee in the cup." Mom's loud whisper echoes from the corner where she stands with arms crossed.

"Fine." I take the cup and step into the mini-bathroom offshoot. This is ridiculous. I've never even been kissed.

After waiting a few minutes for the negative results, the nurse carries in a tray with the loaded injector gun. "There will be a little pinch, and this will sting for only a second. Afterward, you'll feel a bump the size of a rice grain right here." She points at my upper left arm.

"I know." I stare at my feet, biting my tongue to avoid telling her my true thoughts on the subject: *I don't want you injecting things into my body. I want to decide for myself. But that's not possible.*

The nurse gently rolls up my short sleeve, thoroughly swabs my arm, and positions the implant gun. I hear a clunk, feel a stab of pain, and turn away, sick to my stomach. I don't want this implant. I don't want to be like everybody else. Now this stupid thing is going to stay in my arm until I die, when someone like Gus will dig it out and deposit it into a reclaiming canister.

"All done." She sets aside the tray and removes her gloves. "Thanks for coming in on such short notice."

This time I don't hold my tongue. "What was the rush?"

Her glossy smile is meant to reassure me. "It was requested from higher up."

"Why?" I rub my arm. "Did something bad show up in my tests?"

Jen Pringle checks her computer screen. "No. Your tests were fine."

"Good. But I still don't understand why I had to rush in here so fast."

"You're eighteen," says the nurse, as if this explains everything.

"So?" I ignore Mom, who's moved closer so she can glare at me more effectively.

Again, the nurse checks her screen. "It says here you've been putting in a lot of miles while training for the Race for Citizen Glory...with Liam Harmon."

"So?" Why is that anyone's business but my own? My mind flashes back to the previous day. Do they somehow know that I sat on a bed with not one, but two, guys? They can't be watching that close, can they?

"We like to take proper precautions," the nurse says with a polite smile.

I frown. The New Order needn't worry. Nothing's going to happen with Liam, and I've probably ruined my chance with Franco. To him I'll forever be the girl who tried to kill herself—twice.

TWENTY MINUTES LATER, and three blocks away from Family Planning, my mom's still highly annoyed with me. She hasn't said a word, but she doesn't have to. Her flared nostrils inform me she's disappointed in her only daughter—yet again.

After another block of angry speed-walking, she speaks. "Why do you always have to make everything so difficult? It's not like any of this is that nurse's fault. Why did you have to act like she's working against you?"

"Anyone who buys into The New Order is working against me," I mutter so quietly I'm not sure she can hear. "Why can't you see that?"

She frowns. "I guess that includes me, doesn't it? Maybe you can't see it, but everything I do is in your best interest."

"Everything except those Psych sessions you forced me to attend three days a week for a year." I'm edgy, my arm itches, and I still feel sick to my stomach.

Her eyes narrow. "I can't believe you're bringing this up right now, here, in the middle of the street."

But my insides are boiling over and I can't stop. "No matter what, Dad was *always* on my side. Why aren't you?"

She pales. "Well, I'm sorry you're stuck with me, but I'm all you've got. Maybe someday you'll learn to appreciate it."

Our battle of words has brought us to the side door of Medical Facilities Northwest. I yank out my card to scan it, and Mom grabs my elbow.

She hisses in my ear. "Say what you want to me, but don't let the others hear you talk like that. You have no idea how dangerous your words can be." She lets go and hurries away.

I stare after her, my arm in the air, the card poised to strike. Is she talking about Dad and the meetings? No, she can't be. She doesn't know.

Or does she?

19

UNDERGROUND

I scan my work card and descend into the basement, my mind whirling. Mom can't possibly know about the meetings. We were so careful. She must be talking about something else.

I pause halfway down the stairs, remembering a night long ago. The hospital fades away. I grab the railing as the past comes into view.

A few days before his death, Dad and I hovered in the front hallway of our apartment.

"You're my girl, right?" He winked. Everything was a game to him.

"I've got your back," I chirped, excited to be included in Dad's big secret.

"You're old enough to be left alone without getting scared, right?"

I nodded. So very brave. But if I'd known I only had a few days left with him, I would've forced Dad to stay with me that night.

"Your mom will be home in a half hour with the grocery rations." He gave me a quick hug. "And I'll be home soon after. Tell her the light burned out in the bathroom..."

"And I have a cold coming on." I coughed on cue. "So I stayed home while you went to get the replacement."

He kissed my cheek. "That's my girl."

BACK IN THE gray stairwell my hand flutters up to touch my cold cheek. There's nothing left but a memory. Bile rises in my throat when I think about those assholes accusing Dad of causing the fire. That horrible day in the library my faith in my dad faltered for a moment, but now I know better. The Suits lied to me to see how I'd react. Dad had only been to a couple meetings. I still don't have any idea what the meetings were about, but he couldn't have been responsible for the clothing mill explosion after only attending twice. I'm sure of it. Plus, Dad would never hurt anyone. He was wary of The New Order, but he'd never use violence or terror to get what he wanted.

On the other hand, I might not be so passive.

My mind clears as I race down the rest of the stairs and rush into Mortuary Sciences.

Gus glances up from the computer screen in his office. "You're just in time."

"For what?" I join him while Elvis croons in the background. He's one of Gus's favorites.

"For getting out of all the work." Gus smiles. "I finished filling out the last form five seconds ago. It's been a slow day here in the morgue. Nobody wanted to die last night."

"So, now what?" I settle into a chair next to him and glance at the screen.

"Thought you could use a little history lesson." He stands and grabs his hat. "Can you hold down the fort while I run some errands?"

"Sure thing," I reply, already distracted by the article on the screen.

Prior to the establishment of The New Order, one of the most shameful aspects of an early, unenlightened Old America was the slave trade that degraded human life during the eighteenth and nineteenth centuries. Just as The New Order believes in the sanctity and equality of all individuals, the abolitionists at the time formed an Underground Railroad, a secret network of wilderness routes that Southern Black slaves used to escape to the Northern free states.

"Gus, this is fascinating! How come I never heard about this before?" I spin around in the chair, but he's already gone.

I keep reading uninterrupted for another hour. Screen after screen about the travels north, the risks both the slaves and abolitionists took, and the freedom they sought. It all sounds so dangerous, horrible, and exciting.

But it's funny that The New Order acts so shocked and superior regarding the slave trade. Dad always said that everybody is a slave here in Panopticus, even those on top who think they're better than the rest of us.

An hour later Gus returns with a fragrant bag of baked goods, which momentarily disguises the familiar medicinal smell of the Mortuary.

I reach out with a smile. "What's the occasion?"

"Consider it a bribe." He chuckles. "I need you to help me with another exciting excursion out to the Incinerator—unless you're too busy training for that race."

"I'll make it work," I promise. "Just tell me when."

"Tomorrow night."

"Why don't we ever go during the day?"

"They only burn at night. Filling the sky with smoke during daylight hours rouses too much protest from the environmentalists." Gus studies me. "I believe you might know one of the more vocal protestors."

I frown as Franco's outburst at the Incinerator comes to mind. "What do you think about that? Are their objections valid?" I hope this leads to a discussion where Gus will tell me all about Franco's days as Ben's intern.

"I think it's all for show." Gus brushes crumbs off his shirt. "Since ninety percent of this country has gone back to the wild, environmentalism isn't so necessary anymore. All this talk about carbon emissions and pollution is insignificant in the current scope of things."

"But I thought you and Ben were big environmentalists back in the day. In fact, isn't that how you met? At some group event planting trees or something?"

"Oh, yes." Gus smiles, and I can almost see the memories flash across his bright eyes. "But a person can always change their mind."

"You can't fool me, Gus. You're an old stick in the mud."

"I might surprise you."

"Okay." I grin. "Surprise me, then. What have you changed your mind on recently?"

He points. "You."

"Me?" My breath catches. "How so?"

He raises his bushy brows. "When I first got your application, I didn't want you here."

"Why?" A stab of pain pierces my chest.

"I can't say." He smiles. "But I was wrong. Now I couldn't live without you. I hope you realize that. And someday I hope you take this place over."

"Really?"

"But there's more to the job than you think. I want you to keep your eyes open tomorrow night. I've got a lot of things to tell you, some of which you're not going to like."

I can't wait to find out.

2 0

PRESSURE

After work, I hurry to the gym to meet Liam. The yoga classroom is crowded with students. I glance around to discover Liam in the far corner, sitting cross-legged on the bamboo-floor, staring into space. I step up and punch him lightly on the arm.

"What's up?" I ask. "You're in a daze."

He rubs his temples with his hands. "Remember last night how I told you I'm doing this race for my family? My mom in particular? Well, after I got home, she started in on me."

"What did she say?" I settle on my yoga mat in stacked log pose. "But keep in mind that no matter what, it can't be as bad as the argument I had with *my* mom earlier today."

"Moms are trouble." He laughs then sighs. "Anyway, mine said putting myself out there to get noticed is a bad idea."

"Why?" I gently transition into pigeon pose. Running that far yesterday really made my hips tight.

He shakes his head. "I've no idea. She asked me to drop out."

"Is this about the birth control?" I scramble to a crouching position, yank up his short sleeve, and feel his toned upper left arm for a rice-sized bump. There's nothing there.

"I have to go in tomorrow," he replies, pulling down his sleeve.

"Is that it?" I frown. "Is that why your mom doesn't want you near me?"

His eyebrows jerk up in surprise. "No. I don't think it has anything to do with you. Why would you ask that? I'm sure this is all Franco's fault. You know how he likes to talk."

I retreat back to my mat, my cheeks flaming. "Mom hauled me into the Family Planning Center this morning for an A.S.A.P. implantation of birth control because I've been running with you."

Liam's mouth falls open. "Your mom thinks—"

"No. It's worse than that. The *New Order* has noticed we've been spending time together, jumped to conclusions, and 'they like to take precautions,' according to the nurse who injected me."

"Oh." Liam shakes his head. "But I thought—"

"Welcome, everyone." The yoga instructor beams at the class. "*Namaste.*"

"*Namaste,*" the rest of the class echoes. I'm too busy watching Liam.

"What were you going to say?" I whisper to him.

"Never mind. It doesn't matter."

Oh, but it does.

🏃

AFTER CLASS I know it's too late to ask Liam what he was going to say, even though I'm dying to know if it had anything to do with Franco. But it's probably something completely irrelevant, like what Liam's having for dinner.

He offers to walk me home, and I accept. Let the damn New Order think what it wants.

When we reach the bottom of the gym steps, Liam says, "You know, I used to think yoga was for pansies, but my legs feel better after that class. Do you think if I do yoga more often I won't cramp up so much after our long runs?"

I nod. "It definitely should help. And I'm glad you've come to your senses."

He smirks. "So you're ready to run tomorrow?"

"I guess that means you haven't quit on me yet, right?"

"Right."

We merge into the walking lane. It's so noisy this time of day on the streets. Everybody rushing home for their government-approved, appropriately-sized dinner, guaranteed to avoid obesity and type II diabetes.

I smile. "I'm glad you're not quitting, but I can only do a short run tomorrow because I'm working another delivery to the Incinerator."

"That's a bummer. I wanted to get a long run in."

"Yeah, I know. Sorry." I turn to him. "Hey, do you remember learning in school that July Fourth used to be a holiday for people back in Old America?"

"Sure, I remember."

"Gus played me a video of a fireworks show today. Work was slow, so he showed me a bunch of things: The Underground Railroad, the fireworks, and a cool operation on an eyeball."

Liam cringes. "That's gross."

I laugh as we turn onto my street. "How about we meet at the usual time and I'll run however long I can? You can add extra miles afterward, if you want."

"No way." Liam shakes his head. "I've learned my lesson. I'll do what you do. Franco's right about you."

I flush, hoping Liam will think it's from the exercise. "What exactly did Franco say about me?"

Liam chuckles. "He said that if I'm stupid enough to run this race, I should at least be smart enough to keep my mouth shut and follow your lead. Otherwise, I'll only hurt myself."

"Okay, then. Tomorrow we'll save time at the end to work some yoga poses. I'll need to stretch anyway, so I don't cramp up on the long ride out on the truck." Too bad Franco couldn't have said something a little more exciting, but I'll take what I can get. At least now I know he talks about me. Which means I didn't push him away with all my talk of suicide attempts. I try to hide my delight.

"You've got it, yoga-girl." Liam grins. "Whatever you say, I'll do. I'm officially at your beck and call."

"Okay, then. Will you do my laundry?"

"Heck, no. And you wouldn't want me to. I'd probably ruin your clothes. I've never even done my own."

My mouth drops open in mock-surprise. "Are you telling me you're a momma's boy, Liam Harmon?"

"I guess so." He laughs. "That's what Franco says, anyway. Speaking of him, if you're driving all the way out to the Incinerator, maybe you could give him a ride back."

"What?" My steps falter, and the man behind us almost runs into me.

"Franco has to stay out there all night because he can't ride his bike on that road in the dark with all the potholes, and he has some special project going on right now. I'm not going to see him for at least a couple days."

I grimace. "I hope he doesn't see *me*. He hates what the Incinerator smoke does to his crops, and I'm the one delivering fuel for the fire."

Liam laughs. "Well, he'd never yell at *you*."

"Why not?"

He smiles. "Franco said he 'thinks very highly' of you."

"What does that mean?" My mind whirls. Is that a compliment? It sounds kind of patronizing. "That makes me sound like I'm eighty, or a stuffy librarian or something."

"Go ask Franco what it means. I never know what he's talking about."

"Fine. I will." Maybe. Maybe not. Guys are so confusing.

We reach the front door of my apartment. Impulsively, I ask Liam to come upstairs and meet Mom.

"Tonight?" he asks.

"Yeah. Well, you do smell better now than most nights after we work out."

He shrugs. "Good point."

We hike the six flights upstairs. As I put the key into the apartment door, Liam leans close.

"I'll try my best to make a good impression," he whispers.

"Good." The key clicks in the lock.

"I figure it's the least I can do—since you're on birth control now because of me."

"Very funny." I walk inside. "Mom, I'm home. And I want you to meet a friend of mine."

"Really?" She peeks around the corner.

"Yoshe Wood?" Liam steps forward, hand outstretched. "I'm Liam Harmon. I've heard a lot about you from your daughter."

Mom raises her eyebrows. "Ha. I *bet* you have." She shakes his hand, which I hope isn't too sweaty. Mom hates that. "It's nice to finally meet you. Silvia never introduces me to her friends."

"You met Gus once," I argue.

She heads back into the kitchen, waving at us to follow. "Gus is a *grandfather* figure. He's not a friend."

"That's not true—"

Liam elbows me.

"You two must be thirsty." Mom rattles bottles in the fridge. "You're in luck. I got our rations today, and with Silvia training for that race, our allotment practically doubled."

I pretend to grab Liam's arm for support. "I think I'm going to faint. Mom, did you just say that I did something right, or am I hallucinating?"

"Don't be ridiculous." Mom glares at me then pours two glasses of mixed fruit juice and hands them over.

"Thanks. I needed this." Liam glances around the apartment. "You have a nice place."

No, we don't. Our apartment is bland and gray, but I get the impression Liam's trying to be extra polite to my mom. Perhaps he feels the need to make up for my typical rudeness.

Franco's right. Liam is a momma's boy. But maybe it wouldn't kill me to make an effort too.

"Yes, Mom, thanks for the juice."

I puzzle over the sudden brightness in her face. Maybe she needs to get out more. She's happier around company. That's right—I wanted to invite Gus over sometime. Maybe I should get on that.

"Okay, I can't hold it back any longer." Mom beams. "Silvia, I moved up to second chair today. The conductor says I'll be first before the end of summer, but I have to be patient. That is, unless..."

"Unless what?" I ask. Mom always drags things out.

"Well..." Mom pauses, biting her lip. "He said something odd."

"What did he say?" I wait to take another drink.

She shakes her head. "I'm sure he didn't mean it. He was probably joking, but he said that if you win that Race for Citizen Glory..."

"Yes?" *Come on, Mom, out with it.*

She takes a deep breath. "That I'd get into first chair *immediately.*"

Liam lets out a low whistle. "No pressure or anything, Silvia."

EVERY BREATH YOU TAKE

Early the next morning I scurry through the foot traffic to get to work. Upon my arrival, the Mortuary is quiet. No rock music. It takes me a moment to find Gus hovering over the computer at his office desk, his white hair unruly as a dandelion puff. Stacks of papers clutter his workspace. His hand trembles as he reaches for another form.

"What's wrong?" I ask.

"Something's happened," he whispers.

I point at the papers. "What are these?"

"There's a new program we have to use to print out forms." Gus's eyes are wild. "And they changed the time of the delivery to late afternoon."

"That's strange. You've always gone at night before."

"I don't know what happened." Gus gapes at the screen like a lost, scared child. "We've been so careful. Never a mistake. And now, all these changes. How will I manage?"

"Let me help you." I pull up a chair.

"We have to convert over to the new system right away—today." He points toward the Mortuary workroom. "Then we set the new forms on those double-decker carts. Can you believe they're cramming three bodies to a transport bed now instead of two? It's disrespectful."

"Gus"—I squeeze his hand—"it'll be fine. We'll get it done in time. Liam will have to train without me. I'll call the gym later and leave him a message."

It takes hours to make the necessary changes. We recheck each body. We're just finishing up when the Handlers arrive. We've missed lunch, and now it's late afternoon. I rub my grumbling stomach.

"I'm sorry, Silvia." Gus sighs. "I don't even have food for the ride out."

Two Handlers enter the Mortuary, one short and the other tall. Both of them are strangers to me, but I've only done this once before. Gus stiffens but doesn't say a word. I'm guessing he doesn't know them, either.

"Ready to load?" barks the tall Handler.

"Yes." Gus hands him the papers, his face pale.

After the Handlers head for the loading dock, I turn to Gus. "There's something wrong with the Handlers, too, isn't there?" I murmur in his ear.

He silences me with a motion of his hand. I follow him to the truck. The Handlers make quick work of loading the bodies, and then we're off.

As soon as the engine starts, Gus jumps to his feet and jerks open the drawers of his rolling tool box with a loud bang. He pulls out a screwdriver and a Kelly forceps.

"What are you doing?" I whisper from my seat.

He puts a finger to his lips then leans close. "They could be listening to us, right now. Don't say anything you don't want the whole world to hear. Keep your eyes peeled for any signs of a camera."

I begin to babble as Gus traces his fingers along every inch of the truck interior. Getting to my feet, I take the opposite wall. As we search, I talk about the books Gus lent me, the eye surgery we watched together the day before, and how much I'm enjoying the summer weather.

"That must make training for the race more pleasant," he replies absentmindedly.

I pause to stare at Gus as he digs again in his rolling cart. The air seems to press in from all sides. He raises his gaze to mine and gestures that I should keep talking.

I try to swallow, but my throat is dry. "Actually, you wouldn't believe how hard training for this race is."

"Oh?" Gus grabs parts from the drawer and fits them together. The resulting contraption looks very much like a baby monitor. He fiddles with the knobs, the device crackles, and he holds it up in the air.

I back out of his way. "Mom doesn't like all the sweaty laundry, but she's really happy about the extra food rations we get because I'm training."

Gus squeezes through the racks of bodies to wave the device in slow circles around every surface.

"I really hope I do well in this race." I hug myself for warmth against a sudden chill. "It would mean so much to my mom."

Inch by inch, Gus scans the interior of the truck while I talk utter nonsense. In the few years we've worked together, I've never seen Gus upset before. He's always been the calm in *my* storm. Now the roles appear to be reversed. He's more scared than I am, and I don't understand why. But I'm sure I can help him, just like I saved my mother. Only with her, I knew what we were fighting. Here, I'm not so sure. There are a million questions to ask: Why is Gus so scared about these changes? Why does he carry a bug scanner with him out to the Incinerator? What's he worried The New Order will find?

Truck tires stutter beneath my feet.

"We must be getting close," I warn. "Remember the potholes?"

Gus dismantles his bug-detecting contraption with lightning speed, all the while mumbling under his breath. "I think it's clean, but...something's not right. I'm not sure who or what tipped them off."

I help Gus sort the pieces into the drawers. "You know I don't have any idea what you're talking about."

Gus wipes sweat off his brow. "Yes, I know. And let's keep it that way. At least until I can be sure you'll be safe—'safe' being a somewhat relative term, of course."

I grab the key to lock the tool cabinet, and Gus waves my hand away.

"I'm not done yet." He digs in the drawers again. "Not by a long shot. I may be old, but I'm not dead...yet."

Grasping a handful of tools, he kneels next to the nearest body transport cart and fiddles with the wheel. After a moment, he laughs. "Typical. These carts are junk, made on the cheap. This will be so easy; it's almost beneath me."

"Anything I can do?" I watch him work, wondering what the heck he's doing.

"Yeah." He points at the bodies. "Loosen the identification papers here and there. Not all of them. Just more than half. Make it so they come flying off as soon as the bodies are lifted."

Feeling through the metal grate, I slip the papers to one side. Meanwhile, Gus adjusts screws and applies grease, sabotaging the wheels of the brand new transport carts.

After another fifteen minutes, he stands up, satisfied. "This will make them reconsider changing a system that wasn't broken."

The truck bounces through a series of ruts, dislodging one of the identity papers to the floor. I reach for it, and Gus stops me.

"Leave it. Let's just rest." He dumps his gear into the tool chest, locks the doors, then leans back into the side bench and closes his eyes as if taking a nap.

"How can you look so calm?" I ask.

He smiles and opens his eyes enough to wink. "Years of practice."

In less than five minutes, the truck makes a sharp turn, dislodging more papers, then backs up and parks.

Gus leans close. "Follow my lead."

I nod.

The doors clang open behind us.

Gus busts out the open doors, shaking his head. "Either you guys drive crazier than the previous Handlers, or these new transport carts are worthless. Why do they need to crowd six bodies to a cart now? Four at a time seemed more reasonable to me, but what do I know? I've only worked this job for years, but nobody asked my opinion before instituting these ridiculous changes."

The Handler standing closest to the door frowns. "Oh, great. Another complainer."

Gus gives my back a little push. I jump up, dashing around after the loose papers on the floor.

"Just look at this mess!" he continues. "We worked so hard filling out these new forms, and now they're not even attached to the bodies. Using tags worked so much better."

Once I get out of sight behind a cart, I step on top of a couple sheets, making sure to leave footprints to mar the fresh printing.

The Handlers begin unloading the bodies. Within minutes, they're arguing with each other.

"Get out of my way!"

"I can't. The dang cart got stuck on the ramp."

"What the hell is up with the front wheel?"

Gus rolls out his perfectly normal tool cart and gestures for me to follow. As we steer it up the steep ramp, he glances toward the Northern sky.

"Is it weird being here during the day?" I ask.

"Do whatever you can to kill time," he whispers in my ear. "It's important."

Once we reach the main Incinerator Room, I make a slow job of matching up the lost forms with the right bodies, zipping open each bag to check the corpses.

"Your family misses you," I murmur to each body before closing their bag.

Heavy footsteps approach.

"Come on. Come on." The taller Handler reaches out a black-gloved hand. "Let's get this show over with."

I glare at him. "That's not how we usually treat the dead."

He sighs and turns to Gus. "Can you reel in your overly-enthusiastic employee? We're on a schedule here."

Gus shrugs. "She does great work. I understand you're new here, but you'll soon learn that it's best not to interfere with the way things are run."

"What the hell is wrong with you people?" The Handler shakes his head. "Fine. I'll take my meal break while you finish. Just hurry up."

Gus catches my gaze across the room. We continue our work in the summer heat. The main Incinerator Room radiates like an oven. Sweat trickles down my back. As slowly as we can without raising suspicion, we line the body transport racks behind the conveyor belts. Then we stand by the tool chest eyeballing each other, stalling again.

"Aren't you done yet?" the taller Handler calls out as he stomps back into the room.

"Of course," Gus replies. "We were waiting on you."

"Why the heck didn't you come looking for us?" the Handler snaps as the shorter one follows him into the great room, stretcher in hand. "We've been waiting for—oh, never mind."

"Careful with those stretchers," Gus warns. "They don't seem as sturdy as the last ones."

"What the—" The shorter Handler almost loses his grip. "This piece of junk is coming apart right in my hands."

A small smile tickles the corner of Gus's mouth.

"I hope they don't drop any of the bodies," I mutter loud enough for them to hear. "That would be so disrespectful."

Gus turns to me and whispers under his breath. "Desperate times call for desperate measures."

As the bodies travel down the conveyor belt, spaced further apart than usual due to the difficulties the Handlers are having with the carts and stretchers, the Incinerator comes to life with a loud hiss. A heat wave presses against me while flames dance up the walls of the furnace.

I fan myself, melting from every pore.

Gus offers me a water bottle. "Silvia, why don't you step outside and cool off a bit?"

"I'd love that." I turn to go.

Gus taps my shoulder and leans close. "Keep your eyes and ears open."

My legs shake slightly as I leave the room. I gulp down the water, wiping my brow with my arm. The busy Incinerator workers scatter like ants through the hallways. Nothing looks suspicious, not on the surface, at least.

The sun starts to set as I step outside. Purple and pink clouds stain the horizon. I gaze into the warm glow, treasuring this gift. You can't see sunsets very well in the city. The buildings are too tall. The colors fade, and darkness follows. The effect seems so dramatic out here with no streetlights to keep the night at bay.

Sighing, I turn back to scan the dirt parking lot. The overhead lights flicker on, one after the other in each of the distant corners of the lot.

As the last one sputters to life, I see him.

Franco Harmon.

Half-hidden at the far edge of the parking lot.

Glaring at the Incinerator.

And staring at me.

22

FIREWORK

Our eyes lock, the empty parking lot a vast space between us. I hold my breath. Why is Franco here? Is he going to yell at me now?

Footsteps shake the metal ramp of the Incinerator as the Handlers approach.

In the distance Franco backs away from the overhead light, ducking under a cloak of darkness. The trance lifted, I step out of the way of the Handlers rolling out the transport carts. The unruly wheels catch and swivel on the ramp. The Handlers curse and shake the carts as they attempt to load the truck.

"Oops. Sorry about the language." The shorter one catches my eye. "But when I took this job, I was told it was easy." He smiles.

Suddenly, he's a real person. He's not The New Order; he's just an employee. He probably has a family and, under other circumstances, I might learn he is kind or funny or good with children. However, right now, he is the enemy, and my job is to stall for time. I'm a little fuzzy on the details of the war Gus is fighting. All I know is I'll always be on his side. No matter what.

I smile back at him, hoping it doesn't look pained or fake. "I'm new at this, too, but it seemed to me that the other racks worked better." I stand out of the way and make no offer to help as the Handlers struggle through repeated trips up and down the ramp.

Trying not to be obvious, I sneak glances into the dark edge of the parking lot, searching for Franco. Is he still out there? I hope he doesn't launch into another environmental tirade and start screaming at me too.

After the last cart has been loaded, the shorter Handler clears his throat. "When will your Supervisor be ready to go?"

"I'll go ask him." I casually stroll back to the main Incinerator room.

Gus is still fussing with his tool chest. He glances up. "Anything interesting out there?"

Just Franco. "The truck's all loaded. The Handlers are asking if you're ready to leave."

"Why'd they have to move up the schedule?" Gus's shoulders slump. "Oh, well. I guess I can't stall any longer."

I stare at Gus, willing him to tell me what's really going on here. He could at least give me a hint.

I help him push the tool chest outside, making it look more difficult than it is in an effort to fool the Handlers. We ease it down the delivery ramp and onto the truck. Then Gus stands at the opening, tapping his hand on his side. If I didn't know how relaxed he normally is, I wouldn't think anything of it.

I take one more glance toward the spot where Franco stood. Nothing but black sky.

A loud crack and wheeze interrupts the quiet night.

"What the heck?" The shorter Handler steps in front of me and grabs the weapon attached to his utility belt.

I peek over his shoulder as a shower of gold-colored sparks fly through the air.

Alarms wail from within the Incinerator facility. Workers dash around, wide-eyed, yelling orders muffled by the constant booming explosions overhead. But their voices fade in the beauty of the

Northern sky filling with silver and gold fire, spilling from the heavens like a sparkling fountain.

"Well, isn't that pretty?" Gus checks his watch. "Look at the time, folks. Let's get going."

A hazy glow rests on the horizon a moment before another bright flame shoots up into the sky and bursts into a million pieces of light. A chorus of whistles sing through the night air as sparks tumble to the earth. Tearing myself away from the wondrous splendor, I step into the back of the truck.

"Nope." The shorter Handler takes my arm. "You'd better ride up front with me to be safe. We don't know what we're dealing with out here." He points at the sky.

I look to Gus, who settles down with a content sigh. "Best to be safe, I guess. Silvia, I'll see you when we get back. I'm beat. It's time for a good nap."

The taller Handler climbs into the back with Gus. I get down and walk around the truck, staring at the sky, then hop into the passenger seat. We pull out of the parking lot. The wheels catch in a pothole just as the truck headlights outline Franco's tall form on the side of the road. After a long moment, he's lost again in the darkness.

The Handler chuckles. "I hear that guy is a complete psycho. He hates anyone and anything to do with the Incinerator."

"Really?" A smile plays on my lips, because I think Franco just winked at me.

"Yep. That's what the other guys say. But don't worry. If he gives you any trouble let me know, and I'll take care of it."

"Thanks." But your assistance won't be necessary.

"And don't be scared about those explosions in the sky. There must be some simple explanation for it. I'm sure we'll be safe. It'll probably be on the news when we get back into the city."

The poor guy drives as fast as he can over the potholes, gripping the steering wheel until his fingers turn white. For a moment I consider telling him about the fireworks program I watched recently, but I stop myself, thinking that maybe I'd better keep my mouth shut.

The now over-friendly Handler keeps up a nervous chatter all the way back to town. I can barely hear his words over the plethora of questions bouncing around in my head. I need to talk to Gus. Alone. What's his plan now? Why were there fireworks in the sky? How did he know they were coming? That had to be what he was waiting for, but why? What does it mean?

I'm exhausted by the time we finally reach the Mortuary. Even though we haven't been much help to the Handlers all afternoon, Gus starts unloading carts right away. Once we've finished and the Handlers depart, we head back to the office.

The lights are on.

"I thought we turned these off," I say.

"We did."

We step inside a transformed office. Gus's desk has been cleared off. His maps have been unpinned from the wall and folded into a neat pile. His work clothes have been taken off the hooks and tossed over a chair. My gym bag is on the desk, open as if someone rifled through it. An electric teapot is plugged into the wall outlet. There's a foul stench in the air, and I work in a Mortuary so something has to be really bad for me to notice.

"What the heck?" Gus rubs a hand through his wild hair.

Heels click across the floor and a stranger enters. Her bobbed black hair has been teased into the shape of a glossy helmet. Her cool, patronizing tone chills me. "Gus Andrews, I've been waiting for you."

"What's the meaning of this, Edwina?" Gus gestures at his desk. "Where's my stuff? What are you doing here?"

"It's Dr. Wang to you." Her thin lips form a tight, unfriendly smile. "And Gus, you're *far* too old to let yourself get so worked up over nothing. You might have a heart attack and die. Wouldn't *that* be a pity?"

"This is my desk." Gus points. "This is my office. This is *my* job."

"Not anymore. Consider this your retirement party. Starting today, *I'm* in charge."

23

KILLER QUEEN

The already chilled room drops a few more degrees from the loaded ice daggers sent between Gus's blue eyes and Dr. Wang's brown ones.

"I've heard nothing of this." Gus's bushy white brows furrow together.

Dr. Wang scowls, her voice as foul as bile. "Oh, Gus dear, you're positively ancient. You should've stepped down ages ago, but I'll admit it gives me quite a thrill to be the one to kick you out the door."

Gus crosses his arms. "I'll be glad to step down once Silvia is ready to take over. And if I must refer to you as *Dr.* Wang, then I expect the same in return. It's Dr. Andrews to you. Only Silvia gets the great honor of calling me Gus."

"Silvia Wood can't take over." Edwina Wang shakes her head as she hands me my gym bag, which I zip closed. "I've seen her chart. It's marked for 'Special Attention.' She won't be your intern for long."

"What?" Gus gapes. "How did this happen? Who'd you have to blackmail to weasel your way into my job?"

Dr. Wang examines her nails. "I've no idea what you're talking about."

"Oh, yes you do. I know about you and your ways, and don't you forget it."

She narrows her eyes. "Watch what you say, or I'll scream from the highest tower that you're a sexist, racist pig."

"That didn't work last time, did it, *Edwina*?"

"Whine all you want, *Gus*. It won't do you any good. I'm here to stay, so get out of my office!"

"Let's go." Gus places a hand on my back and walks me into the main workroom, his steps dragging like an injured man.

I turn to him and whisper, "What do you mean by 'last time'?"

He breathes heavily. "That evil woman was my intern fifteen years ago. She never did her assigned work. Instead, she used her access to private information to blackmail one of the soft tissue surgeons in the hospital into giving her a coveted medical position upstairs. Somehow, she must've slithered her way up the system to the point that she's here, busy destroying my office!"

I glance back at Dr. Wang, vigorously placing items on Gus's desk. "There's gotta be some way to get rid of her. How can I help?"

Gus rubs his temples. "Have I told you lately what a wonderful young woman you are?"

I grin. "Most every day."

"Good." He bites his lower lip. "Then know I mean well when I ask you a big favor."

"Fire away." I'll do anything to help Gus.

He sighs. "I'm sorry, Silvia, but you're going to have to throw this race."

"What?" My stomach drops. "It's only a few weeks away. What do you want me to do? Drop out or something?"

"No. Don't drop out. That's too suspicious. But don't win it. The dogs seem to be sniffing at your heels, and it all started when you signed up for that race. There's some funny business with this contest. I don't trust it."

"I'm not sure what to say." I clench my jaw.

"Why do you want to win so badly?"

"It's just that…" I sigh. "It's nice to see my mom happy again, and the orchestra conductor told her it would be good for her if I won."

Gus narrows his eyes. "See? What'd I tell you? Sniffing dogs."

"What do you want me to do now? Can I still practice with Liam?" Even at a time like this my first concern is losing my new friend—and my connection with Franco.

"Of course. I don't want to raise anyone's suspicions, but I *must* keep you as my intern. It's imperative."

The sound of a banging hammer draws our attention back to Dr. Wang, who's nailing what looks like official government papers to the wall.

Gus grabs his hat. "Let's go."

"You mean right now? What are you going to tell Dr. Evil?"

He chuckles but only for a short second before his face turns somber. "Oh, let her wonder what happened. I'm out of here but only for the night. I'll be back tomorrow with a plan."

We head for the stairs and begin the ascent.

Gus pauses on the third step. "I changed my mind." He turns to me, a devious look in his eyes. "Let's both take tomorrow off."

"What?" This never happens. Has he gone nuts? "Are you sure that's a good idea?"

"Yes. I think it's perfect." He continues up the stairs. "Silvia, I'll see you in two days. I hope you find the time off to be profitable."

We reach the top without another word, but I can tell Gus's mind is spinning, considering the way his fingers tap imaginary keyboards on both sides of his pant legs.

"Bye, Gus. I'll see you later, then." I call out to his departing back as he heads home, humming a dark tune I don't recognize.

⚡

I SLEEP in the next morning, but due to my tumultuous dreams, I wake even more exhausted than before. After a quick meal alone, I head to the gym for yoga before a long run with Liam.

Pausing at the classroom door, I feel guilty going without asking if Liam wants to join me. But I'm not ready for his steady conversation...not yet. I don't understand what's going on with Gus. I don't like being listed for "Special Attention." And I'm not sure what to do about this upcoming race—if I ever had a chance to win it in the first place. The only thing I am sure of is I don't want to work for Dr. Wang, and I'll help Gus with whatever plan to get rid of her.

I'm tense during Pigeon. I'm tight during Downward Dog. And I can't relax during Savasana. After yoga fails to calm me, I head toward the railway. There, waiting for me at the monorail stop, is Liam.

He waves. "Howdy, stranger."

"Hi. How're you feeling?"

He laughs. "Are you worried I'll cramp up again and prove I'm as big of a wimp as Franco thinks I am?"

I shrug as the monorail pulls into the station. We back up to the metal railing as the passengers pour out, then we board. This time there's no room to stretch. It's so packed we stand pressed side by side, leaning into each other as the train departs.

The buildings pass by in a flash.

"Franco might meet us on his bike after he finishes work," Liam says.

I nod.

Liam frowns. "You're quiet today. Is everything okay?"

I lean close to whisper. "I don't want to talk right now."

"Gotcha."

In mutual silence we watch the other passengers. It occurs to me that very few people actually hold conversations with each other in public places such as this train. Everyone gazes at some arbitrary point, perhaps to avoid making any accidental eye contact. Is this due to customary politeness—or fear? Maybe everyone is afraid of the cameras and the Suits waiting behind them, ready to pop out and haul them away at any moment. Dad always taught me to talk superficially in public and carefully in private. Perhaps this is a lesson we all learn at a young age.

After a few more stops we finally reach our destination: the lovely, hallowed, potholed gravel roads near the greenhouses. I'm free to be myself out here without cameras or microphones recording everything.

"Let's stretch." This time it's Liam who makes this suggestion.

"You really *are* worried about cramping up again, aren't you?" I tease, but my heart isn't in it. My troubles make me feel heavy and old.

We start with a ten-minute slow warm-up run.

"Okay, spill. We're alone now," Liam commands as we run, passing long metallic buildings on both sides. The greenhouses will start on the left soon.

I glance at our government-issued running watches. "That is, we're alone if these watches don't contain microphones."

Liam grins. "Now you're starting to sound like Franco. He checked my watch over for an hour the first night I got it. No bugs."

"Good." I shake my shoulders a little to loosen up. "Here's my problem: I'm really worried about Gus."

"Why? Is he sick?"

"No, but all of a sudden some awful lady came in yesterday and said she's taking over. But nobody told him anything about this, and he's been working there forever. Work is his life. They can't just take it from him. Can they?"

"I don't know. Maybe they can." Liam frowns. "Will you have to work for wench-lady, instead?"

I shake my head. "I don't want to, but I'm not even sure I'd have to. She said I've been labeled 'Special Attention,' whatever that means."

"Really? That's so odd, because today at work they told me the same thing."

"What is going on?"

"I don't know, but ever since we started training for this race, nobody at work will teach me to do anything new even though I'm so bored doing simple tasks. They act like it isn't worth their time."

"Have they told you anything directly?"

"No, but they're acting like I won't be working my job for much longer, so why bother? At first I didn't want to read into it because I thought I might be getting ahead of myself, but now...I'm not so sure."

"What's up with this race?" I ask. "Do you really think we're going to be faster than everybody else?"

"I don't know, but one thing's for sure: we're the only two contestants who petitioned for permission to run off course. The Race Director told me so himself when I saw him at the gym last week."

"Really? Why wouldn't anyone else want to do this? It's so much better than the treadmill."

Liam shrugs. "Maybe they never thought about it. I wouldn't have done it without you and Franco suggesting it."

"I suppose."

"Speaking of mad scientists with paranoid delusions, there he is now." Liam points down the road.

Franco rides up on his bike. I hope the natural redness of my face from running hides the blush rising in my cheeks. While Liam fusses with his watch, Franco winks at me, and I'm suddenly right back in the truck with the firework-frightened Handler. What was that about, anyway? Maybe I should try to get some answers.

"Hey, Liam, did Franco tell you about the fireworks show out here last night?" I ask, keeping my eyes trained on Franco.

"No." Liam shakes out his arms and shoulders to loosen up. "What are you talking about? There was nothing on the news about any fireworks."

Franco rolls his eyes. "That's so you, Liam. If it wasn't on the news, then it didn't happen. So, what's on the agenda today, you pain-loving running freaks?"

Liam details the fartlek schedule: three fifteen-minute pick-ups with ten minute breaks in-between. I welcome the opportunity to focus on something outside my brain. The random tweaks in my hips, knees, or ankles as I dodge potholes aren't enough to worry me. Instead, they help me focus.

Too soon, we finish the workout and slow the pace to cool down.

"So, Silvia," Liam pants. "You wanna tell Franco about Gus losing his job?"

"What?" Franco halts on his bike so fast, he almost topples over. "What's this all about?"

Breathing hard, I give him the details. Once we get to the monorail station, Franco silences me with a look. We ride back into town without the usual banter, as quiet as the others I observed on the ride out. Liam copies all my stretches since the car is mostly empty.

"How do you feel?" I ask him.

"Better." He smiles. "Thanks, Silvia. This really helps."

Franco stares off in space, preoccupied.

"Hey, Franco, you coming over for supper tonight?" Liam asks.

"No, sorry. I have other plans." He glances at me then turns to fuss with his bike. "Here's our station."

Liam walks me home again but doesn't come up. "I'm pretty sweaty and stinky," he says. "I better go home and not ruin the good impression I've already made on your mom."

"All right. See you tomorrow after work for core strengthening class?"

He waves as I enter my building. I head upstairs to shower, eat, and sleep like every other day, one after the other. It's a never-ending cycle that I somewhat accepted until Dr. Wang came along. I can't work under that woman.

But what if Gus can't get rid of her?

THE NEXT MORNING I hurry to work, my nerves on edge. The second I enter Mortuary Services, I want to turn around and head back home. Instead of rock music, opera screeches in the background. And the falsetto singer isn't the only one hurting my ears. It's like a war zone in here.

"So, *Edwina*, I heard that Surgeon you blackmailed eventually killed himself." Gus glowers, his eyes dark and dangerous. "You must be very proud of your accomplishments."

"I had nothing to do with that." Dr. Wang grimaces, bending over a body. "And if you know what's good for you, you'll stop talking about it."

"If you'll kindly remember, *Edwina*, I don't take directions from those beneath me."

She scowls. "You're only here until I get up to speed in this department. I can't believe you didn't show up for work yesterday!"

Gus raises his fuzzy brows. "But, *Edwina*, you said I was retired—"

"Stop saying my name over and over, you aggravating—"

Gus turns to me. "Hey, Silvia, didn't you hear *Edwina* tell me my services were no longer needed here?"

Dr. Wang whips her head in my direction. "So you decided to show up today, too, eh? Why didn't you show up yesterday? I don't recall telling *you* to take a vacation day—"

"No, I did," Gus interrupts. "I told her to take the day off for my retirement party, because *you* said—"

"Oh, just *stop* talking." Dr. Wang wipes her sweaty brow with the back of her wrist. "Silvia, start organizing the carts and bring me some suture."

I hang up my light jacket. "What kind?"

Dr. Wang doesn't answer. Her face pales to a sickly gray. She shudders, her instruments falling to the floor with a metallic clatter. Her gloved hands grab at her abdomen.

"I'm going to be sick." She races down the hall to the bathroom.

"What's wrong with her?" I ask, crossing the room to Gus's side.

"Some people simply weren't meant for this job." He can't hide a smirk.

"What are you smiling about?" I poke his arm. "What's going on?"

Gus avoids my gaze. "Nothing."

"Oh, right," I counter, poking him again.

"Fine." Gus takes a deep breath. "I'll tell you."

I lean in closer. He glances around carefully before whispering in my ear.

"I poisoned her."

24

DANGEROUS

"You *what?*" I glance toward the camera aimed a different direction than usual. "Did you really just say what I think you said?"

Gus whispers. "It's not like I'm trying to kill her. I only need her incapacitated."

"Do you mind if I ask what you're poisoning her with?" I'm standing so close that I'm practically on top of him. I don't want anyone to hear us.

He chuckles. "I knew you'd be interested. Iris root. I ground it up and put it in that foul-smelling tea she's always sucking down. She didn't even notice. Until now."

"Iris root?" I glance around, so sure someone—a Suit, maybe—will barge in at any moment.

"Yes. It causes severe, but not life-threatening, gastrointestinal distress." Gus continues to work, his face a calm mask of dedication and duty. "I've done other things, as well, such as muffling the microphone and aiming the camera on her table to best show her inability to perform her job. Don't worry, you and I remain out of view. But be sure to help her when you can, so that those who are watching see how concerned you are about her well-being."

I take a step back. "I'm beginning to think you're a bit crazy."

Gus smiles. "All the world's a stage, darling. And I intend to play my part in full."

"What if you get caught?" I'm not sure I agree with poisoning people on a regular basis, but this is Gus, and I trust him.

"She's barfing whatever evidence there might be into the toilet. I'm in the clear. I didn't let them film me doing it if that's what you're worried about."

"Shh, she's back," I warn as Dr. Wang slogs through the main workroom, passes us by without a glance, and heads into the office. She drops into a chair and leans her head forward into her hands. I'm surprised I don't even feel sorry for her.

With one last glance at Gus, I hurry into the office. "Are you okay?" I feign concern. "Do you need anything?"

"No. Now, let me be." Dr. Wang winces. Clearly, I'm talking too loud, and her head hurts.

"You look awful!" I speak even louder. "Do you need a doctor? Sometimes people feel nauseous working here. It doesn't bother me, but I've seen a lot of other students come and go—"

"No." She attempts to wave me away with her hand. "No doctor. I'll be fine."

"You don't *look* fine." I can be cruel when needed. "How about something to drink? I could get you some water. It's from the faucet out in the work area, so sometimes it kind of smells like the dead bodies, but—"

She grimaces and points across the room at her electric teapot. "Tea. I'll take tea. Nothing else, please."

As I turn away to pour the steaming drink into her mug, I can't help but smile. "Okay, I'd be glad to get you some tea." I set the doctored tea on the desktop next to her chair and back away as she reaches for the cup.

Throughout the rest of the workday, Dr. Edwina Wang makes

numerous speedy trips to the bathroom. Despite my best attempts to assist her, she scoffs at my repeated suggestions to go home and sleep it off.

"Nonsense, girl." She scowls as she grabs the teapot out of my hand to pour her own cup. "Now go back to work and leave me alone."

I bow to concede then hurry back to my table.

When the job is done for the afternoon, I pack up, expecting Gus to join me outside for a private consult. He grabs his lunch bag and heads for the door, walking at my side.

"Wait a minute!" Dr. Wang rushes out of her office where she's been resting for the last half hour. "Where do you think you're going?"

Gus turns to her with a patient look on his face—courtesy of his days in the theater, no doubt—and says, "If you want to be in charge, you're going to have to accept some responsibility."

"Don't you dare go and leave me with all this mess of yours!" she wails, yanking on his arm.

Gus moves back into the room, strategically placing both of them in full view of the camera.

"If you don't think you can handle the job, you should resign." Gus doesn't pull away from her reptilian grip on his arm.

"You're an evil man," she growls.

"Takes one to know one. But since others depend on a job well done in this department, I'll stay and help you. Bring everything out onto this table."

Again, he chooses a location in full view of the camera. Dr. Wang hustles into her office to gather a stack of papers. Gus glances at me, raising his brows. I gesture slightly toward the camera overhead and then back at his table.

He smiles and says, "There's no need for you to stay, Silvia. You hurry on over to the gym to practice for your big race."

"Yes," Dr. Wang agrees. "Do us proud, Silvia."

The two enemies bow their heads over the paperwork as I head out the door. Taking the steps two by two, I reach the top quickly to discover that it is raining outside. I dash through the heavy drops to the 37th Northwest Street Health and Productivity Gym. My hair drips onto my shoulders and shirt as I hurry inside.

"Where is your umbrella?" asks Liam, waiting for me at the door.

"It's invisible, can't you tell?" I reply.

"You look like you just took a shower. With your clothes *on*."

I squeeze out my hair. "I'll dry off in the locker room."

"I thought maybe we should lift some weights today."

I hedge. "I'm not big on weights."

"But it would be good to build strength to help us with our endurance, right? Listen, I'll only make you do this once because we have to taper soon, anyway. Besides, I did yoga with you, remember?"

"I can't believe the race is only two weeks away." I tense with anticipation. "I guess that's what we get when we only have a couple months to train. It doesn't seem like long enough."

"Are you kidding?" Liam shakes his head. "I can't wait for this to be over. I've never been so tired in my life. I want to kick back and relax."

"You sound lazy, and I'm freezing." I head for the locker room and call back over my shoulder. "I'll meet you in the weight room."

Getting dressed in a hurry, my mind spins. Am I going to get caught? What's going to happen to Gus if we—and, yes, I do mean *we*, because now I'm truly involved too—can't get rid of Dr. Wang? What's going to happen to me if she wins and I lose Gus?

Oh, I can't think about this right now, I tell myself, heading for the weight room.

"I think I'll mostly do lunges with handheld weights," I tell Liam. "I suggest you do the same."

"Yes, master." He makes a face and bows.

We spend the next fifteen minutes in silence, focusing on our form so as not to get hurt right before the race.

"So, how's work?" Liam asks.

I immediately search for the cameras above us.

"Oh. Never mind." Liam follows my gaze. "But promise me something—don't let yourself get as paranoid as Franco."

"I don't want to talk about it here," I mutter, turning my back to the cameras so no one but Liam can read my lips.

"Hey, after we get done with yoga, Franco wants to meet at the Library to view that big model of the race."

My stomach clenches at the thought of visiting that building. "I suppose it would be a good idea for planning purposes."

"Okay." Liam glances at the clock. "I figure we have five more minutes here before we'd better head to that core yoga class you like."

I set down the weights. "I'm done now. I need some water." I head toward the drinking fountain, trying to calm myself. I can handle going to that library. I know I can.

As I lean down to drink, an image of the Suit slapping my face hits me. I choke on the water, sputtering all over myself. A chill shakes my body as I'm sent back in time, back into that room, back into that chair. I rub my wrists, glancing around to see if anyone's watching.

But I might as well be alone in this crowd. Nobody's watching for once.

Yoga class doesn't relax me like it usually does. I can't concentrate on my breathing or form. There are too many images flashing through my monkey brain. After a quick change, Liam and I rush over to the library, huddling close together under his wonderfully big umbrella.

The comforting smell of books and sound-absorbing carpet hits me the moment we walk through the doors. Hardly anything has changed. The librarians' smiles are so familiar. The quiet beeps of books getting scanned at the checkout sounds exactly the same. I can't help but glance toward the elevators. No menacing Suits stand guard there today.

"There he is." Liam heads over to Franco, who watches us from a distance.

Next to Franco is the scaled-down version of the race. I circle the spectacle, which takes up half the room. The detail is amazing. Every building in Panopticus seems accounted for. Small plastic human figures run, frozen in place, with an audience cheering them on from every street corner. Miniature flags hang still from most of the buildings as if the wind has forgotten them. Children eat plastic ice cream cones. Colored balloons float above their wrists.

"I've never seen anything like this," I say. "It looks like one big, giant party."

Franco points at the tall New Order Offices. "The race both starts and ends right here."

"Oh, man," wails Liam, causing a librarian to shush him. "We have to run that giant hill *twice?*"

I smile, noting that the race starts at the bottom of the hill, in front of the government offices, then winds all around the city before coming back and ending at the very top of the same hill.

Franco laughs. "You're the one who signed up for this torture, you fool."

There are bleachers next to the finish line and volunteers handing out medals, drinks, and bananas.

I shake my head. "I wonder how long it took to make this. I can't believe how meticulous it is."

"Yeah." Franco points to a balcony on the Government Building. "They even have the Representatives watching the race from above."

Following his gaze, my stomach drops. There, in exquisite detail, stands an exact replica of the red-haired girl who had been dragged into the Citizen Family Planning and Reproductive Services Building.

Right in front of me.

On my birthday.

When everything bad happens.

2 5

THE LADY IN RED

The red haired replica holds me in a trance.

"Silvia, are you okay?" Liam waves his hand in front of my eyes.

"Uh...do you know who that is?" I point at the small plastic figure.

"Representative Waters-Royce, of course," Franco replies then pauses. "Why?"

"Wait a minute...is she the pregnant one?" I flash back to watching the news with Mom over a month ago. I'm getting confused. Is everyone with red hair pregnant?

"Yes," says Franco. "Silvia, is something wrong?"

"Um...not really." I cock my head. "She looks too young to be a Representative. I...I thought she was someone else for a moment instead—someone our age."

"Do you mean *our* age or Franco's?" Liam slaps him on the chest. "He's practically ancient."

"Oh, be quiet." Franco's gaze catches mine. "I'm not *that* old."

I chuckle, but my mind is busy with other, more disturbing things. I turn back to the race model. "I can't get over the resemblance," I mutter. But I only saw that strange girl for a moment. What if I'm remembering her wrong? Maybe they look nothing alike, save for the long, red hair.

"She's older than she looks." Franco leans close to whisper. "Rumor is she's had a lot of age-reducing surgery. And she probably requested that the model designers make her look young."

"Plastic surgery?" Liam laughs. "Are you mad? You've got more conspiracy theories than brains in that head of yours."

"It's why her skin is so tight, especially around her eyes, and why she always looks so awake," Franco argues, his warm breath on my skin. "I'm telling you—she's had reconstructive surgery."

I frown. "But that's impossible, isn't it? Surgery's only done to save lives and ease discomfort. Gus said people aren't even trained in cosmetic surgeries anymore as it was ruled a waste of resources."

"I wouldn't listen to Franco if I were you." Liam crosses his arms. "He's full of crap."

Franco smiles to himself and steps away. My side suddenly feels cold. He runs his hand along the railing around the race model as he walks away. He grabs three sheets of orange paper.

"Here we go." Franco turns back, handing us each a copy. "Now you can study this at home. It's got a map, elevation, and expected weather forecast. Although, I truly doubt they can know that so far ahead."

I take the sheet but keep staring at the model, my gaze drawn toward Rep. Waters-Royce. Whatever happened to that red-haired girl? Is Waters-Royce related to her somehow?

The library fills with the excited voices of school children on a field trip. We're no longer the only observers. They swarm around the spectacle, their short little bodies bumping into my sides until it finally breaks my concentration. I turn to the left and right, but all I see are kids. Where did Franco and Liam go?

I glance toward the exit. They wave at me with grins on their faces like they're sharing a joke. About me, no doubt. I hurry over, slightly embarrassed but too preoccupied to care much about it.

"What took you so long?" Liam asks.

"Why didn't you tell me you were leaving?" I say in return.

"We did, but you obviously weren't listening." Liam pushes the door to go outside. "Man, I'm starving. How about you guys?"

Once we step into the foot traffic, Franco puts a light hand on my arm. "Silvia, are you okay? You seem off today."

"Something's wrong at work." Liam digs in his gym bag. "Oh, sweet. I found a snack bar."

"How can you eat that?" Franco cringes. "It probably tastes like your socks."

I laugh, and Franco turns his attention back to me.

"How's work going?" he asks. "How's Gus?"

I hesitate and glance around, but I'm pretty sure no one can hear us in this crowd. "I really like working for Gus, and I'm pretty sure I won't get along as well with his replacement." That's only a very small portion of the story, but I'm not sure how much to tell without implicating Gus in wrongdoing.

Or myself for that matter.

"I still think it's weird," says Liam. "Like I've said before, work hasn't been the same for me either since this race thing started. It seems like everybody's getting shuffled around a lot, but maybe it's a coincidence."

"My mom says to never trust a coincidence." I veer to the side of the walkway since we're nearing the tall apartment complex where I live.

"What's left if you can't trust anything?" asks Liam. "Just be suspicious all the time about everything and drive yourself nuts? Like Franco?"

"Those are deep thoughts, especially coming from you, little cousin." Franco rubs his knuckles over Liam's head, making his golden hair stand on end.

"Stop that!" Liam backs away, almost running into a woman behind us. She hurries around our group without a backwards glance.

In a few steps, we're at my front door.

"Do you want to come up?" My cheeks warm as I wait for their answer.

"Sure," says Liam. "You got anything to eat?"

I laugh. "I'm sure Mom would be more than happy to feed you."

We head into the building, hike up all six flights of stairs, and discover that Mom is, indeed, more than happy to serve up some of her special cookies and soymilk for my friends.

"I suppose your family is also enjoying extra rations for the race?" Mom asks Liam, a big smile on her face. "It will be hard to get used to regular portions once this is over."

"Yeah, only two more weeks." Liam eats fast. He sure is hungry.

Franco hangs back. Mom eyes him, some reservation in her eyes. I'm not sure if it's because of the memorial video that I showed her or due to the fact that Franco seems more interested in the contents of our apartment than in filling his stomach. He wanders around as if our small home is a museum. At one point, he disappears from the combined kitchen and living area entirely. Mom throws me a look, and I hurry after him.

I hover in my bedroom doorway, watching Franco examine my room. Fortunately, I didn't leave any embarrassing underwear or bras lazing about on the floor. I'm not sure whether to be flattered by his interest or feel like some new plant specimen he's investigating.

Franco looks at everything, touches nothing, and then stops short in front of my dad's photo hanging on the wall. As Franco stares at my dad's red hair and blue eyes, I find it hard to breathe.

We both remain silent and unmoving.

My ears hum. I start to sweat. The banter from the kitchen sounds muffled and far away.

The longer Franco stands in front of my father, the faster my heart races. It's beating so hard, I barely hear the words he speaks as he runs a finger along Dad's picture frame.

His broken voice comes out in a whisper. "I'm sorry."

I catch my breath. He's *sorry*? What the hell does that mean?

"What are you sorry for?" I burst into the room.

Franco jumps a foot away from my dad's photograph. "I...I meant I was sorry for your loss."

I cross my arms. "That's something you say at a memorial service, which was eight years ago, you may remember? That's not something you say now."

"But look at this." He gestures at the picture. "Your dad's face is the first thing you see when you wake up every morning, isn't it?"

I slowly nod, hating that he's right.

"It's just..." Franco can't rip his gaze away from my father's image.

"Am I depressing you?" There's nothing I hate more than being the subject of someone's misguided pity. "You'd think that, with all I've told you already, you'd almost expect this, but...I guess maybe not."

"Please don't get mad, Silvia." Franco averts his gaze. "I certainly don't mean anything against *you,* of all people."

"You think I'm weak, don't you?" My tears threaten to burst like a storm cloud. "You're no better than all those psychiatrists, looking down on me and telling me I'm pathetic."

He grabs hold of my arms. I don't even fight back. I'm so mad at him for making me cry and so angry with myself for not being in better control of my emotions.

"That's not what I think," Franco assures me. "In fact, I'm pretty sure you're a lot stronger than the rest of us. If I lost someone I loved I'd hide or destroy every picture. I don't think I could bear seeing them at all if that was all that was left for me."

I swipe at my streaming eyes. "You'd rather live in denial?"

"Oh, denial's not such a bad place to live." Franco half-smiles and half-frowns. "Sometimes, it's the only way to survive."

"I can't live like that."

Franco's grip tightens. "I can see that. And that's one of the things I admire most about you."

"You admire me?" I sniffle. Great timing for a runny nose.

Steps approach in the hall. Franco drops my arms and takes a step back right before Liam pokes his head in my room.

"Hey, you guys," Liam says. "What are you doing in here? Yoshe's asking about you. so get your butts back in the kitchen before you freak her out, will ya?" He spins around and strolls away.

Franco raises an eyebrow. "I don't think your mom likes me very much."

"Sure she does."

"Thought you didn't believe in denial." He offers a tiny smirk.

"Okay, fine. She just likes Liam more for whatever reason."

He shrugs. "I'm used to that. Everybody likes him more than me."

"Is that so?" I tease, refusing to admit I might feel differently. "Maybe it's because you label your clothes—"

He narrows his eyes. "What are you talking about?"

"There's a 'Property of Franco Harmon' label on your jacket. That's kind of weird, you know."

"So?" He scowls but appears amused instead of irritated.

"I haven't seen those kinds of labels since the Early Grades in school."

"I happen to like my coat. I don't want anyone to take it."

"Or maybe it's the way you dress. First of all, I swear you must wear that jacket all year long because even when it's blasted hot out, you've still got it on."

He rolls his eyes. "Again with the jacket."

"And those combat boots are a bit intimidating."

Franco grabs my arms again. He's so close I can feel his breath on my face. "You don't seem to mind them."

He's got that right. We stare into each other's eyes long enough for my heart rate to accelerate far above any pace induced by running.

Franco breaks off his gaze, and my stomach jumps like it's full of bouncing balls.

"Let's go back to your mom before she bans me from your apartment altogether," He tugs on my arm, and we leave the room.

I frown. Things were just getting interesting.

2 6

WELCOME TO THE JUNGLE

In the morning I force myself down each step to Mortuary Sciences. As the glass entry doors swish open, cool air strikes my face and loud music blasts my eardrums. Out of dueling speakers, a rocking guitar-solo battles with glass-shattering opera notes. Gus and Dr. Wang work back-to-back in the middle of the room, their shoulders tense. Once again the overhead camera is aimed at Dr. Wang.

Her face is wan and pale. Her previously over-groomed, shiny, bobbed, black hairdo is rumpled and dull. She leans against the table and closes her eyes. The scalpel in her hand wavers and falls into the open chest cavity of the body lying in front of her.

I drop my gym bag, yank on gloves, and extract the scalpel, holding it up in the air to glisten for the camera before handing it back to Dr. Wang.

She shakes her head. "No...I can't. You'll have to finish for me." She rushes out of the room, moaning and clutching her side.

I turn to Gus. "What should I do?"

"You heard her. Finish it up and make a show of it." He glances toward the camera. "And turn off that shrieking opera. I can't hear Slash."

I click off Dr. Wang's music. "He's from the band Guns and Roses, right?"

"Yes, of course. Only the best for your auditory enjoyment, my dear." He focuses on his autopsy, a smile playing at the corners of his mouth.

I laugh and grab the chart Dr. Wang was working on before she became "ill."

By the time I sew up the abdominal cavity, we have unexpected company—although, perhaps not so unexpected for Gus. The doors swish open, and two Suits step inside Mortuary Sciences. I tense, my heart leaping into my throat.

"Gus Andrews?" A third Suit says as he enters the room but keeps a safe distance from our tables of death. "I need to speak to you in private. We can use the office."

"Of course." Gus sets down his instruments with great finesse and removes his gloves. "Silvia, you can finish up for me, can't you? This one only needs closing. I'm done, otherwise."

I nod, still rendered silent by the presence of the Suits.

After filling out the chart for the first body, I move to Gus's. I hate turning my back on the two remaining Suits, but I don't like watching them either.

"Listen to that guitar solo," one Suit murmurs to the other.

"If you'd prefer, I could turn the opera back on," I reply.

"Opera?" the second Suit protests. "Just shoot me now. My wife makes me listen to that crap. She says it's romantic, so what's a guy to do?"

I smile and relax. These two aren't the bad guys.

Gus must have successfully schmoozed the third Suit, because within the hour, Dr. Wang is removed from the premises, swearing that all men are despicable and asking if she could please have a female doctor for once in her life because her insides feel like they're being ripped in two. After her noisy departure I clean the work area, and Gus moves into the office, singing along to his music. Once the trash cans are emptied, I'm done for the day.

Gus waves me inside the office. "Don't worry. It's safe to talk in here. I checked."

I glance at his desk, comforted by the presence of his familiar penholder and paperweight. "It didn't take you long to get rid of Dr. Wang. I'm amazed—stunned, actually."

"What do you mean?" He smirks. "It took three whole days. That's long enough. I couldn't have taken much more of her."

"How'd you do it? Besides that awful tea, I mean."

"You're right. That wasn't enough. It took a little finagling, but I managed to contact the favorite niece of the surgeon she blackmailed years ago. I'd heard she'd climbed her way rather high up in influential circles, so I knew she'd have the ability to get rid of Edwina. And I was pretty sure she'd still hold a grudge since her uncle killed himself over the deal."

"You're a tricky man to figure out sometimes."

"It's how I keep so young at heart and mind." Gus waves airily, stapler in hand to fasten his maps back on the wall. "Don't you need to go run now or something? No need to wait for me. This could take hours."

"Yeah, I'm going running, but we're starting to taper, so I'll probably be home early tonight."

"Good. Your mom probably gets lonely without you."

"So...regarding the race." I pause. "Do you still think I should throw it? Because if you do, I need to tell Liam so he knows what to expect from me race day. Otherwise, it isn't fair to him."

Gus turns to me, an urgent tone in his voice. "Don't tell Liam anything. And I'm not sure about the race. I've got some feelers out, trying to figure out if Edwina was right about them taking you away from me, but I haven't heard back yet. I'll have to let you know."

"Okay, I'll wait, then." Why are things getting so weird around here? "I'll keep practicing like I'm trying to win, although I have to say, this puts a cramp in my focus. I like to know what I'm doing."

"I understand." Gus pats my shoulder. "But I don't have an answer for you yet."

🏃

As I HEAD to the gym, everything in my body feels heavy—my legs, my head, and my heart. Why can't I just be happy that Dr. Wang is out of my life? But what if what she said is true? What if there are plans for me? Plans I don't get a say in? A life I won't get to choose? I don't want to leave Gus behind even if it is my mom's dearest dream. She wants me to win the race to move her up in Orchestra. But Gus might still ask me to lose. When do I get to choose? And what options do I really have, anyway?

"Did you hear what happened to Liam?" a familiar low voice interrupts my question-packed reverie.

"Wh-what?" My head pops up to discover Franco strolling next to me—for once without his bike. He looks upset. Not quite crazy-man-screaming-at-the-Incinerator-workers upset but very unhappy, almost distraught.

"Liam got hit." Franco shakes his head as if, somehow, this is his fault.

"What?" I turn the corner with Franco close to my side. "Who hit him?"

"Some guy on a bike. That's all he said in his message. I just got here."

"Is he all right? Where is he?" I realize I'm still headed to the gym, and Liam could be at the hospital for all I know. But then why would Franco be walking in the same direction as I am?

"He's waiting for me at the gym. He said not to worry, that he's all right, but he won't be able to run today, I don't think."

We reach the 37th Gym steps and jog up them. Liam lounges in a chair near the entry door, a harem of young women fussing over him. They scoot back as Franco pushes to Liam's side.

"What happened?" demands Franco.

"Holy crap." My gaze falls on Liam's scraped legs. His right knee is swollen, and both legs are bruised and bloodied. "Have you cleaned your wounds yet? Did anyone check your knee? Can you walk on it?"

"Listen to the doctor over here, Liam." Franco chuckles then turns serious again. "Tell me what happened, every detail."

Liam waves his hands. "I'm going to be fine. Superficial wounds, mostly. I landed on my knee, but I should be back to normal after a day or so."

"I hope you didn't tear your cruciate ligament." I cross my arms. "Let's see you stand. Do you need a crutch or anything?"

"No, I don't need a cane," Liam grumbles as he struggles to his feet. "I'm fine, see?"

"You should go home and rest," Franco instructs. "Plus, Linda's going to blow a gasket if she can't keep an eye on you."

"Yeah, I figured Mom would be upset. Right before the race, too. I'm so sorry, Silvia."

"There's no need to apologize," I say. "I'm sure it was just an accident. Let's get you home."

Franco and I each take one of Liam's arms and assist him down the front steps. He can bear some of his own weight, but flinches and groans with each step.

Liam scowls. "I can't believe this happened. Training was going so well. I really thought we were getting somewhere."

"We're tapering, anyway." I reassure him. "Focus on getting that knee back to normal size, all right?"

"What did the guy look like who hit you?" asks Franco.

Liam glances around and lowers his voice. "Like he was homeless."

"What do you mean 'homeless'?" I ask. "Aren't the Representatives always saying that housing is one of the basic rights guaranteed by The New Order? The homeless don't exist."

Liam shakes his head. "I know it doesn't make sense, but I swear he looked and smelled like he hadn't showered in weeks, months maybe. His teeth were dirty. I swear they were brown. I've never seen anything like it. I guess I never realized how clean everyone is, normally."

"Was he drunk?" asks Franco.

"No. I mean, he acted a little bit crazy, but he didn't smell like booze or anything."

I frown. "Did he at least apologize and make sure you were okay after he hit you?"

"That's the funny thing." Liam pauses. "I think he hit me on purpose."

"What? But why?" Franco tenses. "Did you recognize him?"

"No, I've no idea who he is. But he knew *me*, that's for sure."

Franco's eyes widen. "What do you mean?"

"Like I said, he probably ran me over on purpose. Then he jumped off his bike, grabbed my arms, breathed his rotten meat breath right into my face, and said, 'You're a dead man if you run that race. Did you hear me? A dead man.'"

Franco tenses. "He *threatened* you?"

Liam shrugs. "Maybe he just wants somebody else to win."

I sigh. "I don't know why everyone assumes we're going to win. It's starting to bug me."

Franco stares at me a second then breaks his gaze. "Maybe he's right, Liam. And at least you'd have an excuse to back out now. You could show them your leg."

Liam shakes his head. "But I don't want to quit. And I can't believe you'd want me to give in to some freak-show bullying me into giving up on something I want."

Franco frowns. "This guy sounds dangerous. Who knows what else he could do to you?"

"I'm not afraid of him." Liam turns to me. "Silvia, what do you think? What would you do if this happened to you?"

I pause to consider the question. "I probably would've been so pissed that I'd have grabbed his bike and rode off with it. See how he liked it. That is, if I could do it with a bum knee."

"You see, Franco?" Liam laughs. "Silvia's got more balls than both of us put together."

Franco rolls his eyes. "That's very flattering, Liam. I'm sure Silvia is thrilled to hear it."

"At any rate, I'm with Silvia. I'm going to rest up, fix this knee, and run the race to win it–no matter what anyone else has to say. I hope that guy doesn't show up and breathe his deadly breath in my face again. It was *awful.* Thank goodness I floss."

2 7

COLD AS ICE

Liam's mom, Linda, hovers at the apartment door as we approach. She points to the couch where a soft blanket awaits. As soon as we have Liam situated, she brings over a small tray crowded with ointment jars, bandages, and wet cloths. Linda opens two jars, and the room fills with the smell of camphor and lavender.

"What do you think?" Franco asks his aunt. "How bad is it?"

Liam gestures at me. "Oh, hey, Mom, this is Silvia Wood."

"Yes, I know," Linda answers without even a glance in my direction. Instead, she focuses on Liam, who winces as she flexes and extends his swollen knee.

"He can bear partial weight on that leg," I add, trying to be helpful.

"It's too swollen for me to say how much permanent damage has been done." Linda grabs a fragrant jar and begins to rub a greasy yellow ointment around the affected knee. "We'll have to try to get the swelling down and see what happens."

I cross the room, grab a few pillows, and bring them over to the couch. "Do you want to elevate the leg? Should I get you some ice?"

Linda turns to me. Her frosty gaze makes me feel like I've done something wrong. I'm just not sure what it could be.

"I can take it from here," she says. "Thanks for bringing him home." But her gratitude is aimed at Franco, not me.

For some reason, she doesn't like me. Maybe it's something stupid, like how Citizen Family Planning wants to inject everyone with birth control the second they come in contact with a member of the opposite sex. Perhaps they aren't the only ones who believe I'm sleeping with her son.

"Ouch!" Liam squirms on the couch. "Come on, Mom, that hurts!"

Franco elbows me. "We'd better hurry away if you don't want to see Liam turn into an infant. He's not good with pain."

Feeling a bit dismissed, I head for the door. Franco and I exit the apartment, head down the hall, and turn a corner before either of us speaks a word.

"Listen, I have to ask." I pause, wondering if I really want to know why Liam's mom instantly disliked me. I couldn't possibly have done something wrong. "Why does your aunt hate me so much? I don't even know her."

He frowns. "She doesn't really hate you."

"It sure feels like it."

"Yes, I'm sure it does. You have to understand—Linda's not the happiest person on the planet. Liam's a lot different than her. He's more like my Uncle Jack."

Liam's more like his dad. Now, I understand.

"Is it because I remind her of the accident?" I ask. "Is that why she doesn't want me around?"

"Yes, I'm sure that's it. So don't take it personally."

"I've never understood that saying. It doesn't make any sense. How do you *not* take something personally when it's about you—which is personal, right?"

"I guess so." Franco changes the subject as we enter the elevator. "What do you want to do now? Are you still going running?"

I sigh. "No. I don't really feel like using the treadmill, and if I go outside on my own I'll worry that freaky guy on the bike will run me down too."

Franco shakes his head. "He's probably long gone by now."

The elevator door opens on the first floor, and we stand in the entryway, staring through the windows. The sun beckons us outside. Now what?

"What are *you* going to do?" I glance at Franco, wanting to stay with him though I have no idea what he's doing next or if he'd even want my company.

"Well...we're both done with work, I guess." He squints at the sun as we step outside. "And your mom isn't expecting you home for a while, right?"

I nod, full of hope.

"How about the park? You like plants, right?"

"Yes, of course." I smile. Finally, a moment alone with Franco. Not that it isn't a shame Liam had to get hurt in order for me to spend some time alone with his cousin.

We hurry our steps to the Northwest Citizen Park. A couple times, Franco's fingers brush mine, and I hold my breath, wishing he'd take my hand. But he doesn't. As we reach the tall metal gates leading into the garden, a flood of people rush out of the park.

"Oh, no," I exclaim. "Is it closing-time already?"

"No. Everybody's heading home for supper. These are just the day pass people, but you can go at night anytime."

"Are you sure?"

"Yeah. I come here a lot." Franco gestures at the lilacs. "It's peaceful here."

"Yes. It's like home... Or what my home used to be like."

Franco pats me on the back twice then quickly removes his hand. I wish he'd put his arm around me and leave it there.

"Are you hungry?" he asks.

"No." Food is the last thing on my mind.

"Good. Me neither." He smiles. "Let's walk around and pretend this is what the whole world looks like. Forget there's row after row of identical gray apartment buildings outside the gates."

I smile. "You've got yourself a deal."

We head down the nearest trail. Franco points out which plants he's researched—which is the vast majority of the fruit trees, herbs, and vegetables on display.

"This one's mine too." He points to an apple tree, heavy with immature fruit.

I glance at the placard label stuck in the ground at the base of the tree. "Wow. Your name is actually listed on there."

He chuckles. "Did you think I was lying?"

"No, but I guess I didn't realize—"

"Actually, if you look, my name is on a lot of these signs."

I smirk. "Oh, I see. Now it's braggity-bragster time."

He smiles. "Let's just say I'm highly interested in the subject matter."

Franco raises his gaze to mine. I begin to drown in his eyes. People walk by, but I don't see them. My heart races, and yet, he doesn't say a thing. He doesn't step any closer, and I'm afraid to move. I don't want to break this spell.

A small girl crashes her bike next to us on the path, interrupting my brief stint in wonderland. She whimpers, hunched over on the ground.

"Are you okay?" I bend down, noting her scraped knees and tear-stained face.

"Marissa! Don't go so fast." A short man rushes toward us as I help the girl to her feet.

She tentatively tries out both legs.

"See, you're okay," I reassure her, and she rewards me with a smile.

The guy finally reaches us, puffing hard.

The little girl runs up to him. "Did you see me, Daddy? I was *super* fast."

"Yes. That's the problem, dear. Daddy's *not* super fast. Here, let me have a look at your legs. Oh, no. Your mom's gonna kill me."

I stand up. "I think she'll be fine. She's a toughie. She barely cried."

The girl's dad glances at me, worry etched all over his face, then pauses. "Wait, I know you. You're Silvia, right? From Mortuary Science, Northwest sector...with Dr. Gus Andrews?"

It takes me a moment to recognize the shorter Handler who drove back with me in the front of the truck through the fireworks-studded night on July fourth.

"Yeah." I smile. "Sorry I didn't remember you at first. You look so different in street clothes."

"It's Marissa's birthday today," he explains. "I got a work pass."

I wave at her. "Well, happy birthday, Marissa."

She grins. "Thanks."

"I'm here after work today myself," I explain.

We both turn to Franco, who appears to be intensely studying the tree he'd just pointed out.

"Hey, aren't you the guy who–" The Handler takes his daughter's hand and quickly moves away. "Never mind. Have a nice evening, you two."

After they disappear around the next heavily mulched corner, I murmur, "I think he recognized you."

"Yep." He chuckles. "Pretty sure he did."

"Why do you hate those guys so much, anyway? They're just doing their job. If you really have an issue, you should go above them."

Franco avoids my gaze, still smiling to himself.

"At least you didn't go after him in front of his kid," I continue. "In fact, that's probably why he took off right away, so you wouldn't freak her out."

"I wouldn't do that." Franco's face turns serious. "Believe me."

"I don't get you. Half the time you seem so pissed off, and the rest of the time, like right now, you act like you've just heard some joke I don't understand."

He shrugs. "I don't know what to tell you, Silvia."

I narrow my eyes. "It's like you're a chameleon or something."

Franco nods. "Let's just say: I find it useful that no one really knows who I am."

2 8

LIKE A VIRGIN

We walk a bit further on the path before Franco halts, a cringe on his face. "Hey, don't kill me or anything. But I just remembered that I've got to be somewhere else right now."

"What?" You've got to be kidding me.

"Yeah. I've got a meeting tonight."

My stomach drops. "And you remembered this very moment?"

"Yeah. Sorry. I'll walk you back to the gates, and then I've got to go, okay?"

My shoulders slump. Maybe Franco really doesn't want to spend time with me. It's also quite possible the guy is nuts. I shake my head as we approach the gates.

Franco frowns. "I really am sorry, Sylvia." Then he ditches me.

Once he's gone, I hurry through the gates before nearly sprinting across town. That counts as running, right? It shouldn't matter whether or not Franco's comfortable being alone with me. It shouldn't matter whether or not he likes me. At least that's what I tell myself with every step I take.

"Mom, I'm home!" I call out once I reach the apartment.

She greets me in the narrow front hallway. "I'm so glad you're here. I see you have another appointment with Citizen Reproductive Services tomorrow morning." She holds out a card. "They're more concerned about the time you're spending with boys your age than I am."

"Again?" I scan the writing. *Silvia Wood, 6:30a.m.* "I'm so sick of that place. What do they want now?"

I SIT on an exam room sofa in Reproductive Services, this time without my mother. A nurse types with lightning speed into the computer at the desk.

"Pre-race jitters?" She glances over at me with a supportive smile.

"Not really." She's caught me off guard. How does she know about the race?

"That's why you're here, of course. You knew that, right? Every female contestant must have a pregnancy screening, among other things, before the race. It's for everyone's safety."

"But I just had a pregnancy test not that long ago."

She holds out a cup. "We have to be sure. It won't take long, I promise. And our newest tests are so sensitive, they can detect a pregnancy only seven days along."

"But last I heard, a person actually has to have sex before they can get pregnant."

She holds the cup closer. "Just pee in the cup. It will only take ten minutes out of your day, I swear."

"Is this really necessary?"

She raises her eyebrows. "No pee. No race."

I grab the cup. "Boys get off so easy."

"Well, usually I'd agree with you, but they have to provide samples, too—not checking for pregnancy, of course. We just have to check to make sure no one cheats during the race."

"How can you cheat in the race? Not that I intend to do it. I'm just curious."

"There are ways. Certain drugs or blood doping. The New Order wants this contest to be clean."

"Fine, I'll go pee." What a total waste of time.

Twenty minutes later, instead of the promised ten, the nurse comes back into the room.

"Guess what?" she says with yet another smile. "You're not pregnant."

"Well, that's a relief," I mutter.

The nurse eyes me. "Don't forget about all the benefits you receive for your participation in this race. It's not that hard to comply with the few rules and regulations that go along with it."

"I guess not, but since I'm not even sexually active, *and* you've already shot me up with this long-acting form of birth control"—I point to my upper arm—"whether or not it's 'standard procedure,' this appointment still seems pointless. Can I go now?"

"Of course." She turns back to her computer, her smile gone. "Good luck at the race."

I'M STILL GRUMBLING about the pregnancy test when I get to work. My duties today include processing all the implants—meaning a lot of tedious entering of names into the computer while the noisy machine grinds the hormone capsules to bits. Then I get the joyous task of dismantling all the microchips into pieces for recycling. Usually I don't mind either of these jobs, but today, everything grates on my nerves.

"What's wrong with you?" Gus asks. "You're wearing the ugly scowl of an old, German woman, and I don't like it one bit."

I sigh. "I can't believe how many times a virgin has to have a pregnancy test in order to run this damn race."

He chuckles. "Which part is it that you're mad about?"

I flush. "Good grief, Gus. Get your mind out of the gutter."

"It's a fair question, I think." Gus smiles. "You've got to declare yourself a homosexual if you want to get Reproductive Services off your back. Well, that's not exactly true, either."

"At least you wouldn't have to keep peeing in a cup."

"I wouldn't be so sure about that. There's still lots of tests they want to put you through to determine if you're genetically sound or, perhaps, even superior."

I roll my eyes. "I'm guessing you were deemed 'superior'?"

"You have to understand, with fertility rates so low, sometimes Reproductive Services runs tests to determine if someone's eggs or sperm is a better match or more viable."

"Did you have to donate?" I ask. Now I'm the one getting overly personal.

He makes a face. "Sometimes I wish you'd just take the hint without getting so inquisitive about things."

"So you have kids? You never mentioned any."

"That's because they weren't ours to raise. You have to get permission to have children, whatever your preference, and, I guess, we never got around to it. I did wish afterward that we'd thought more on the subject, but then Ben got sick, and it was too late."

"I'm sorry, Gus." I touch his arm. "You would've been a great dad. And I'm sorry I never met Ben. Franco totally idolized him."

"Yes, I'm aware of that." Gus clears his throat. "Are you still spending so much time with that boy? You know he's too old for you."

I turn back to entering in names, the machine growling and grinding next to me. "Yeah. Mom thinks so too. But she *adores* Liam."

"Everyone always has." Gus turns away.

"Really? You think so too? Franco says everyone always prefers Liam over him."

"Then, for once, I agree with the man."

⚘

I ENTER the gym through the sliding glass doors, dreading the thought of working out alone.

"Silvia Wood?" The front desk worker waves me down as I enter. "Liam Harmon left a message for you."

She turns the monitor toward me. I lean over the computer screen.

Hey, Silvia. Sorry I can't train with you today. The good news is: I can walk now but with a cane (you were right). I came in earlier for an ice bath and some physical therapy. Not sure when I'll be running again, but even if I have to limp along the sidelines, I'll still cheer you on.

I smile and leave my electronic signature to prove I received his message.

"That poor guy." The front desk worker clucks. "I hope they figure out who ran him over."

"You'd think that with all the cameras—" I freeze and slam my mouth closed. Should not have said that.

She leans forward in a conspiratorial whisper. "I heard that none of the cameras caught it. He's like a ghost who can't be seen on tape."

I bite back the words that want to spill out about hiding from view, darting around cameras—everything my dad taught me. Instead, I go with, "I hope Liam gets better in time to run the race. It won't be as fun without him."

"Fun?" She shakes her head, laughing. "I'm sorry. I admire you all, but running thirteen-point-one miles is *not* my idea of fun."

THE NEXT THREE days spin by on robotic pilot: work, gym, home. Work, gym, home. Treadmill-racing those running next to me even though I'm supposed to be tapering, but running hard usually calms my mind. That and an hour of yoga after each run.

And yet, no matter how fast I push my legs or how long I hold each pose, my mind still jumps about like a bouncing ball.

On day four I enter the gym to find Liam leaning against the counter, chatting up the front desk worker.

"How was your ice bath?" I ask.

"Torture." He scowls. "I hate them, but today was my last time. Look, my knee is back to normal size."

"Bend it," I command.

He winces as he bends his knee.

"You've got pretty good range of motion, but it obviously still hurts."

"I'll be fine. I've got to be. I'll just rest up a few more days then join you on a few shorter, easy runs. You're tapering already, aren't you?"

Crap. I'm so busted. "Uh. Not exactly."

"Are you kidding? What are you waiting for?"

I grimace.

"Lost without me, huh?" He smiles, and the front desk worker giggles.

"No," I say. "I've got a lot on my mind, but you're right. I'll start tapering now."

"Good. Oh, and one more thing: you're invited over to my house the night before the race to carbo load."

"Whose idea is this?" I cross my arms. I don't like the idea of his mom glaring at me all night across the table.

"What's the matter with you?" He laughs. "Hey, Franco told me Mom kind of freaked you out, but don't worry about that. She tends to rub new people the wrong way. It's nothing personal."

"Yeah. You Harmons keep saying that."

"You *have* to come," he wheedles. "We're having pasta. And bring your mom."

"Are you sure your mom wants us invading her privacy?"

"She insisted. She's forcing Franco to come too. He didn't want to at first, because he wants me to drop out of the race altogether. But she told Franco he had no choice in the matter."

"Then how can I refuse?"

29

CLOSE MY EYES FOREVER

The next day at work, everything appears back to normal. Gus's office is organized in its usual untidy but organized fashion, his maps on the wall and a picture of him and Ben resting on the desk. In that way, Gus and I are the same. We always want our loved ones with us, no matter how much it hurts to remember the past. I wipe a speck of dust off the top edge of the silver frame then head back out into the main workspace.

Gus gestures toward the speakers. "You'll like this song. 'Respect' by Aretha Franklin. Man, she had a great voice."

I listen a moment. "I *do* like it."

"I knew you would." Gus points to a bagged body across the room. "And I haven't had a chance to check out that poor soul over there, yet. Do you mind?"

"Sure, but...first I have a question for you." I position myself so the cameras can't read my lips.

Gus pauses mid-suture to peer over his glasses. "Okay, then. Shoot. And don't worry; I've already upped the volume with my handy-dandy remote so the only words they hear are Aretha's."

"Okay, good. I need to know what you want me to do about the race."

Gus shakes his head. "I can't believe how many people have entered that stupid race. Did you know there were so many?"

"Yes, Liam told me—seven hundred fifty runners."

He raises his brows. "And you're sure you can beat all of them?"

I shrug. "I don't have any idea."

He sighs. "Here's the deal. I've asked around, and no one seems to know anything about you leaving this position. So I think we're safe. I'm not sure Dr. Edwina even looked at your chart. It might've just been a ruse. She has a sick mind, that one."

I place a hand on the cool table. "Okay, so, what do you want me to do?"

He frowns. "Maybe the more important question is, what do *you* want to do?"

I picture Liam running beside me on the treadmill, on the potholed roads, and downward-dogging next to me during yoga. My mind fills with memories of Franco biking alongside us, watching me stretch on the monorail, and making fun of Liam.

I know what I want.

"To run."

"Okay," Gus replies. "Then you should."

I take a deep breath. "And I want to win it."

He raises his eyebrows. "May I ask why?"

"It sounds horrible, I know, but I want to be better than everyone else for at least one moment in my life."

Gus snorts. "How egotistical of you."

"Yes, I know it is."

"Well, even if you're fast enough to be in the top ten, all the fastest runners attend the Championship Ball afterwards. You can meet all the Representatives. Would you like that?"

"I'm not sure."

"Yeah, I'm not sure I'd like that, either." Gus turns back to suturing. "Meanwhile, that body over there is getting cold, so to speak."

"Right. I'm on it." I cross the room and grab the file.

Female, White European Descent, nineteen-years-old, died in childbirth. Simple processing requested. No diagnostics required.

That's odd.

"Hey, Gus. What do you think of this? This girl's only a year older than me and died in childbirth. Isn't that strange? I mean, nobody gets pregnant that young anymore, and I've never heard of anyone dying during childbirth."

I unzip the black bag starting at the feet then up the pale white legs, past the purplish C-section incision, over the chest and shoulders. A long red curl falls out.

No.

It can't be.

In a fast, fluid motion I peel off the rest of the bag.

Red hair.

Lying before me, dead, is the same girl the Suits dragged into Reproductive Services on my birthday. I'm sure of it. Absolutely sure. It's her.

The metal clipboard clatters to the ground.

"I won't do it!" she had screamed as they dragged her away.

And look what happened.

Gus hurries to my side and gathers up the chart. "What are you doing?"

"Where is it?" I dig through the long bag, frantically searching. "Where is it?"

Gus places a firm hand on my shoulder. "Silvia, calm down. Remember who's watching."

"Where's the baby?" I ask, jamming a hand into every empty corner of the bag.

Gus glances at the chart. "You'll never find the baby. It's not here."

"You mean it's alive?" I ask, hopeful.

"Actually, it doesn't say." He shakes his head. "I'm sorry. It's hard to see someone so young dead."

"That's not all of it." My hand pauses at the incision from the C-section. Black sutures stand at attention along the long scar. "Gus..."

His gaze follows mine.

"Doesn't that chart say she died in childbirth?"

"Yes."

"Then can you explain why this incision is at least two weeks old?"

3 0

TRY NOT TO BREATHE

"Here's what's going to happen," instructs Gus. "I need you to move around to that side of the table, so no one can read your lips. Have you got a grip on yourself now?"

"No, Gus, I don't." I do as he directs and stand on the opposite side of the table to face him, my back to the camera. "In case you haven't noticed, I'm actually kind of freaking out."

"Then can you fake it?"

I gulp a deep breath. "Yes."

"Good." Gus pauses. "Now, explain to me why you're so upset. Did you know this young lady from school?"

"No. I recognized her from the street." I try to calm my breathing, but I'm close to hyperventilating. Not good. I won't be able to hide that from the cameras.

"Silvia, you pass hundreds of people a day—"

"I know, but this was different. On my birthday, my mom brought me to Genetic Counseling—"

"Nice birthday present. If I'd known you were getting the day off for that, maybe I would've raised more of a fuss."

"That's beside the point." I take a deep breath. "She took me to the park afterward, so it was fine. But on the way there was a holdup in traffic because this girl was screaming and trying to get away while the Suits dragged her into Citizen Family Planning and Reproductive Services."

Gus tenses.

I narrow my eyes. "You still haven't answered my question about the scar."

He takes a deep breath. "That's because I don't know, and I'm afraid to guess."

"Maybe she was in a coma afterward, and the chart is incomplete," I offer. "Maybe they used some advanced tissue adhesive I've never seen before and it speeds healing. Maybe there was an accident..." I come up empty.

"Maybe. Maybe not." Gus stares at the chart. "Process her and be done with it. I don't want you getting into trouble over someone you didn't even know, so don't make a fuss. It's too late for her now, no matter what happened."

Can Gus really be so cold inside?

Breathing deeply, I pretend I'm in yoga class instead of Mortuary Sciences and pick up the scalpel. I incise the skin on each upper arm to release the microchip and birth control capsule, setting them both to the side. Then I clean away any traces of blood, smooth her hair, and zip the bag closed over her body. There's nothing else to do for her.

Except...

Cupping the capsules in my hand, I cross the room to the tall metal disposal chambers. Using the scanner, I record the microchip. As her personal information flashes across the screen, I commit the home address to memory. Then I crack open the birth control capsule, ready to sprinkle the contents in the containment chamber.

But it's empty.

THE RED-HAIRED GIRL's name was Amelia Brown. She lived in the Southeast sector of the city. After work I head straight to the gym, but that's not where I intend to stay, no matter if Liam is there or not.

It's a relief when he's a no-show, so I don't have to explain myself. I hurry to dress in the locker room, careful to wear all race-appropriate clothing, including a white training baseball cap with green stripes across the bill. The hat will keep the sun off my black hair, and the bill will hide the top half of my face from the cameras. I leave the running watch in the small side pocket of my bag.

Tightening my ponytail, I approach the wall displaying the training-approved routes. I grab one of the fliers. There are several paths leading into the Southeast sector, but only one will take me within a half mile of Amelia's home. The route is several miles longer than I should be running this close to the race, but I don't care. I need to see that the baby is okay. It's the least I can do.

After a few active stretches, far less than I usually do, I'm on my way, carrying a printed map in my pocket in case I get turned around. But somehow my feet seem to know right where they're headed. Alone in the car lane, which has temporarily been approved for race training, I forge ahead. Ten minutes in I spot two other runners far ahead of me. I speed up.

As I pass them, the girl calls out, "Hey, don't you know you're supposed to be tapering?"

I don't respond. Even though the walking and biking lanes are full, all I can hear is the sound of my own breath and the slap of my shoes on the pavement. The world spins around me, but I'm the only one here.

When it feels like I've run about three miles, I search for an overhead camera. Once I'm positioned right, I glance down at my wrist then fake that I'm upset I forgot my watch. I only do this for a second because I don't want to overplay the ruse.

Approximately six miles in I spot 35th Avenue Southeast and hang a right. I need a drinking fountain. I scan both sides of the street then slow to a stop when I spot one. There's another camera overhead.

I stretch and drink, massage my left calf muscles then rotate the ankle on that side. Now I'm walking. As soon as possible, I melt into the crowd. A half mile later I turn onto Amelia's street and pause. What should I do? I need to find that baby.

The sound of children playing attracts me to a small park a half block down. Kids scamper around, kicking balls, jumping rope, all within the confines of a tall fence. Half the park is pavement; the other half grass with very few trees.

I see brown hair, blond, and black. But no red. Amelia Brown's survivor list included two younger sisters, a mother, and a dad. Maybe they're eating supper.

I pass the park and keep walking, all the way up to the front door of their apartment building. I stop. What could I possibly say to these people? I stare at the entrance until I have to step aside for another occupant hurrying home with rations.

Biting my lip, I turn away, retreating slowly until I reach the busy park. All at once, my legs feel too tired to go on. I enter the park and approach the nearest bench with a good view of Amelia's apartment. Before sitting, I stretch my legs, which are starting to ache.

An older woman rests on a bench across from me, a red balloon tied around her wrist. Her watery eyes don't seem to focus on anything.

"Is it time for bed?" she asks.

I'm not sure if she's talking to herself or me, but I answer, "It's more like supper time, really."

"Why aren't you eating?" She shakes her head. "You're too skinny. Girls are too skinny nowadays."

A woman rushes over, tucking a stray curl behind her ear. "Oh, I'm so sorry. Don't pay any attention to her. Please don't be offended. She'll say anything to anyone, her mind the way it is, but she doesn't mean any harm."

"It's fine," I assure her. "She isn't bothering me."

The woman rubs the elderly lady's hand. "I wanted to bring her to the park today. It's her birthday. But my hands are already full with my granddaughter." She points at a young girl digging in a sandbox.

The little girl picks up a shovel and begins to spoon dirt into her mouth.

"Oh, no." The woman sprints back to her. "Spit that out, Claudia. You know better than to eat dirt."

"It does look like you have your hands full," I call after her, sitting down by the elderly woman. "Happy birthday."

"Life and death," she replies.

"What about life and death?" I ask.

"Everyone thinks they're enemies, but they're not. They're friends. They walk hand in hand."

I nod.

"Such lovely hair." She touches my long, black ponytail.

"Thank you."

"Be glad it's not red. Red is a bad luck color." She scowls at the balloon tied to her wrist and shakes her hand as if to be rid of it. "Black is good luck. Such good luck."

"My father had red hair."

She frowns, tugging on the balloon. "Then he's dead."

I tense. "Yes, he died eight years ago. But how could you know—"

"They're all dead. Girl. Baby. All dead."

Does she know what she's talking about? Or is she just crazy?

Her bony fingers grip my shoulder. "Don't trust anyone. They'll kill you and cut you to pieces."

The daughter rushes back. "Oh, dear. I better get her home. I'm so sorry. She doesn't know what she's saying. Her mind goes in and out like a worn-out light bulb."

I stand and move away. "I'm afraid she doesn't like her balloon. Something about the color red bothers her."

"Yeah. Ever since our neighbors—that poor family—lost their daughter in childbirth."

"That's so sad." Part of me knows it's wrong to keep pushing, but I do it anyway. "What about the baby?"

"The baby died too. Poor little thing." She helps the old lady to her feet.

I drag over the walker standing nearby.

"Oh, thank you," she says. "You'll have to excuse me. Claudia, we're leaving. I said *right now*, Claudia."

I let them pass, empty inside. If the baby is dead, then where is it? Why didn't it get sent to the Incinerator like all the others?

Glancing at a nearby overhead clock, I realize I'd better head home if I don't want to get in trouble with Mom. I've got a long way to go and not much in the way of answers. My feet swiftly take me back the same route I used to get here. This time of evening, most people pass me with end-of-the-day exhausted work faces. I hurry along the inner edge of the walk lane for a short while, and then jump back into the designated race-approved car lane as soon as I reach it. I press onward, trying to focus on my form. Force myself to lift my legs higher, use my glutes more, utilize my core—anything to take my mind away from my thoughts. What does a stupid race matter, now? Why does everyone always have to die?

Miles churn by, and it's all a blur. I make my way back to the 37th Street Gym without even trying. I go to my locker, grab my gym bag, and speed home without changing. I just want to be alone. In the shower. In my bed. Somewhere where I can cry, and nobody has to know about it.

It's a relief to find our apartment empty although it's odd for Mom to be out this late. I shower and go immediately to bed without eating or stretching. I don't care about all that tonight.

I WAKE up stiff and sore the next morning—not good, considering the race is only a couple days away. The apartment is empty again, but by the dishes in the sink, I can tell Mom had hot cereal for breakfast.

One teacup sits upside down on the countertop. She'll be back later, alone, as usual. I hurry to work, rush downstairs, and fly through the open doors of Mortuary Sciences.

The gurneys shake with the beat.

Gus points to the speakers. "You're just in time for another classic —'November Rain' by Guns and Roses. You need to pay special attention to the ending. It's important."

I position myself alongside him, pretending to examine the body he's processing, my back to the cameras. "I gotta talk to you."

"What's up?"

My eyes well. I'm not sure why. I don't even know these people. "The baby's dead."

"Yes...but how do you know this?" He frowns. "I hope you didn't look it up. They can trace that, you know."

I shake my head. "No. I went there."

He leans closer. "You went *where*, exactly?"

"To where they live, and I talked to some crazy lady in the park."

Gus hands me a suture scissor. "Make yourself useful. You need to focus. Now keep talking."

My hands shake, clenching the scissor. "The lady was really old. She said she liked my hair. That black was lucky and red was dangerous. That everyone with red hair dies."

Gus purses his lips. "Silvia, she wasn't talking about your dad."

"She could've been. Then her daughter rushed up and, with some prompting on my part, told me about Amelia's family."

"I wish you wouldn't have done that." Gus finishes his continuous line of suture then leans back for me to cut the ends. "You don't want anyone to accuse you of invasion of privacy and terminate your position here."

"I had to do it. I needed to know."

"You could've asked me."

"I did. You didn't say anything."

"Goodness, girl. You have to give me a little time. If you'd been patient, I was going to tell you today that the baby's body was processed in the Southeast Sector two weeks ago."

"So, it did die during childbirth. But what about the mother? Why were they processed two weeks apart?"

"That question I can't answer with a simple computer search."

I cock my head. "Wait a minute—I thought you said not to look it up in case it gets traced."

"They can't trace me. Not the way I do it."

3 1

EVERYBODY HURTS

Gus sends me home early from work, promising to watch me race tomorrow. The walk home should relax me, but my legs are so tired from my long run yesterday that all I do is worry I've ruined my chances at racing well.

I collapse into bed, scrubs still on, staring across the room at Dad's picture.

Hours later, Mom shakes me awake. "Hurry up, Silvia. We haven't got much time to get ready."

I groan, throwing an arm over my eyes. "For what?"

"Dinner at Liam's."

Oh, yeah. I sit up in a flash.

Without thinking much about it, I change out of my scrubs and slip on jeans and a long-sleeved green T-shirt. I don't want Linda to see my scars. She dislikes me enough as it is. Or, at least, it sure seems that way.

"Let me fix your hair." Mom pushes me into the bathroom and positions me in front of the mirror. She pulls out my ponytail, rubs in some styling cream, and brushes my long black hair down over my shoulders.

As I face my reflection, I realize I'm wearing the same outfit I wore on my birthday. I hope that's not a bad omen.

"There. You're perfect." Mom smiles at me in the mirror.

"You always could work my hair better than I can," I answer.

She pats my shoulder. "Time to go."

We rush downstairs and into the street. Masses of people trot along with us. I try to keep my eyes averted so I won't see anyone with red hair, but it doesn't work. A tall man with short red hair hovers at my right side.

"Why are you so jumpy tonight?" asks Mom. "Pre-race jitters?"

My stomach clenches, my back is stiff, and my legs are sore. I'm doomed. But it's not the race that bothers me. The red-haired man matches my footsteps, his arms swinging back and forth. I slow my pace in hopes he'll pass by.

"Come on, Silvia," Mom urges. "We don't want to be late."

I don't lose sight of the red-haired stranger until we make the last turn to Liam's apartment building. My hands tremble, but at least he's gone now.

Mom and I enter the complex. She fidgets as we wait in the hallway outside Liam's apartment. Why is *she* so nervous tonight?

Linda opens the door, an unreadable expression on her face. "Yoshe Wood. I've heard you play. You're a magnificent violinist. Please, come in."

Mom enters ahead of me. Nobody seems to notice that I don't receive the same warm welcome. Liam sits on the floor of the small living room, both of his younger sisters vying for his attention. Lydia is nine, and Lucy is eleven. I'll bet neither of them really remembers their father.

A comforting fragrance of tomato and basil fills the air. Franco stands next to the stove, stirring the pot. He says something I can't hear over the wild living room banter, so I step closer.

"I'm sorry. What did you say?" I ask.

He smiles. "I was merely informing you there aren't any gelatin-based protein cubes on the menu this evening."

"Thank goodness." I grimace. "I hate those things."

His smile grows. "Yes, I remember."

"Experimental alternative sources of protein, then?"

"Perhaps." He chuckles and gestures toward his cousin. "You might be interested to know that Liam over there has already assured us of your double victory tomorrow."

"Oh, has he?" I glance at the three siblings, laughing together. They seem so happy.

"Yes, but I was wondering how *you* feel about the big race." Franco watches me closely.

I shrug. "I'm not so sure, I guess." Instead of focusing on the race plan Liam and I devised weeks ago, I'm obsessed with the death of Amelia Brown. I can't escape her red hair and pale skin. The image of her cold body lying on the mortuary table blends with the portrait of my father hanging in my room. Back and forth, the pictures flicker and fuse until the two become one. It's not like they're the only people in Panopticus with red hair, but their deaths have bonded them together in my mind.

I'm starting to hate red hair.

Franco tests a noodle with a fork and announces, "I hope you all are hungry because it's time to eat."

We gather around the table, the two younger girls chattering non-stop on either side of Liam. Franco serves, Linda bustles around, handing out plates and drinks, and my mom keeps asking if she can help.

"No, you're the guest of honor," Linda assures her.

So, Mom is the guest of honor, not me. How nice.

"I propose a toast," announces Liam.

Franco clamps his mouth shut but picks up his glass after Linda glares at him.

Liam stands and pushes back his chair. "First, I'd like to thank Mom and Franco for this wonderful dinner."

"You're very welcome." Linda's face transforms when she smiles at her only son. She almost looks like a nice person, for once.

Franco only grunts in response, a storm brewing in his eyes.

Liam turns to me. "And secondly, I'd like to thank Silvia for training with me, teaching me about yoga—"

Franco laughs, and the storm clouds disperse.

"Shut up, Franco." Liam makes a face. "And, finally, I'd like to pre-thank Silvia for racing with me as Team Win tomorrow. I know we can do it." He lifts his glass.

I'm not as confident as Liam but lift my glass in return. "And thank you for getting me off the treadmills. How will we ever go back?"

While everyone else drinks, I realize this is the end. No more limited, government-issued freedom. No more extra passes, increased food portions, and special attention. And, quite likely, there will be no more time with Franco.

I turn to him as he settles into the chair next to me. My mother and Linda sit next to each other, bending their heads together in conversation. Franco focuses on his food, and I try to do the same but find it hard to eat. I want to sit still and do nothing. I remain silent and hide my thoughts in the company of others.

Franco is as quiet as I am, but Liam glows with excitement, bantering back and forth with his sisters. My mind is too numb to follow their conversation.

My mom laughs and smiles. She seems so happy. Is it a show or for real? I can't tell anymore.

And then there's Linda. I watch the woman who, simply because she had a fight with her husband, caused me to try to kill myself. Twice. When she returns my gaze briefly, I wonder if she's thinking similar things about me. I tug at my sleeves to cover my wrists. I don't want her to see my scars.

At the end of the meal, Linda stands. "And now, Liam, I have a small gift for you hidden in my room. But first, let's clear the table."

Everyone carries their own plates to the sink except for Lydia and Lucy, who fight over the honor of waiting on Liam.

Linda eyes me as she clears my mostly untouched plate. "Don't you like spaghetti?"

At my side, Mom hurries to make excuses. "So sorry, Linda. The meal was delicious. I'm afraid my daughter has a nervous stomach."

"Yes," I agree, to appease everyone. "I'm sorry. I don't think I could eat anything tonight." I walk away.

Dinner plates clink in the sink. Voices bubble around me. I wander over to the couch and pick up a cushion. It's red. I want to rip it apart, throw it on the floor, and jump on it until it's destroyed. I feel so sad and angry at the same time and can't make any sense of it.

My stomach convulses, and I glance around for signs of a bathroom. There's a dark hallway past the living room. I rush toward it. There are four doors in the hallway, and all of them are shut. I'll have to guess which one's the bathroom. I reach for a doorknob.

Muffled voices freeze my hand in mid-air.

"She knows." Linda's tense voice whispers from behind a closed door. "I tell you she knows. I can see it in her eyes."

"She doesn't know," Franco murmurs.

"Well, she at least suspects."

"She's smart, Linda. She can tell you're edgy around her. Maybe you should try to act normal for a change."

"I want you to stay away from her," Linda pleads. "We have to be safe. They're still watching us. They're always watching, waiting for us to screw up."

"We *are* safe. I've spent my life making sure of that. But if you want to be invisible, you never should've let Liam sign up for that race."

"Are you going to stay away from her or not? I see the way you look at the girl."

My heart hammers in my chest as I wait through a long pause in the conversation.

Franco clears his throat. "I'm just keeping an eye on her. I feel bad about things. Have you seen her wrists? That's because of *us.*"

"Don't you think I know that?" Linda sighs. "At least Liam and the girls had you. That poor child had no one. No wonder she hurt herself. Everyone else hurt her too."

"Silvia?" Mom calls from the living room. "Where are—"

I bolt out of the dimly lit hallway.

"There you are."

"We should go." I interrupt her, heading for the front door.

"What's wrong?" She narrows her eyes. "Oh, dear. You look sick. And you hardly ate anything for supper. No, it couldn't be... You're not—"

I turn away and head for the door, Mom close behind me.

She grabs my arm and pulls me close to whisper in my ear. "Silvia, *please* tell me you're not pregnant."

"*Are you kidding me?*" I roll my eyes. "Of course not. Don't be ridiculous." I wave at my running partner, eager to get far, far away from his family. "Bye, Liam."

"Where are you going?" he asks. "The party's just getting started."

"Pre-race jitters or whatever. Sorry." I return my attention to my mother. "Let's go." I open the door, but Mom doesn't move. "Please can we go? I don't feel well, and I want to go home *now*."

"Okay." Mom sighs and turns to Liam. "Please make our excuses to your mom. I'm sure it's just a case of the nerves. We'll see you tomorrow."

Liam grabs me into a hug I don't want, especially not right now. "Come on, Silvia. You know you're going to be awesome. There's no reason to be nervous. See ya tomorrow."

I break away and flee down the hall. Mom hurries after me.

I punch the button for the elevator. "I can't believe you think I'm pregnant. You, of all people." I spin around to face her. "What is everyone's obsession with that topic lately? I swear I've taken more pregnancy tests—"

"What?" Her eyes fly open wide. "Why are you taking pregnancy tests?"

"Every frigging time I go to that stupid Citizen Family Planning Center, they force me to pee in a cup."

Mom pauses. "Okay, calm down. That's probably standard procedure at your age."

I point to my upper arm. "But they've already injected me with their government-issued birth control. So what's their problem?"

Mom lowers her voice. "Well, there *have* been rumors."

My hands begin to shake. "Really? What rumors? About me?"

"No." She covers her mouth with a hand, so no one watching the cameras can read her lips. "About girls getting pregnant. At first, there was talk that The New Order should lower the birth control mandate to fifteen, but then I heard that the girls who'd gotten pregnant had already been injected. So then the rumor was that some of the capsules were faulty."

My eyes widen. "I know. Sometimes they're empty when I remove them."

"Really?" Mom grimaces like she does any time I mention dead bodies.

I nod. We step into the open elevator and remain silent until we get back in the relative safety of the noisy outdoor traffic.

"I suppose no system is perfect," Mom says once we're on the street. "No vaccine is a hundred percent effective. No chemotherapy works for all cancer patients. This is the same thing. Maybe some people's bodies absorb the hormones too fast, rendering them ineffective."

"Maybe. I suppose that's possible." That's a reasonable explanation, but it doesn't explain the discrepancy in dates between the deaths of Amelia and her child. I shiver despite the summer night's heat. "But why would that kill them?"

"What are you talking about?" Mom leans in close to whisper in the midst of the street traffic.

"Well..." I check for overhead cameras. "When you heard these rumors, did all the pregnant girls die?"

"Of course not. The babies did, but we're used to that." Mom gives me a little hug. "You don't know how discouraged your father and I felt after all those miscarriages. Then came you, our lucky charm."

I frown. "I don't feel so lucky tonight."

Mom rubs my shoulder. "I'm worried you're coming down with something. You know you don't have to race tomorrow if you don't want to."

"No, I have to." I flinch as a red-headed woman passes us by, rushing in the other direction. "I just need to take a bath and go to bed."

Mom bites her lip. "I know you're used to getting extra treats because of this race, but you shouldn't get in the habit of being wasteful."

"Come on, Mom. The last time I took a bath was six months ago when I had a cold. Otherwise, I never use more than my allotted five-minute shower a day."

We reach our building. Mom opens the front door, and I head for the stairs.

Mom takes my arm. "Let's take the elevator this time. You look exhausted."

Up we travel. I trudge down the hall to our home and lean against the wall as Mom unlocks the door.

She frowns. "Why don't you use my water allotment for today? You need it more than I do."

I give her a grateful smile. "Thanks, Mom."

Once inside the apartment, I run a bath, holding my hand in the stream of scalding water without flinching, forcing myself to become numb. It's safer that way. Must not feel too much.

Inside the bathroom cupboard, I find a lavender satchel and drop it into the steaming bath. I climb in, welcoming the heat, willing it to dissolve the chill inside. Sighing, I lean my cheek against the smooth white tile. My sore, overused muscles relax in the warmth as my mind races. What is Linda so scared of? Why does she hate the very thought of me? And she doesn't have to worry about Franco. It's obvious he just feels sorry for me. There's nothing I hate more than that. I don't want people's sympathy. I want their respect. That's why I'm running tomorrow. To prove I'm tough. To show there's more to me than what those doctors said. Despite their doomsday predictions, I will survive. I've figured out that hurting myself doesn't harm them. More likely, it's exactly what they want. When The New Order put a suicidal patient to work in Mortuary Services, their intentions became obvious.

On the other hand, my motives are hidden.

They'll never get into my mind.

It's the only escape I have.

MY FINGERTIPS RELISH the softness of the beautiful red dress Dad made for me to celebrate Mom's big concert. I sway slightly, side to side, and feel the swish of the fabric against my legs. The sky darkens, and I lean against my father.

He hugs me with a wink. "Don't fall asleep yet, hon. You have to wake up."

My eyes fly open. I flail in the now-cool bath.

"Wake up, Silvia. I'm counting on you." His voice again.

So close to my ear.

"Dad? Where are you?" I jump up, splashing water over the bath edge. "What's going on?"

But he's not here.

It's just another cruel dream.

I dry off and go to bed, still shivering. The city lights filter through the bedroom window and settle on Dad's face, forever imprisoned in a picture frame on the wall.

Tears spring to my eyes. "Dad, I could really use some help."

3 2

LET'S GET PHYSICAL

"Hurry, wake up!" Mom shakes my arm.

I groan as the sunlight hits my eyes. "Is it morning already?"

"How do you feel?" She peers into my face. "Are you okay to run? I let you sleep as long as I could."

"Of course I'm fine to race. I told you, I'm not sick. It's just nerves." I throw off the covers, jump out of bed, and change as fast as possible.

Skipping breakfast, we rush down the street to the race's check-in site. New Order flags in red, white, and blue flutter above each doorway in celebration of the event. Mom and I arrive, out of breath, at a tent. Long rows of runners wait to reach the tables inside. The place is a mad house. Lots of serious faces and attitude. Plenty of bulging leg muscles. A few splashes of face paint like ancient warriors. I wonder where they got the paint. Gus would probably know.

Liam pushes his way to us in the mob. "Hey there, Silvia. Time to hurry up and wait, eh?" He gestures to the line ahead of us.

"Did your family drop you off?" I ask him.

He nods.

I turn to Mom. "I guess you don't have to wait with us, either, if you don't want to."

"What else do I have to do today?" She puts her hands on her hips. "You can't get rid of me that easily. I want to be here."

"Okay, then. Stay." Why does every conversation with my mother turn into an argument?

We creep ahead in line as the runners check in, one by one. Each entrant leaves with a red shirt and blue baseball hat in hand.

"Are you kidding?" I sigh. "We have to wear red today?"

"What's wrong with it?" Liam shrugs. "I'll bet you look nice in red. I've never seen you wear it."

Mom smirks, averting her eyes.

"I don't like that color," I explain.

"Why not?" Liam asks. "I thought your dad's hair was red—Oh gosh, I can't believe I just said that. I mean, Franco told me about that picture in your room, and—"

Mom puts a hand on Liam's arm. "That's okay. I'm sure you didn't mean any harm, but when Silvia was a little girl, Daniel—her father—made her the most beautiful red dress. Then he died, and she's never worn the color since."

"I haven't?" I ask.

"No," Mom replies. "Don't you remember?"

"Yes, I remember the dress, but I don't recall ever having made the decision—"

"Name please!" A voice barks. I've reached the front of the line.

"Uh...Silvia Wood."

"Give me your arm." The check-in attendant scans my identification then hands me a standard red shirt and blue hat. "Good luck. Next!"

"Thanks," I mumble and turn away.

Liam signs in, changes into the uniform shirt in a flash, then stands, holding his discarded green shirt in his hand. "What am I supposed to do with this?"

"I'll take it," Mom offers, and Liam hands it over. They both turn to stare at me.

"I've got to change out here in front of everyone?" I ask, flushing.

"You're wearing a sports bra, or at least I hope so. What's the problem?" asks Mom.

Liam chuckles. "Don't worry. I'll turn around."

Once he does, I first make sure Franco isn't anywhere nearby, then I quickly change and hand my mom my extra shirt. Now I hate looking at myself. All I can see is red. I slip my ponytail through my hat.

"Okay, I'll let you two get to the starting line. Good luck! And don't worry—you'll both do fine. You've worked so hard." Mom gives me a quick, tense hug and disappears into the crowd.

Liam elbows me. "You ready for this?"

I shake out my hands to try to get rid of the nerves. "Yes. How's your knee?"

"Good as new. You're gonna have trouble keeping up with me."

"Oh yeah?" I smile. "So much for all your talk about us running this together as a team."

He grins back. "I'm just kidding. I'd probably die out there without you egging me on. Franco's right. I'm letting you be in charge today. So, do you want to use hand signals to let me know when you're going to pass somebody?"

"How about we point ahead? Keep it simple and work from there."

"Okay." Liam leans in close as we approach the starting corral. "I like it. Where do you want to start?"

"Not right in the front, because I don't want to get trampled, but not too far back so we get stuck. How about a few rows in, on the left side, because the first turn is to the left?"

Liam nods once. "This is why I let you make all the decisions. Okay, let's go."

The runners wait in the starting corral. Everyone leans back to watch footage on an overhead screen near the Capitol Center. Each Representative gives a short speech encouraging the runners.

Liam whispers in my ear. "Are they seriously going to make us listen to all these speeches right before we take off? What a killjoy."

I try to smile but can't. I feel like I'm going to puke.

Representative Nielsen, an older man with a bad cough, attempts to speak from his hospital bed. "Congratulations to all of you young people, for putting forth such effort..." He coughs. "And determination." Again, his speech is interrupted by a wet cough. "We are...saving the planet and saving ourselves... One step at a time."

The crowd claps, and I follow suit to not stand out. Not when eyes and cameras are recording everything.

The announcer steps up to the podium and declares, "And now, the one you've been waiting for—Representative Waters-Royce and her new baby!"

I flinch as the crowd starts cheering and her image floods the screen, her glossy red hair flowing over her shoulders, her skin tight with no sign of wrinkles. She holds her newborn like an accessory. The people grow quiet as she begins to speak.

"This is the time to be proud of what you have accomplished," she says. "A time to appreciate our New World. A time to move ahead. Expect great things from the future!"

The overhead screen goes blank. A cheer rises up from the crowd of runners again.

"Well, if that just doesn't get me in the mood," Liam jokes.

I can't smile. My nerves are too on edge.

I shut out everything but the announcer's voice. "On your mark, get set, GO!"

And we're off.

The thunder of feet.

The erratic sound of my own breath.

People everywhere, both in the road and lining the streets. It's elbow to elbow. There's a scramble for placement. I keep pointing and surging.

I've got to get away from the crowd. It's the only way I'll be able to settle in.

Liam follows my lead.

A half mile in, sweat breaks across my upper back. The crowd thins slightly, but it's still hard to maneuver to the front. Then we're at the first mile. A 6:30 split.

Okay. We just need to keep this up. There are aid stations every two miles with water and sports drinks. Mentally, I break down the race by aid stations.

I keep pointing. We pass person after person without overdoing it. There's still a long way to go.

Mile two. 13:01. We can't get sloppy. Need to stay on track. Only the people ahead of us matter, not the exact time. But we can't get slower with each mile, or we'll lose our focus. I grab a sports drink, swallow, and toss.

We pass more people, picking them off, one by one. Once I can see we're in the top ten, I settle in to ride it out. All I have to do is keep them in sight. Let them reel me in.

I relax my shoulders into the mountain yoga position then clench and release my hands. Can't waste energy in the upper body. Use the core. My head sweats under the cap.

Miles three and four. My eyes start to water. The wind tunnel between the tall buildings grabs at my hat. With one swift move, I tighten it. Liam races beside me. So far, he isn't favoring the leg. If he does, I'll have to forge ahead alone, but I don't want to do this by myself. I shove the thought away.

Miles five and six. More sports drink. I wipe my brow, get the salt out of my eyes. We're in the top pack. Our times are on target.

"Silvia!" Mom screams from the sidelines. "Go, Silvia! And Liam, you too!"

Then she's gone from view. We press on through mile seven.

A flash of red hair distracts me. I see my father pushing through the crowd and almost trip. Then the stranger bends down to hand a little girl some ice cream. I force my gaze back to the road.

Get a grip. Focus. Your father's dead. Forget about him.

My right calf spasms. I wince. Why does it hurt? I've never had a problem with it before.

Never mind. Ignore it. Doesn't matter.

We're pulling up to mile eight. I need more sports drink. The electrolytes will fix my leg; I'm sure of it.

The refreshment table is up ahead. Volunteers hand cups to the few runners left in front of us. A red-haired girl dashes out to hand me a drink. Amelia had two younger sisters. What if this is one of them?

It is. She's wearing a black scarf of mourning. I veer away, almost tripping over Liam to escape her.

"What are you doing?" he sputters, grabbing two cups from the girl and handing one to me.

As I take the cup, my vision clears. The girl's not wearing a mourning scarf. She just has a black T-shirt on. I've got to relax.

No, I can't relax. We're only halfway into the race. Got to focus. Forget about the red hair, for once.

A half mile later, I notice that my leg stopped hurting. Now, pain shoots across my back instead. I raise and drop my shoulders, stretch my neck side to side, do what I can to alleviate it. Despite the screaming crowds, my own breath echoes the loudest in my ears.

Mile nine is history.

Mile ten at 1:04:50. Another refreshment table. This time I force myself to approach. No more surprises. As I reach down for a glass, the table wavers, transforming to a gurney. Amelia Brown's body appears, surrounded by glasses of water and sports drinks. I yelp.

It's not real. I know it's not real.

I force myself to grab a glass.

Amelia reaches up to grasp my arm.

I scream and flail.

Liam grips my shoulder and steadies me. "What's wrong? Come on, let's go."

We drink and toss. I point, and away we go.

"I see we're picking up the pace," gasps Liam.

By mile eleven, we're in the top five. My feet burn. There's a crick in my neck. My right Achilles tendon feels tight. Just in time for the last 2.1 miles, all a gradual uphill.

I lean into the incline, my hamstrings on fire. Semimembranosus and semitendinosus muscles twang in unison. We're almost there but still not in the lead.

At mile twelve, I see them along the sidelines—a red-haired mother with two younger girls, all wearing black mourning scarves. I'm not sure if they're real or my imagination. I tear my eyes away and surge ahead.

Liam grunts from behind me. "Are you crazy? You can't flat-out sprint the last mile!"

"Just watch me."

My feet falter, then I regroup. No. Mustn't think of Dad. Mustn't think of anyone. Not Franco. Not Linda. Only this race matters.

The wind swoops down and blows off my hat.

I leave it behind.

We're nearing the end. Only a few blocks left.

I blaze past three other runners, no idea if Liam's with me or not. I can't see anything but the road. Can't hear anything but my breath. Can't feel anything but the wind.

The flags are in sight. The clock's overhead. 1:21:08.

I'm almost there. I've got this.

"And our winner is..." the announcement comes over the loudspeaker.

Representative Waters-Royce steps forward, a medal in her hands. She's all I can see. Her sharp suit gathers at her small waist.

Mom's voice rings in my head: *How do famous people manage to look so good pregnant? No bloated faces. It's not fair.*

No woman could look that good right after having a baby. Maybe she had more plastic surgery? Or maybe—

No. Not that.

I stop.

Right in the middle of the road.

My mind flashes to the pre-race speech, the red-haired baby, less than a month old.

It can't be.

What if Representative Waters-Royce stole Amelia Brown's baby because she couldn't have one of her own?

I think she did. In fact, I know she did. I want to pull out her hair, punch her in the nose, and demand to see her stretch marks.

"What are you doing, crazy girl?" grunts Liam, who grabs my arm and drags me across the finish line.

"Our winner is...Liam Harmon!"

33

STAND BY ME

Representative Waters-Royce narrows her eyes. "She's in shock. Take her to the medical tent, immediately."

"Liam, will you go with me?" I ask, but he's already gone, whisked away by Representative Waters-Royce herself. They climb up the stairs to a podium and wave to the crowd.

"Come with me, please." A race attendant offers his hand. "You need to get out of the way of the other runners."

I shake my head, stubborn. "But I don't want to—"

"I've got her." Franco swoops in, puts an arm around my stinky, sweaty back, and hauls me away.

"I'm fine," I argue. "I don't want to go to the medical tent."

He raises his brows. "You don't *look* fine."

There it is again—his sympathy. He feels sorry for me, that's all.

I pull away from his touch. "I can walk by myself. I'm not an invalid."

"Suit yourself." Franco points. "There's the aid tent, right over there."

I shake my head. "I don't see why I have to go in there."

He stops walking and turns to me, his face grave. "Okay, then explain to me why you stopped running less than a hundred feet short of the finish line?"

"Well, I—"

He leans in close to whisper. "Your choices include: exhaustion, dehydration, and disorientation...*or* an open protest against the most popular Representative in The New Order party. Which is it going to be?"

I pause. "Disorientation sounds nice."

"I knew you'd see reason." Franco puts his arm around me again, guiding me into the medical tent. As soon as we step inside, he declares, "We've got a fainter."

Everyone swarms me, pushing me down on the medical bed and touching me everywhere. Franco steps aside to watch my humiliation.

"Are you thirsty?" someone asks.

"Yes." Of course. I just ran a half-marathon.

"Is your mouth dry? Does your tongue feel swollen?" someone asks from the other side.

I turn but can't figure out who's talking. "Yes. And no."

"Do you feel weak or dizzy?" a third voice pesters me.

"Uh...yes, sort of. I'm kind of tired." After all that running. Duh.

A freezing cold stethoscope slides up my shirt. I flinch.

"Does your heart feel like it's pounding?" the med tech asks.

I take a deep breath, trying to avoid telling her exactly *where* she can shove her frigid stethoscope. "Yeah, well, I recently raced a half-marathon, and I really think I should go stretch instead of lying here. I'm going to stiffen up."

The stethoscope is removed. "She's hyperthermic, her heart rate's elevated, and she's babbling. We need to cool her and perhaps start an IV."

I try to stand but hands hold me down. "Are you kidding? I don't need IV fluids. I just need lunch."

"You called?" Gus, my savior, appears in the tent, one of his fabric food bags in hand. "I've got her."

"Please, step aside." An assistant puts a hand on Gus's shoulder. "We're medical professionals here."

"Really? I couldn't tell." Gus pushes through to sit by my side.

A pale-faced runner staggers into the tent and vomits all over the floor.

Gus gestures at the prostrate man. "Looks to me like that fellow over there could use your assistance. Why don't you help *him* instead and leave *us* alone?"

The crowd around me disperses.

"Sandwich?" Gus asks, handing over his lunch bag.

"You're a total life-safer." I eat a banana first then the sandwich. At the same time, I stand and stretch my super-tight quads.

"Franco..." Gus growls. "Why did you bring her in here?"

Franco cowers. "I'm sorry. I thought it was best."

"Why don't you act out of character and go do something useful —like finding Yoshe and bringing her here."

Another vomiting runner enters the tent.

Gus cringes. "Scratch that. Bring Yoshe to that bench across the way. We're out of here."

Franco disappears as Gus helps me hobble over to the bench. I'm still eating. I can't get enough food.

I drain his drink canister and nod toward the refreshment table. "I'm still thirsty. Do you mind?"

"Your wish is my command." Gus strolls over to the stand and returns with two water canisters and two sports drinks.

"Oh, *thank you*." In one hand, I hold up the drink. With the other, I lean against a pole to ease my tight IT bands.

Gus peers into the crowd, a hand over his eyes. "I see your mother approaching. Are you okay to walk home?"

I nod. "I better walk now, or else I'll regret it later."

Mom races toward me. "Why aren't you in the med tent? Are you okay? Did you faint? I heard you stopped right before the finish. What happened?"

"Yeah, I got disoriented. You know, I skipped breakfast and then did all that running. I just got confused. Thank goodness Liam was there to help me."

"Yes. He's off with Franco, Linda, and the girls now." Yoshe cocks her head. "But you need rest; I can see that. Let's go home."

She slips an arm around me, Gus takes my other side, and we retreat slowly back to the apartment, one step at a time.

34

WE ARE THE CHAMPIONS

Hours later, after a long soothing salt bath—Mom doesn't even raise an eyebrow this time—and an even longer nap, I wander into our tiny living room to discover Gus and Mom having tea.

"Hey, Gus." I rub my weary eyes. "I'm sorry I've been sleeping. I didn't realize you were still here."

Gus stands, glancing at his watch. "Well, now, look at the time. I'm afraid I've kept you from your day, Yoshe."

"No need to apologize." Mom takes his cup and sets it on the kitchen counter. "And thanks so much for your help with Silvia today. It's good to know her boss is so considerate."

"Wow." I place a hand on my heart. "That's the best thing you've ever said about my job."

Mom sighs. "Silvia, would you *please* try not to embarrass me in front of our guest?"

Gus chuckles. "Don't worry, Yoshe. I'm familiar with your daughter's tactics. I'm quite sure she gives me just as much heck as she gives you."

Mom groans. "Oh, no. Now I'm even *more* embarrassed." She glares at me behind Gus's back as he heads for the door.

I trail after him. After that race, I can't walk as fast as usual. "You don't have to leave—"

"I'm afraid I do." He turns back and pats my shoulder. "It appears you've got quite an evening ahead of you. You'd better prepare yourself." He points to Mom's open bedroom. A mountain of fancy gowns covers her bed.

My eyes widen. Am I seeing things? "What in the heck is that?"

"Your new uniform if I'm not mistaken." Gus waggles his eyebrows. "Now, have fun, and *be careful*. There's bound to be powerful people at that ball. Watch what you say and do. And it's probably best if you don't drink any so-called 'adult beverages' while you're there. Drinking makes people do stupid things."

I roll my eyes. "Don't worry. I'm not interested in drinking. In fact, I'm not even interested in this ball anymore. I'd rather just eat and sleep some more."

"I'm afraid that's not an option." Mom crosses her arms as she enters the now-crowded small hallway. "Thanks again, Gus. And you are more than welcome here, anytime."

Wait, really?

He tips an imaginary hat, and then he's out the door.

My mind buzzes as we enter Mom's room together. I knew she'd like Gus if she just gave him a chance. The idea that they might even become friends makes me smile like a kid at a carnival.

Inside, I count ten fancy ball gowns in various colors on her bed. Grimacing, I discard the two red ones without even trying them on.

"Isn't this amazing?" She runs a hand along the shimmering fabric. "I've never seen such dresses. Your father would've—"

"I won't wear the red ones."

"I expected that." She hands me an envelope of soft paper. "This came with the gowns. I already opened it."

I slide out the invite.

Silvia Wood and guest are invited to an evening of celebration at 7 p.m. at The New Order Tower, Penthouse floor. This party is invite only.

Mom smiles, her eyes alight. "I've always wanted to go there. The view is supposed to be amazing from the top floor. I mean, you don't have to take me, or anything. I realize that you might want to bring someone else."

"Of course you'll come with me. I don't want to go alone." And Franco is *not* an option at this point, because all he does is pity me. "I bet one of these frou-frou dresses will fit you too."

"Yes." Her face flushes with excitement. "Three of them do, actually. I already tried them on while you were sleeping."

I laugh. "Which one will you wear, then?"

"Gus liked this one." She points at a slender black gown with sequins highlighting a lower neckline.

"He did, did he?" This is new.

"Be nice, Silvia," Mom warns. "I admit that you're right—your Gus is a lovely man. And I'm sorry I've given you so much grief over your job. Now I understand why you enjoy working for him. And I promise not to bother you again on the subject."

"That will be a nice change," I reply warily.

"I'm serious, Silvia. I don't suppose you could understand this because you're not old enough to have any kids of your own, but I felt that your not getting into Plant Production was *my* fault."

I pause to look Mom in the face. "*Your* fault?"

She squeezes my arm. "I know I let you down after your father died..." Tears threaten to take over her newly found happiness.

I can't let this happen. "Don't worry, Mom. Everything will be fine from now on. I promise."

Mom wipes her eyes. "That's quite the grand promise."

"I mean it." I smile, hoping she'll return the expression. "Now, help me try on these dresses."

I squeeze into every dress, except the evil-colored red ones, and trudge up and down our small hallway, seeking Mom's approval. One by one, I toss them to the side in a crumpled mound of lush fabric and move on to the next. While Mom waits for me to decide, she gets ready. She's all set before I even wrestle into the fourth gown.

"Why do you have to tromp around like that?" Mom complains as I slump past her in yet another tight, scratchy dress. "It sounds like you're going to bust through the floor!"

"I'd be more comfortable in my own clothes."

"But you never minded the costumes Daniel made for you from the leftover scraps at work." She turns to her bed. "In fact, this red gown looks remarkably similar to the one—"

"I know. Like the one Dad made. It's eerie."

She bites her lip. "Do you want to try it on?"

No. Yes. Maybe. Why does it have to be red?

My hands shake at my sides. Is this some sort of warped test by The New Order? Or am I getting as paranoid as Franco?

I sigh. "Okay." I take it from her and slip into the silky-smooth fabric.

It fits perfectly, like it was made with me in mind. I stare at myself in the mirror, entranced by my image. If only this was eight years ago, when life was still fun.

"You look lovely," Mom whispers in my ear. "And it doesn't look like a little girl's dress at all. In fact, I've never seen you look so grown up before."

"That decides it. I'm wearing this one." I grab a small purse. "Let's go."

"Not so fast." Mom shakes a finger at me. "First, we have to do something about your hair."

⚘

Twenty minutes later, we leave the apartment. A long, black car waits outside the building.

The driver gets out and interrupts us as we approach the walkway. "Silvia Wood?"

I nod. Why is he talking to me?

"Please get in." He bows and opens the shiny passenger door.

I glance at Mom. Her eyes are huge. I've never ridden in a car before, only taken the monorail. The finish on this car is so glossy; I hate to touch it, worried I'll leave a smudge behind.

I pause for a moment at the car door, not sure whether my butt or my feet should go first, but Mom slides in ahead of me like she's done this a million times.

"To The New Order Tower," announces the driver as he enters the car lane.

The walkers and bikers gawk and move aside in a fluid motion as we pass by. It feels so funny to be in a car. So unfamiliar. I stare out the window as the buildings sweep by, towering far above us.

"Isn't this wonderful?" Mom clasps her hands in rapture, her eyes wide, taking in everything. "Such an honor. I'm so proud of you, Silvia."

"Yeah. It's nice. But my feet are antsy. I'd rather be walking, so I don't get so nervous. I'm not sure I belong at this ball."

"Oh, Silvia," groans Mom. "Why do you always have to find something to dislike about everything?"

"We're here!" The driver jumps out to open our door.

I glance up. The New Order Tower is the tallest building around. Mom and I head inside and wait in front of the elevators, listening to the floor bells ring as the elevator cars rise and fall. Finally, it's our turn. The climb lasts forever, my ears popping as we travel to the very tippy-top.

"Top floor," announces the overhead, robotic, female voice.

The mirrored doors slide open. I'm reluctant to step out of the safe, small enclosure. The open room ahead is filled with people milling around in all their finery. Voices bounce off the walls, none of them distinguishable. The smell of unfamiliar food makes my stomach rumble. Running makes me so hungry.

"Come on," beckons Mom.

I follow, trying to take it all in. Chandeliers hang from the ceiling —huge explosions of twinkling lights. The penthouse appears to be one huge room, the outer walls made of floor-to-ceiling windows. We're so high in the sky. Even from here, I can see the city of Panopticus spread out before me.

"Oh, my gosh! Look at that view!" Mom rushes over to the nearest window.

I pause a few steps behind her and stare at the rows of identical gray buildings, all lined up as if someone drew them with a ruler. The streets are so far below, all at right angles. We're above the rest of our world, looking down on everyone else. People hurry through the streets on foot. They seem so small, so far away. Like worker ants, busy for their queen. And this place is as fancy as a palace, meant for such a queen.

I glance back at a chandelier, so beautiful and delicate and gargantuan all at the same time. This place is overwhelming. I didn't know this kind of glamor even existed anymore. I mean, I guess I should've known. I've seen pictures of the olden days in Gus's videos, but I didn't realize how overdone and ritzy the Tower would be. But Mom doesn't seem the least bit bothered by all this excess. She's as comfortable as I am edgy.

"I've never seen so much sky." Mom points towards fluffy clouds in a sea of blue air.

"Yeah. You can't see sunsets much in town, but out near the Incinerator you can."

She turns to me. "I wanted to ask: can you keep running outside now? After this is over, I mean? Do you still get to train with Liam?"

I shake my head. "No, I don't think so. It's back to the treadmill for me."

Mom frowns. "That's too bad. Maybe you can petition—"

"You made it!" Liam rushes over to pull me into a hug. "Where were you? I searched for you everywhere today."

"I went home, ate something, and took a nap."

"You totally missed out." Liam's face glows with excitement. "I've been all over today, meeting tons of people. Winning this race is going to turn into something big for me. But Silvia...it should've been you. I mean, you were there first, but you didn't cross the line. What stopped you? Representative Waters-Royce asked me, but I didn't know what to tell her." He pauses to take a drink from the brown bottle in his hand.

My mouth opens, but nothing comes out.

"Once again, Silvia's the smart one." Franco speaks from behind me.

I force myself not to turn around. Make him come to me for once.

"Liam, you should've been resting," Franco continues. "You'll never make it through this party. You'll crash for sure."

"Will not." Liam takes another drink. "This party's going to be awesome. Look at all the hot girls, for starters."

"The prettiest one's right here." Franco touches my arm.

I swing around. "What?"

"Actually, I meant your mom, but"—he cocks his head—"you look nice too."

"Oh, please." Mom giggles, flashing the biggest smile I've seen in years. I forgot she had that many teeth. She's having the time of her life, and I don't want to ruin it. She deserves to have fun for a change.

I turn back to find Franco staring at me. My stomach lurches. *He just feels sorry for you,* I remind myself. But it's hard to ignore the fact that Franco looks amazing in a black tuxedo. Makes me go all mushy inside. My heart races, and my legs feel like butter. I wish I could blame this on the race, but I know better.

I need to stop staring at him, so I turn to Liam, who looks rather spiffy in his own black tux but doesn't confuse me nearly as much as Franco does. Plus, he doesn't pity me.

"I'm hungry." I rub my growling stomach. "Where's the food?"

"That's what I like about you, Silvia." Liam grins. "You've got your priorities in order."

We approach a long, wooden table, laden with a feast. The

heavenly fragrance of warm, fresh bread tickles my nose. I reach for a bun, but Representative Waters-Royce intercepts my reach with a firm grip on my arm.

"Just the young woman I've been looking for!" She swings her hawk-like gaze to my running partner. "And, Liam, you should come along too. So many important people want to meet you both tonight. Try your best to make good impressions, children. This is your time to shine." Her eyes flash without a hint of crow's feet on either side. Maybe she *did* have surgery.

We march across the floor, away from the luscious food. My stomach growls in protest, and these borrowed heels pinch my feet. Representative Waters-Royce has a death grip on both our arms. There's no getting away from her, now. If only I could've eaten something first. I'm starving. I glance back longingly at the bowls heaped with fresh fruits and the plates of warmed vegetables.

Franco interrupts my view, smirking before he takes a huge bite of the bun I'd been eyeing a minute before. I scowl at him.

"Here we are!" announces the red-haired politician as we approach a small gathering of well-dressed individuals. "Fellow Representatives, I have the great honor of presenting to you the top finishers of the Citizen Race for Glory—Liam Harmon and Silvia Wood."

"Nice to meet you," I say without meaning it. Why do I suddenly feel like an insect trapped under a glass? Everybody's staring at me like I'm a painting in an art museum they've been hired to critique.

"Oh, look, the announcements have begun." A tall Representative points to an overhead screen.

Footage from the race flashes across the screen. I watch myself passing the other runners, Liam always following just behind. The red-haired girl hands me a drink, and I swerve right into Liam to avoid her. From that point on, my eyes appear to take a manic glow on the screen. I tense, wondering what the very end of the race will look like, but the video skips from mile twelve straight to Liam crossing the line with me in tow.

A round of applause breaks out from the penthouse. Who are all these people, anyway? They can't all be Representatives. I scan the room and find Suits in every corner. Scrumptious bread or not, now I want to leave.

Political speeches follow the race footage. My interest wanes until a female representative from a different city is announced. I wonder if she'll look different somehow, but instead, she looks like...*me*. Idly, I wonder if her mother was full Japanese and her father of red-haired European descent.

Liam elbows my arm. "Hey, that's you in twenty years or so, don't you think?"

I nod, not even listening to the speech itself.

The coughing man who spoke before the race comes back on the screen. That's when I realize this must be live footage because they catch him at a bad time. He's coughing so hard the announcers give up and move on to the next speaker.

"Poor guy." Liam takes another swig from his bottle. "Looks like he's in a hospital gown. He must really think this race is important. I've heard he's having surgery soon, a lung transplant or something."

After the overhead screen goes blank, Representative Waters-Royce steers us around the room, introducing us to loads of people whose names I'll never remember. Occasionally, we swing near a buffet table but never close enough for me to grab any nourishment.

I halt, causing the representative to jerk to a stop, her hand still clenched on my arm.

"Listen, do you mind if I eat something?" I ask. "I'm kind of hungry after that race."

She frowns. "Not yet, dear. It's easier to make a good impression if your mouth isn't full." She introduces us to yet another cluster of her so-called "quality people."

As Liam eagerly proclaims his undying loyalty to The New Order and his gratitude at being given the chance to prove himself, I watch other people eating my food. I'm not the least bit interested in meeting all these strangers, but Liam is as energetic as a news reporter. Whenever the conversation turns to me, about the only thing I care about is what's on their plate.

"Yes, I enjoyed the race today. Thanks for asking." I smile politely, trying not to drool. "Say, how are those cinnamon rolls? They look *divine*."

The red-haired politician sighs, shakes her head, and moves us on to the next group. She doesn't even pause to greet Franco and my mother as we make another loop around the crowded room. I make another attempt to reach for a roll, but she slaps my hand away.

"Try to pay attention, Silvia," she snaps. "I'm attempting to improve your future. It would serve you well to show some interest."

I sigh and glance back to catch Franco winking at me. While I suffer through two more rounds of forced introductions, that crazy botanist parades back and forth behind the people I'm supposed to focus on, smirking and eating the whole time. He's mocking my hunger. I'm not sure who pisses me off more—Representative Waters-Royce for not allowing me to eat the feast presented supposedly in my honor, or Franco for his maddening methods of torture.

A middle-aged man asks me, "Silvia, do you plan to continue your training, now that you've discovered you have a natural talent for it?"

What do I say? Here's my chance to push for the opportunity to keep running outside, but is now the time? "I, uh—"

"Wow, these strawberries are *so* good." Franco's voice projects across the room. "They simply *melt* in your mouth."

I pause for a moment, distracted. But this is a question I want to answer.

"Actually," I clear my throat. "You bring up a good point. Running outside brought my physical fitness to a new level. I think it's in the best interest of all athletes if Panopticus continues to permit these opportunities for their citizens. Is that a possibility, Representative Waters-Royce?"

The red-haired woman shakes her head. "That's not going to happen."

"But why not?"

She counts off the reasons on her fingers. "It's a safety issue, primarily. Congestion of traffic. Risk of being hit by cars."

"But there are barely any cars on the roads," I protest. "Why shouldn't someone use those lanes?"

Her nostrils flare. "I'm telling you, accidents happened all the time until The New Order made safety a high priority for the citizens. And if a person has a heart attack running while at a gym, there are health professionals there ready to assist you."

"But what's the point in taking away every freedom if you take away every happiness along with it?" The question shoots from me before I consider the ramifications. I don't even like discussing politics, but here I am, challenging the most popular Representative of the courts.

"You're young, Silvia." The Representative narrows her eyes. "So very young. It takes a level of maturity you haven't yet achieved to appreciate that happiness comes from security, not freedom."

She grabs both my and Liam's arms, steers us away from the others, and calls back over her shoulder. "Excuse us, please. Miss Wood is exhausted, I fear, and needs her rest." She lowers her voice. "Liam, why don't you take Silvia to your room? She should lie down for a while before returning to the party." She relaxes her grip, drops our arms, and walks away.

"What room?" I ask. This is the first I've heard of this.

"Oh, it's awesome." Liam grins. "Just wait until you see it."

"Okay. Lead the way."

We pass by a rapidly emptying buffet table on our way to the elevator. Liam sets down his empty bottle while I manage to grab a handful of crackers and a banana. Thank goodness the red-haired politician doesn't notice. She'd probably have a hissy fit.

Liam cocks his head. "Are you seriously that desperate for food?"

"Yeah, aren't you? We ran the same race, didn't we?"

He hits the elevator down button. "I'm fine, really, but I don't know about you. Why are you acting so strange? Winning this race is a great opportunity for us, but you don't seem to see that. Why are you deliberately ruining any chance you have for advancement?"

I roll my eyes. "I don't see why winning a race should change anything else in my life. I just wanted to prove to myself I could do it."

We step into the quiet elevator. Liam frowns, and his voice drops to a low growl. "I don't get you. Are you purposely trying to annoy everyone here for some insane reason?"

"I don't like her," I whisper in his ear, covering my mouth with my hand, not ready yet to admit this out loud to the rest of the world, including whoever might be watching.

"Who? Representative Waters-Royce?" he mutters back.

I nod.

He turns to me, talking quietly. "Why not? She's been super nice to me, introducing me to tons of people. I think she's only trying to help us."

We face off in the elevator, arguing in hushed voices, our faces hidden from the camera in the corner.

"I've got my reasons." I cross my arms. "But I don't wish to discuss them, especially not here."

"What reasons? That she's got red hair? Because you supposedly don't like the color red, even though you're wearing it right now?" He gestures at my dress.

"That wasn't my choice. They sent it to me. It was the only one that fit right."

He scoffs. "You're ridiculous. You know that?"

The elevator doors slide open. Liam fishes a key card out of his pocket. We step into a small black-and-white lobby. There are three doors to choose from. Liam steps up to the middle one and enters his key card. His movements are sharp and angry, but he says nothing until we get inside.

He spins around to confront me. "I don't get you. If you want to get ahead in life—like, for example, if you want Yoshe to get into first chair—you have to play their games."

"And why is that fair? Why should Mom get first chair because I can run fast? How is that fair to whoever is in first chair now?"

Liam raises his hands like he's giving up. "Do you want your mom to be happy or not?"

"What kind of question is that? You *know* what we've been through!" I snap, showing him my scars like they're some kind of weapon.

Liam clamps his mouth closed.

I glance around the room. One wall consists of floor to ceiling windows; the other three are covered with a soothing, metallic blue fabric. Pushed against the far wall is the biggest bed I've ever seen, covered with at least a dozen blue pillows. In the far corner are two small doors.

"Did you take a nap here?" I point at the bed.

"No, I didn't have time." He sits down on the bed, rubbing a hand over his face.

I walk over to explore what's behind the doors. The first is a luxurious bathroom the size of our kitchen and living room combined. The other holds a fancy closet the size of my bedroom.

"Why on earth did they give us this room?" I ask. "There's only a bed here."

He laughs. "Don't worry, Ms. Sanctimonious. I can sleep on the floor."

"What are you talking about?" I cross over to the windows as darkness falls outside, this time pushing myself to the edge. I place both hands on the cool glass. The vision is captivating, like watching the inner workings of some vast machine. "I'm not staying here tonight."

"Why not?" He stands next to me at the windows. "I don't get you. When else are you going to have the opportunity to sleep in such a fancy bed?"

I glance back at the mountains of pillows. "I still don't get why there's only one bed."

He shrugs. "They must think you like me more than you do. After all, they put you on birth control."

I sigh. "I hate all those appointments at the Reproductive center and the automatic birth control. I should be able to make these decisions for myself."

"The New Order is just trying to do what's best for the people."

I narrow my eyes. "I have my own mind. I don't need it made up for me."

He huffs. "What is your problem, Silvia? Why are you acting so high and mighty?" He gestures around the grand room. "This is a gift, you know. Try to appreciate it."

I point at the bed. "I have no intention of sleeping on that bed or doing anything else there, either, if that's what you're implying."

Liam crosses his arms. "Trust me, I'm not that desperate. I can get a girlfriend any time I want. I would've liked to run this evening together as a team. To make the most of the opportunities presented, together. To move ahead, visit other cities, whatever comes our way. But if you'd rather remain stuck where you are, then suit yourself. I'm done with you."

A lump forms in my throat. "And here I thought we were friends." I gaze down at the streets below. "But we're not. You're just like one of them."

Liam's voice hardens. "All my life I've wanted to be someone important. And I'll do whatever it takes to get there."

"I'm sorry to hear that." I push myself away from the window, my heart hard and cold. Thick carpet muffles my steps back to the entrance door. "I sure hope you don't lose yourself in your pursuit to become someone else because I liked you better before the race. Now, I'm not so sure."

I let the door slam shut behind me.

35

STAND BY YOUR MAN

I ride the elevator alone. Loud music welcomes me back to the party, muffling the overhead robotic announcement that I've reached the top floor. I scan the crowd for Mom, hoping I can convince her to leave early. Parties are supposed to be fun. This is more like torture.

I skirt around the dance floor, which opened up in my absence. A small orchestra plays an upbeat tune that I might appreciate if I wasn't in such a hurry to escape. It takes three sweeps of the giant, open room to find Mom. She's deep in conversation with an older gentleman wearing glasses and carrying a cane. She waves when I catch her eye but doesn't invite me to join her. And so I wait, leaning on the nearest wall.

The room spins and swirls with busy activity. Only I am as unmoving as stone. Once I realize Mom has no intention of ending her conversation any time soon, I search for food. But the buffet tables have all been removed, save for one, which has been picked over. As I gaze in disappointment, several white-coated servers come and remove the serving trays.

I sigh. My feet ache and my stomach growls. And my head and

heart are sore. I'm pretty sure none of the Harmons like me now. Franco only feels sorry for me. Linda has always hated me, and now it seems Liam's decided to join her in that opinion.

But who cares? I don't need them anyway. I don't need anybody but myself. And food. Food would be nice here.

"Hey, Silvia, I saved you a plate." Franco startles me with a tap on the shoulder.

I swing around. A gorgeous man in a black tux hands me a heaping plate of cinnamon rolls and fruit. I swear I can feel my stomach smile. I grab the plate out of his waiting hands.

"Oh, my gosh, I love you." I flush. "I mean—thanks. This looks great."

He laughs. "Thought you might be hungry."

"You're right." I don't even have the patience to not talk with my mouth full. "I'm starving."

"Plus, I figured you are one of the few people I think deserve this level of extravagance." He waves an arm around the room.

"Yeah, isn't this place crazy?" I lick frosting off my fingers.

"Yes. Feast your eyes on another government-run, so-called-non-profit organization. Or, as they say, see how the other half lives."

I shrug. "Well, if they only do this celebration every five to ten years or however often they have this race, I guess it doesn't bother me."

"Oh, no, my innocent little Silvia."

I cringe, suddenly feeling like a four-year-old at a big kid's birthday party.

He scowls. "They eat like this all the time."

I stop chewing for a moment, swallow, and then speak. "They couldn't. It's so wasteful."

"But they do." He cocks his head. "I've been talking with the servers. They work at shindigs just like this at least once, if not twice, a week."

"While the rest of us are on rations?"

"Now you're catching up. Don't you know that the real motto of

The New Order is 'Liberty and Justice for None, and Thievery and Gluttony by a Few?'"

I lower my voice. "How can you talk like that so openly in here?"

He gestures toward the orchestra. "Who's going to hear me over that mambo? And you're the only one I want to talk to here, anyway."

"What about Liam?"

His face tenses. "I'm not sure I trust him anymore."

"Really? Then I'm not the only one who thinks he's changed."

He frowns. "I'm afraid not." In a flash, the dark mood covering his face vanishes. "Are you done eating?"

"Yes."

"Then let's dance." He takes my hand, leads me to the dance floor, and puts his arms around me.

I'm too stunned to object. And, sure enough, it's a slow dance. He holds me close. I can feel the heat from his body radiate into mine. I try not to hold on too tight. I don't want him to know how much I care about him. There's no point.

He whispers in my ear. "I wanted to ask you: what happened today? Why'd you freak out on the course? What made you stop just before the finish line?"

I consider what to say and decide to be brief, blunt, and honest.

"I thought I saw my father," I whisper back. And that's the truth. Let's see how he likes it. "Along with some other dead people."

"I suppose that's a job hazard for you." He holds me tighter.

I tense. I can't do this. Not if he thinks of me as a kid. Not if he pities me. Not when my entire being urges me to kiss him. I can't stand this close and still be so far away.

I take a step back, causing him to release his hold on me. "Franco...I—"

The orchestra goes silent.

"Quiet everyone!" Representative Waters-Royce demands over the orchestra microphone. "I have an announcement to make."

A drumroll begins. The titan-haired politician gestures into the crowd as Liam steps onto the platform beside her.

She holds his hand up in the air, her chin raised proudly. "Liam Harmon has just accepted a high level position in Argos, our fair Great City to the south!"

The room erupts in applause. Except for Franco. His face pales.

I whisper into his ear. "I knew I hated her for good reason."

He leans on me as if he's lost all strength to stand on his own. "Silvia, you're the only one here who makes any sense. Please, take me home. I can't watch any more of this charade."

I wave my mother over. She rushes up, takes one look at Franco's face, and helps me escort him into the elevator. I try to calm my racing pulse as I hold Franco upright, his body held tight against mine. At the bottom, we shuffle out of the building and to his home, his shoulders slumped and his head hung down.

"You should be happy for Liam," encourages Mom. "This sounds like a great opportunity for him."

Franco rubs his face with his hands. "Linda's going to kill me."

"But why?" Mom pats him on the shoulder. "Surely she'll be proud of what he's accomplished."

"You don't understand." He shakes his head. "Linda will go nuts, losing her husband and now her son. I don't know how to tell her he's leaving."

"Why don't you let Liam tell her instead?" I place a tentative hand on his shoulder. Even if he only pities me, all I want is for his sadness to end.

Franco sighs. "No. I have to prepare her before he gets home. She won't want him to know how she really feels."

Mom frowns. "I see. You better head over there right now, then, so you get there first."

"I know." He groans. "I should've stopped him from racing, but I never thought he'd win, especially after that bike accident, but that hardly even slowed him down." He covers his face with his hands. "Oh, man, how am I going to tell her? She's going to blame me. I know she will."

"Tell her to blame me, instead," I suggest. "Why not? She hates me anyway."

We've reached Liam's building. Franco gazes up to their apartment window and releases a deep sigh. "She doesn't hate you," he says.

"Yes, she does."

Franco turns to stare at me a long moment before wrapping me in an unexpected hug.

My heart almost stops beating, and I find it impossible to breathe. I don't dare glance over at my mother. I don't want to see the disapproval that's sure to be in her dark brown eyes.

He releases his grip. "Thanks for the offer of taking blame, but it won't make any difference. The result is still the same. Liam will move to another city, and Linda may never see him again. Just like all the others Chosen before him. Goodnight, both of you, and thank you."

Franco half-heartedly waves as he heads inside, leaving us hovering under the street lights.

Mom turns away before I do. "I wonder if you'll ever see him again."

I don't ask if she means Franco or Liam.

I don't want to know.

36

BITTERSWEET SYMPHONY

The following two weeks crawl by. Liam leaves town in a hurry. I never even get a chance to say goodbye, but maybe that was his choice. He made it clear at the party that he was disappointed in me. And that goes both ways.

Any worries I might have had about never seeing Franco again have vanished. Ever since the race, he's popped into Mortuary Sciences on a daily basis, the same question on his lips every time.

"Have you heard anything from Liam?" Franco asks, a hopeful light in his face that I don't wish to crush.

But I must.

"No. Sorry." I shake my head. I'm sure Liam would never contact me before his family, but I don't tell Franco that.

"Linda's getting worried." He frowns. "It's been five days, and not one word from him. We were told that, although transportation between cities is treacherous, once a person gets there safely, communications are still good."

Gus zips up another body bag. "I'm so sorry, Franco. This must be hard for your family."

Franco turns away, either unwilling or unable to talk. His shoulders sag, and he wanders from the morgue like he just lost his best friend—which I suppose he did.

Gus and I share a long look. I'm not sure what he will think when I rush after Franco, but he doesn't say a thing as I dash out the sliding glass door.

"Franco, wait!" I catch him at the base of the stairs.

He turns to face me, his gaze on the floor. "I'm sorry to keep bothering you."

"Don't be silly." I reach out to touch his arm and pause, my hand held in mid-air. "It's no bother. I'm worried too."

His eyes water. "What happened to him?" he whispers, finally raising his teary gaze to mine.

I drop my hand to my side, my stomach sinking. "I don't know, but I'm sure he's fine." If I truly believe this, then why does my voice catch?

He gives me a slight smile. "You're sure? Could I get a guarantee with that?"

I shrug. "I don't know. I *want* him to be all right, so that's what I'm going to believe." I know why he doesn't contact *me*, but I've no idea why he'd hold out on his mom and sisters.

Franco sighs. "Well, he's mad at me, so I'm not shocked he hasn't messaged me, but you're his friend. He'll write you eventually. Maybe he's just gotten lazy."

"Yeah. Maybe." *Maybe not.*

He chuckles, rubbing a hand through his hair. "I'm sure you think all we did was fight, but I miss him."

"I know you do."

"Anyway...thanks for listening." He turns as if to go then spins back, grabbing me into another hug. And this time, my mother isn't watching.

My heart jumps to my throat. His arms grip so tightly around me. It takes me half a second to respond, and then I tentatively encircle my own arms around him, my hands resting on the back of his jean jacket. Within my arms, he tenses and shudders then relaxes. My heart hammers and breaks at the same time. He's in so much pain, and I'd give anything to take it away.

We stand in silence except for the sound of our breaths in the cool air. The door at the top of the stairs slides open, the wind whooshing through it.

Franco stirs. "Will you check at the gym again tonight?" he murmurs into my hair.

"Yeah, of course." I nod.

And then he's gone, taking any last shred of happiness I had with him.

$\dot{\chi}$

AFTER WORK, I head toward the 37th street gym for yoga class. I haven't run since Liam left town. I tell myself I'm taking rest days, but it's more than that. I glance between the tall buildings lining the streets. The sun doesn't even seem to shine right anymore.

I hurry inside the gym and get stopped at the check-in desk.

"Silvia Wood?" a male attendant inquires. "That's you, isn't it?"

"Yep."

"You have two messages." He turns the electronic reader so I can read them.

Message #1:

Keep running. I'll be back for the next race. -Liam Harmon

Message #2:

You have an appointment tomorrow at 6 a.m. at Citizen Family Planning Services.

I groan. "Not again."

🏃

I PERCH on the edge of one of Family Planning's chairs, ready to leave as soon as they're done with me. The nurse scans my arm then hands me a cup.

I stare at it. "Another pregnancy test?"

She smiles. "Yes. Just taking normal precautions."

"Fine." I go to the bathroom and pee in the cup, just like they want me to. It's not worth the effort to fight it, but this is getting ridiculous.

Thirty long minutes later, a different nurse enters the room, a puzzled look on her face. "You're negative."

I stand, grabbing my gym bag. "I could've told you that when I walked in here."

"But..." She pauses.

"Can I go now?" I gesture toward the door. "I really need to get to work. I didn't even have a chance to warn my boss I would be late."

The nurse doesn't answer. She taps her fingers on the test result sheet.

"Do you need anything more from me?" I really don't want to pee in a cup again, especially not twice in one day.

"No...unfortunately. You can go."

I rush to work, excited I finally have something to say to Franco when he asks if I've heard from Liam. He'll be happy. He might even smile again—which would be wonderful.

Now I'm the one who pities him instead of the other way around.

There's a backup in Mortuary Sciences when I arrive.

"Sorry, Gus." I set my gym bag on the floor and grab a coat. "I had a last minute appointment."

"You're having a lot of those lately." Gus's hair sticks up all over the place. It's even messier than usual. He hurries around the room, checking bags and tags. "We've got to get everything ready for the Incinerator tomorrow."

"I can stay as late as you want. I don't have anything waiting, and Mom has extra practice for Orchestra."

"That would really help me out. Thanks, Silvia."

Hours later, we're all caught up. Gus leans back in his chair, drinking a juice, and I'm scanning a computer article about ankle reconstruction.

"Got another body for you," announces a Handler, rolling in a cart.

Gus sighs as the Handler parks the dead body and leaves. "I'm plain worn out today. I'm getting too old for all this, but don't tell Edwina Wang that."

"Don't worry." I jump up out of my chair. "I've got this one."

I cross the room and search for the chart. It's not attached to the cart, and it's not tucked under the body bag. I dart out in the hall to see if it fell when they made that last turn. Nothing.

I head back into Mortuary Sciences. "Gus, there's no chart."

He groans but doesn't get out of the chair. "Those Handlers are getting really slack lately. I'll call upstairs for it."

"Okay. I'll get started." I unzip the bag, starting at the feet. The toes have running calluses.

That's strange. The Citizen Race was two weeks ago. I unzip further. Blond hair covers well-muscled lower legs. Ones I've seen before.

I start to tremble. Slowly pull the zipper to the top. My hesitant gaze follows the long incision that runs from the waist up to the chin. To the blue eyes I'd seen almost every day for weeks before the banquet that took him away.

I back away from the cart, bile flooding my stomach. I cling to the table behind me, my legs useless beneath me, my breath in gasps.

Liam.

Dead.

He's not in Argos.

He's here on my cart.

Maybe the city of Argos doesn't even exist.

All I know is that *Liam* no longer exists. No wonder the sun doesn't want to shine anymore.

"No!" My scream echoes, hitting off every metallic surface.

"No!" I grab everything I can find and fling it across the room. Charts, surgical instruments, and chairs smash into the walls.

Gus narrowly misses being hit by a flying scalpel as he rushes to my side. He grabs my arms and pins them down. "Keep it together, Silvia," he whispers in my ear. "They're always watching. *Always.*"

The doors slide open behind us.

I spin around, expecting the Handlers. Or maybe the Suits. At least this time I might have a weapon or two I can use.

But it's worse than that.

It's Franco.

My heart tears in two as tears slide down my cheeks.

"Hey, have you heard from—What's wrong?" His face blanches as he glances behind us.

Franco glides to the gurney like a ghost, reaching out a shaking hand to brush back the hair above Liam's ear. He tries to close the eyelids but can't. Liam's eyes remain hauntingly open, revealing a blank, empty death-stare.

Franco's face crumbles.

I reach out to him. "I didn't want you to see this."

He backs away. "Don't touch me. Not now. I want to kill somebody, and I might hurt you."

"Franco, you'd better think hard before you do anything rash," Gus warns. "Or Linda will be left with nobody."

Franco glares at Gus. "Give me some scissors."

"What for?" I ask.

"Just do it," he growls.

I place one in his quivering hand. He snips a curl from Liam's head, shoves it in his pocket, and turns away.

The scissors clatter to the floor as he sweeps out of the room.

I rush after him. "Where are you going?"

"I'd say hell, but I'm already there, aren't I?" Franco's voice cracks, and he pauses on the bottom stair. "Take care of yourself, Silvia. I'll probably never see you again." He sprints up the stairs, away from me.

I collapse onto the cold, hard floor, silent tears spilling into my hands. Gus follows me into the hallway, sits down next to me, and puts an arm around my back.

"There now. Cry all you want."

I lean into him and sob harder than ever before. I don't remember crying this hard for my dad. Probably because it took me so long to realize he really wasn't coming back. With Liam dead and Franco off to do something crazy, I feel all the bad at once. Every person I've ever truly cared about—with the exception of Mom and Gus—has been ripped away from me. The pain in my chest is overpowering.

"Get it all out." Gus pats my shoulder. "We still have to process the body."

I tense.

"I'm sorry, but it has to be done."

"I can't—"

"It's the only way to figure out what happened to him."

I suck in deep, shaky breaths. Yes, we need to find the cause of his death. "A live body can hide so many secrets, but a dead body never lies, right?" I murmur.

"That's right." Gus stares at me, waiting for me to be ready for this.

I sit up, clench my jaw, and wipe my eyes. "Let's get started. I need to know the truth, the real reason The New Order lied about Liam going to Argos."

AN HOUR LATER, I know four things:

1. Liam was alive this morning.
2. His lungs have been removed.
3. His birth control capsule was empty.
4. According to the evening news report, Representative Nielsen is recovering nicely from lung transplant surgery performed earlier today.

37

LOVE IS A BATTLEFIELD

I rush up the hospital stairs, heart pounding, throw open the door, and gasp for air. But it's no use–I can still smell Liam's dead body, his liver, his blood.

Glaring streetlights make a false day of night and block out every star. Even at this late hour, the streets still teem with life. All the worker ants hurrying to and from their places of employment.

The New Order feeds off its citizens twenty-four hours a day. Always taking whatever it wants. Babies. Organs. Whatever they want, they take.

And they give so little in return. Just enough to keep our hopes up. Just enough to make us try harder, give more, with empty promises that we can get ahead.

That's what Liam wanted. That was his dream.

And in return, The New Order cut his life into little pieces and fed them to the Representatives.

My mind fills with painful pictures.

Liam's pale body bathed in the blue lights of the mortuary. His blond hair on the table. His feet lifeless, wrinkled, and cold.

Franco's face when he saw Liam on the gurney with a fresh incision down his chest.

My stomach heaves, and I fall to my knees, gagging in front of the hospital for all the cameras to see. But I no longer care. Did they show me Liam's dead body as a warning? Or a threat? Are they trying to push me over the edge again? There has to be a reason for this. I don't believe it's an accident his body ended up here at my hospital.

I rise to my feet, gulp in metallic air, and brush away the tears flowing freely down my cheeks. I've got to keep it together, or they'll come for me next.

I finally know the truth, and it hurts even more than the lies.

I fly over to Franco's apartment, running even faster than on race day. Some force pushes my finger on the elevator buttons and empties me on his floor. My steps clatter down the hushed, empty hallway to his door.

I knock, my legs trembling beneath me. They don't even feel like they belong to me anymore. Nothing does. Everything I have, everything I am, belongs to The New Order. At least, that's what they think.

I knock again. Silence. Nothing but silence from inside his apartment. Why isn't he home? Where is he? How is he?

I jump when the door three apartments down swings opens. I take a deep breath and try to calm my racing heart. It's obvious Franco's not home. Why did I even come here? He's probably with Linda and the kids.

As I turn to leave, the door handle to Franco's apartment shudders and turns. The door creaks open slowly. Franco and I stare at each other.

He sighs. "Silvia, what are you doing here?"

"I wanted to see if you're okay." My hands clench.

"I'm fine." His voice is wooden and gravelly like his throat has been scratched raw with sorrow.

"No, you're not. Your eyes are bloodshot. Your hair's a mess." He's not wearing a shirt, either, which is rather distracting, even now.

"What does it matter?" He runs his hands through his nest of hair, his voice cold and empty. "It doesn't. Nothing matters anymore."

His slumped shoulders and dead eyes convince me to make a move.

"I'm coming in," I say.

"Suit yourself." He backs up and lets me pass.

His place is a disaster. Papers, clothes, and food everywhere. He plops down on the couch, and that's when I smell it—booze. There are bottles all over, empty, tipped on their sides.

"You've been drinking?" I gasp. "I didn't know you drank. Where'd you even get this stuff?"

Franco shrugs. "I just started. But what do you care? Why should anyone care what I do anymore?"

"I care." My gaze catches on another drawing of the pony-tailed girl. Not the same picture as before. But perhaps the object is the same.

I grab the sheet and examine it.

The pony-tailed girl is me.

Not some other girl.

She's definitely me.

And I look...beautiful.

My breath catches in my throat. Why did I have to find this out right now?

"Why should you care? You don't even know who I am." Franco drops onto the couch. "Nobody does. It's better that way. But I'm not holding back anymore. I'm taking it all down. Everything. The whole city of Panopticus—where there is Liberty and Justice for none."

"What are you talking about?" He's talking crazy again. I set down the picture. It doesn't matter right now.

Franco's dark eyes hide something dangerous under the surface. "Never mind. You're innocent. Just like Liam. Neither of you have any idea what happened to your fathers."

I sit next to him on the couch. "What do you know about my dad?"

But it's like he can't hear me. "None of you know the truth. I wanted to tell Liam when he was old enough, but Linda wouldn't let me." He hides his face in his hands.

"You can tell me." I scoot closer. "Linda doesn't have anything to do with me."

He scoffs. "That's how little you know. She has *everything* to do with you."

I put a hand on his arm. I'm torn between shaking the truth about my dad out of him and grabbing him to force his lips to mine. Maybe then he'd stop panicking for a second.

"Tell me," I beg. "Please."

He drops his hands and glares. "Why are you here anyway? Why don't you just leave me alone?"

I narrow my eyes but keep my voice calm. "I was worried about you. Now, tell me about my dad." I move even closer to him, trying to ignore the fresh smell of his skin. He must've recently showered.

Franco slides further away down the couch, increasing the space between us. "Silvia, you should be at home with your mom where you belong."

"Franco, I'll go home once you tell me what you know."

He shakes his head, seeming at war with himself, then his eyes widen and he grabs my arms in a frenzy. "No, don't go home. They'll find you there. You'd better escape. Now. Go far away from here." His eyes are wild, unrecognizable.

My heart races. He's crazy. He's absolutely nuts. "What are you talking about?"

"Go," Franco insists. "Run away before they take you too."

My stomach drops with sick fear. "Who, the Suits? Why do you think they'll come for me?"

Franco loosens his grip on my arms. His eyes fill with tears. "I didn't protect him. I promised Jack I would."

"Liam's father? When did you—"

"What if you're next?" He points at me. "What if something happens to you?"

I cross my arms. "I can take care of myself."

He turns away. "You should go. I don't want you seeing me like this."

I take a deep breath, glance back at the door, and consider leaving Franco alone with his crazy talk.

But I can't. Because something in my gut tells me Franco isn't simply paranoid.

"I'm not leaving."

Franco sighs. "Why are you here? You should hate me. You should go home."

"Don't be stupid. I don't hate you."

He shakes his head. "You might, if you knew—"

"Knew what? *What* are you talking about?"

He looks me straight in the eyes. "Why are you still here?"

"Because I'm in love with you, you idiot," I snarl—and then gasp. Did I really say that out loud?

Neither of us blinks.

My heart beats so hard, it might break my ribs.

My lungs breathe in booze-tinged air, making my mind dizzy. The skin on my arms still burns from his touch.

He pushes me back on the couch. He's sprawled on top. The warmth of his skin radiates through my scrubs.

His hands are in my hair, on my face, touching me everywhere at once. I can't keep track.

His lips are on mine. I follow his every lead.

My eager hands explore his hair, his face, his skin.

His breath flutters on my cheek. White sparkles dance before my clouded eyes. I can't see anything. I can't hear anything. I can only feel his skin on mine.

Please don't stop. Let this go on forever.

His hand travels downwards to my thigh. It becomes impossible for me to focus. The real world has gone fuzzy and distant.

"Stop!" Franco rips his lips off mine and jerks away, flattening himself against the far end of the sofa. "What are we doing?"

"What's wrong?" My voice sounds small and child-like.

He lurches to his feet and stumbles away from the couch. "Go away, Silvia! You shouldn't be here. Go home!"

My eyes burn. "Why? I want to be here. I want to be with you."

"No. You can't." He pauses in the doorway. "I shouldn't have done that. You're just a kid. This is wrong."

"I'm not a kid!" I stand, my legs weak and untrustworthy.

"You don't know the truth. I've done something you'd never forgive."

"Don't judge for me." My temper flares. "Tell me what it is and let me make up my own mind."

"I can't." His voice cracks. "Just go. Please." Franco flees the room, retreating into the back hallway.

I brace myself on the closest chair. The world spins, and nothing makes sense anymore. I glance toward the hallway to Franco's bedroom. He won't come back until I'm gone.

I'm not about to follow him. Not tonight. Not after what happened to Liam.

I turn to leave and again spot the picture of me on the table. After a tiny moment of hesitation, I fold it in half and take it with me out the door.

The walk home takes forever. My mind spins like crazy. Why does he say I would hate him if I knew the truth? What is he still hiding?

Eventually, I reach my apartment building, head up the steps, and slip my key in the lock.

The door swings open before I even turn the key.

The apartment is filled with voices.

"Oh, you're here!" Mom pulls me in from the hallway, her face filled up with light. "You won't believe what's happened. It's so wonderful!"

She hugs my shoulders as she leads me toward the voices.

I stiffen. Our living room is filled with Suits.

"Oh, honey!" Mom hugs me tight. "Isn't it wonderful? You've been Chosen!"

My stomach drops, and my hands fall open.

Franco's drawing falls to the floor.

He was right.

They've come for me already.

DON'T FEAR THE REAPER

What am I going to do? How do I get out of this?

"No. I'm not going with you." I tear out of Mom's grasp and back away from the Suits.

"Silvia, what are you doing?" Mom gapes. "Isn't this what you wanted?"

"It's not what you think it is, Mom." My voice shakes. "I know what happens to those who get Chosen. I work in the Mortuary."

Mom pales and collapses on the nearest wall. I flashback to the night Dad died. It's going to happen all over again. No matter what I do, I can't save her from herself.

A Suit approaches. "Silvia Wood, there's no reason to be unpleasant. This is an honor for someone in your position. You should be grateful. It's your chance to do something good for society."

"You ask too much," I mutter through gritted teeth.

"Let's not upset your mother. You know how fragile she is." He grips my arm so hard I know I'll develop bruises tomorrow.

If I'm still alive.

The Suits encircle me, forcing me out of the living room.

I reach back for my mother. She's still leaning against the wall.

The light in her eyes is fading. I can't be this helpless. There must be something I can do. If not for me, then at least for her. She's got to get angry, wake up, not just fade away again with no one to take care of her. She'll die, too, if I don't do something.

As the Suits drag me through the kitchen, I grab a teacup and smash it upside down on the counter.

Mom's eyes rise from the carpet. They flash and catch mine.

Save yourself, is my unspoken message. I will her to understand.

She nods.

The Suits yank me around the corner, toward the front door. A sharp pain jabs my right arm. I watch the syringe pull away and know they've got me now. They march me down the hall, toward the elevator. I can't help but glance behind us. As if Franco might come and save me.

But my legs have turned to jelly and fail completely as we enter the elevator.

The lights black out before I can even start to fight.

39
LIGHT MY FIRE

I wake to the soft clink of metal on metal.

I'm so tired. Better go back to sleep. I hope it's not time to get up for work yet.

Something shakes my arm.

"Silvia," Gus's gruff voice whispers in my ear. "Can you hear me?"

My eyes flutter open and then close. "What's up? Is it morning already?"

"Hold still. I'll get you out of this," he promises. "Don't make a sound."

I try to move my arms and realize I'm handcuffed to a gurney.

Panicking, I start to flail.

Gus pushes my shoulders back down on the bed. "Stay calm and lie still. I slipped a sedative in the guard's drink, muffled the microphones, and hijacked the cameras, but we have to hurry before they catch on."

They. The Suits. The New Order.

They're all out to get me.

I'm not pregnant with Liam's love child, so they've probably sold my internal organs instead. Because, to them, I am merely disposable goods.

Now I'm both angry and scared. I have to escape before they kill me, so I can figure out how I'm going to kill them instead.

Wait a minute. How did Gus know I was here? What's his plan? What's going on?

"Gus," I whisper, holding as still as I can, "How did you know I was here?"

"I'll tell you everything, but right now there's no time. I've got to get you out of here."

"Aren't you going to get in trouble?"

The first handcuff releases with a clink against the hospital bed.

Gus hurries to the other side to work the other lock. "Someday, I expect I will get in a whole heck of a lot of trouble, but I don't care about that anymore. I'd rather be killed for doing the right thing than die inside by turning the other cheek."

The second handcuff opens, and I rub my wrists. Gus helps me off the gurney. My legs are weak, but I manage to stand.

"Hurry. Put these on." Gus pulls out some scrubs from a bag slung over his shoulder. "And give me back your hospital gown. Sorry I don't have any shoes for you. Couldn't risk bringing them in here."

When I switch outfits, Gus slips the robe over a long pillow and carefully arranges it to look like a body under the sheet.

"Let's go." He covers his face with a surgical mask and hands me another one along with a scrub hat to hide my hair.

We duck out into the dimly lit hallway, checking each corner and evading every camera we can. We scurry to the back stairway where Gus has somehow managed to turn out all the lights. He hands me a flashlight and down we go, all the way to Mortuary Sciences.

The gurneys are all lined up and ready to go to the Incinerator.

One is empty.

Gus hands me a black body bag. "This one's yours. I'm sorry, Silvia. There's no time to explain. You have to trust me."

Shaking, I climb onto the empty gurney, slip into the body bag, and watch the room disappear as Gus zips it over my head.

"Don't move or talk," Gus warns. "The Handlers will be here soon."

Metal carts clang together. Papers shuffle. Body bags rustle.

I'm in the middle of one of the triple-wide gurneys Gus hates so much.

The gurney creaks and shudders, and then I'm sandwiched between two cold, dead bodies, one on either side.

"I'm sorry, but it's the only way," Gus whispers under his breath.

The back door opens with a bang.

"You ready to go?" hollers a Handler.

"Yeah," says Gus. "I've been ready and waiting for over an hour."

"Then let's go."

Carts squeak and roll past. When another cart jolts the one I'm on, I brace myself, biting my lip so as not to make a sound.

With a sudden jerk, I'm on the move, sliding back and forth in the bag. The wheels whine and complain beneath the weight, catch on the grate of the ramp, and then the gurney steadily inclines into the truck. The cart bangs into the next one in line, and we halt.

Doors clang shut. The truck engine comes to life. And we're off, headed for the Incinerator.

I hear Gus's monitor crackle to life. The hum moves from side to side around the truck. I wait in silence. After what seems like forever, Gus unzips the bag.

"How're you doing in there?" He frowns. "We should be out of the main part of the city and onto the outer-lying roads soon."

"Then what, Gus?" I ask. "Do I jump out and run for it?"

"No." He shakes his head. "Where would you go?"

"I don't know." I can't sit up, the upper metal rack is right over my head. I'm trying so hard not to cry, but it's no use. A few tears squeeze out. "They're going to kill me, Gus. And what about my mom? What's going to happen to her?"

Gus sighs. "At the moment, your mom will have to fend for herself. But she *could* be in trouble."

I wipe my eyes. "She started freaking out when I was taken. And now there's no one left in our family to take care of her."

"I'm afraid things might be even worse than you think, now that Franco talked to her."

"What do you mean?" I can still feel Franco's kisses on my lips, but that seems unimportant now and so far away. "What does he have to do with this?"

"Franco went looking for you this morning when he woke up," Gus explains.

"He did?"

"Yeah, he said there was some misunderstanding between you two." Gus waves his hand. "I don't need to know the details. But when he didn't find you at work, he went to your home and found your mother instead."

"So, what does my mom think happened?"

"Franco told her everything. In fact, now she knows more than you, and we'll get to that. But my point is, that's how I knew where to find you."

"I'm glad you found me, and I don't mean to sound unappreciative, but what do you plan to do with me at the Incinerator?"

Gus chuckles. "Well, I don't plan to turn you to ash. That's for certain."

The truck grinds to a sudden halt.

"What the hell?" Gus exclaims before zipping the bag back over my head.

I hold still in the stale darkness.

The back doors of the truck slam open.

"Truck's overheated!" yells a Handler. "Do you have any water?"

"Yes." Gus swears under his breath, fusses with his tool rack, and clambers out. I strain to hear the voices outside the truck, but they're too muffled to comprehend.

Finally, Gus clambers back inside and shuts the doors. The engine starts again, and I take a deep breath. The zipper opens to reveal Gus's sweating face.

"Stupid piece of crap truck, trying to carry too heavy of a load. Damn thing overheated, but some water did the trick. Unfortunately, you'll need that water later, but there was no other way. I have to get you to the Incinerator."

"What am I going to do at the Incinerator?"

He points toward the floor. "You'll be going out the sewer."

"What?"

"The sewer drain. It's there in case the building catches on fire. There's an overhead emergency sprinkler system. I'll unscrew the drain cover, down you'll go, and then you'll run till you reach the woods for cover."

My heart races. "The woods outside the fence? But there's wolves and man-eating creatures out there."

"Silvia, don't be scared of the wilderness. That fence was built to restrain you, not protect you."

"But I'll starve." I rub my stomach. I'm hungry right now.

"No, you won't." Gus shakes his head. "I'll give you the supplies you'll need. All you have to do is find the others."

"What others? What are you talking about?"

"After the War, some people resisted the move to the cities." Gus takes a deep breath. "Ben's brother was one of them."

I gasp. "*Your* Ben?"

"Yes. His name's Harry. He's the one who sets off the firework show every fourth of July, just to let me know he's still out there."

"So, that's why we waited for the fireworks. But I still don't understand."

"Don't you get it? I'm the Underground Railroad for getting people out of this Godforsaken city."

"Why? Because of what they did to Ben?"

"Yes, it started with Ben. When I realized that The New Order basically enslaved the survivors of WWIII to serve their own needs, I knew I had to do something."

A cold chill races down my spine. "Holy crap, Gus."

"I wanted to tell you. I was working my way toward it. My plan was for you to take over for me. I'm getting old, Silvia."

"To take over?" I feel dizzy. Good thing I'm already lying down. "But where do these people go exactly?"

"Don't worry. Once I set the Incinerator on fire—"

"Once you *what?*"

"Don't interrupt; there's no time. I hid explosives in one of the body bags. That will start a fire once it hits the Incinerator. Then you've got to get out of this bag and jump down into the sewer system. I'll drop down all the supplies—maps, compass, and the like. They're hidden in another of the body bags, in case you're wondering. Oh, and I have some stuff stashed in my tool chest."

I'm shaking all over. "I don't know if I can do this."

"Sure you can. You're smart—plus you have no other option."

"But what if I want to come back? Then what do I do?"

Gus shakes his head. "You're never coming back, Silvia. It's hard enough getting you out."

"No, I'm coming back. I'll find all the others and convince them to join me."

"Join you in what?"

"Overthrowing The New Order just like Franco said when he was drunk. I thought it was crazy talk, but now I know he was right. It's time to destroy it. Blow it to smithereens."

Gus's eyes widen. "Franco was drunk? No wonder he smelled— oh, never mind about that. But, Silvia, put the thought of coming back out of your mind. This is goodbye."

"No, I'll see you again." I get up on both elbows, so he can see my face. "I swear it, Gus. I'm coming back for you and my mom at the very least."

Gus chuckles, but he grabs at his chest like it hurts him. "That's what they all say, that they'll come back. But it never happens."

"No, I'm coming back!" I protest. "I'm not like the others."

He holds up a hand, and I fall silent.

"Silvia, that's exactly what your father said. And he never did come back, did he?"

"W-what?" I can't breathe.

"That's what else I had to tell you. Your father was in the accident along with Jack, Liam's dad. Neither one of them died. And it was no accident, either. It was staged by The New Order, trying to get rid of the rebels working in that sector of the clothing industry. Your father and Jack were unconscious when they were brought to me, but not dead."

"He's not dead?" My heart ricochets in my chest. Now that I finally have proof, I can hardly believe it's true.

"No. The accident didn't kill him. But I knew the Representatives had their eyes on them, so I drugged them to make it look like they'd been killed in the fire. They were covered with soot when they arrived, and I used my stage makeup to make their injuries look worse than they were. I fooled the examiners, who were just a bunch of politicians anyway. Not a real doctor in the bunch, thank goodness."

My hands shake. "What are you telling me, Gus?"

"Your father's alive. And you're going to see him again."

"That's impossible," I mutter breathlessly, as if someone has just punched me in the gut.

The truck halts with a bang and a wheeze that echoes the commotion whirling in my overwhelmed brain.

"You'll find that what's impossible often comes true. Now be quiet!" Gus zips me back up.

Trapped once again inside the bag, I force myself to take calm, shallow breaths as the truck backs up to the Incinerator. Dad's alive, and I'm getting out of here. I have to find him. *I have to.*

The back doors bang open. The metal gurneys roll off the truck, one by one.

I'm moving, bouncing off the truck, rolling up the incline and into the sweltering Incinerator.

The air inside the bag is stifling. Sweat trickles into and stings my eyes, but I can only blink. I can't wipe it away.

Voices shout out commands. Metal clanks. Papers shuffle.

I remain still as a stone, so they won't find me. I know what a body bag looks like when a corpse is inside.

The Incinerator flares to life.

Gus directs the Handlers.

The body on my right is removed.

Terror splashes acid in my stomach.

My hands tremble, and I press them flat to my sides.

More voices. More clanging.

The grinding of the conveyor belt rings in my head. Smoke chokes me.

I carefully stuff a hand in my mouth to keep from coughing, then tremble with the possibility that somebody noticed the movement within my bag.

The overhead sirens wail.

Heavy footsteps race across the floor. People scream and shout.

Drops of water pelt the body bag.

My cart rolls over to the side. Gus unzips the bag. The room is filled with black, cloudy smoke.

"Get ready." Gus clanks open his tool chest and unscrews the drain cover. It bangs to the side. "It's open. Now, jump."

I scramble through the dark smoke, find the opening with my bare feet, and pause.

"Go," he orders. "You don't have time to think."

"Visit my mom," I beg. "Turn two teacups over on the kitchen counter. She'll know what it means. Do it, Gus. I'm counting on you. And this isn't good-bye. I'll be back for both of you."

When he nods, I jump down the rabbit hole.

Two bags drop down beside me. A lit flashlight clatters on the ground, near my feet.

I grab the light and dig inside the first bag.

The drain cover clatters into place far above me.

I'm alone now. It's up to me.

Voices shout overhead as I pull out Franco's jean jacket. I check for the *Property of Franco Harmon* label to make sure. It's still there. Why do I have his jacket?

I dig in the pockets. They're filled with small books detailing what plants are safe or toxic to eat. But I still don't know why he would give me his jacket. Then on the last page of one of the books, I discover a handwritten note: *Please wear this jacket at all times. I need to know you made it out alive.*

My empty, aching stomach clenches. If they find me wearing Franco's coat with his name branded across it, they'll know he was in on my escape and come for him too. This means he's risking his life for me. And it also means he's in on Gus's Underground Railroad scheme.

He knows about my father.

That's why he said I'd hate him if I knew the truth.

But he's wrong. I don't hate him. I only hate one thing: The New Order and every Representative that enforces it.

And I'm coming back with an army to take it all down.

Smoke scratches my eyes as I scramble into travel clothes and running shoes, then I zip open the stuffed backpack Gus tossed down. The corners of my mouth twitch in a short-lived smile. Gus even made me a sandwich. Quickly, I cram the scrubs in the backpack in case anyone comes down here. I can't leave any clues behind.

The flashlight catches on remnants of other bags, scraps of food, and small bone fragments as I creep along the sewer floor. The beam of light scatters small rodents and one tiny snake.

None of it bothers me. I'm only afraid for those left behind. What if they discover Gus saved me? What will they do to him? Or Franco? Or Mom?

Together, they saved my life.

And I don't know if they'll be alive come morning.

Reaching the end of the huge drainpipe, I peer out of the sewer into the night.

Fire climbs into the heavens. Smoke billows far into the distance. Wailing sirens blast my eardrums.

It's the perfect cover for my escape.

I take off the backpack and shove it through the rusted metal rungs before squeezing through myself. Franco's jacket catches on a sharp edge, holding me back. With one more pull, I yank free and stumble away.

Breathing hard, I race across the field, into the trees. The ground is rugged, but my pothole-trained feet never slow their pace. I push through the thick smoke until branches and leaves scratch my face and catch in my hair.

Hidden in the brush, I'm tempted to look back at the Incinerator, but I force myself to continue onward without slowing. I must cover as much ground as I can before morning.

My chest expands with each deep breath, the fire in my heart burning stronger than the one behind me.

I must stay alive in order to save Franco and the others.

So I run for all our lives.

GLOSSARY OF TERMS

Clavicles = Collar bones

Core muscles = Think beyond the stud-muffin six-pack. Core muscles involve your spine, pelvis, abdomen—everything that's not your arms and legs.

Downward dog = Similar to a dog stretching post-nap, downward-facing dog is a yoga position shaped like an upside down V, with the hands and feet both touching the ground and the butt up in the air. If your hamstrings are tight like mine, it's a bit difficult to get your heels on the ground.

Dragon pose = This yoga pose begins with kneeling upright, then extending the front leg out, setting that foot down and leaning forward to stretch the hip flexors, leaving the back leg in the kneeling position for leverage. (see lunge)

External Obliques = The large side abdominal muscles closest to the surface.

Fartlek = A workout with periods of fast running varied with periods of slower running. The word itself means "speed play" in Swedish. Runners can choose time periods to vary speeds or to race from mailbox to mailbox, etc. It's adult playtime.

Gastroc/gastrocnemius = Calf muscles of the leg, preferably bulging.

GPS watch = A running watch with a global position system that allows the runner to track mileage, current pace, overall speed, and probably some other things I haven't figured out yet.

Hamstrings = Muscles from butt to knee, on the backside. Generally tight in runners. They will spend their whole lives trying to loosen them to no avail.

Hip flexors = The muscles responsible for the motion of bringing the knee up to the waist.

IT bands = The Illiotibial (IT) band is the tough connective tissue connecting the ileum of the pelvis to the tibia bone located in the lower half of the leg. This band is often tight in runners, resulting in pain either at the outer side of the knee or the outer side of the hip, or somewhere in between.

Lunges = A stretch or exercise where the athlete's weight is thrust forward on the front leg with that knee bent and foot flat on the ground. The rearmost leg is also bent, with either the foot up on the toes (to work on strength) or the leg from knee on down set on the ground (to work on stretching the hips).

Mountain pose = A basic standing yoga pose, where all is aligned, hips over knees over ankles, a position of power and centering.

Namaste = The customary greeting to others at the beginning of a yoga class, but in the United States is often used as the closing greeting at the end of a class after Savasana has finished.

Pectorals = Chest muscles

Pigeon pose = A lovely (or painful, depending on how you look at it) yoga stretch for the hips done on the floor, pretty much twisting your legs into a pretzel where one leg stretches straight back flat on the ground with the top of the foot resting on the floor and the other leg bent and curled around so that the opposite foot is in front of the other hip. Makes total sense, right?

Run up tempo = Running faster than comfortable, the goal being to increase one's endurance and stamina for future races.

Savasana = The corpse pose, lying flat on the floor and relaxing, meant to give enough time for the body to absorb the benefits of the practice and allow the mind to calm back down. However, my mind never calms down, and I find it impossible to remain still because there is always something else to do (laundry, pick up the kids, walk the dogs, etc.).

Semimembranosus/Semitendinosus = see Hamstrings

Stacked log pose = One of my favorite sitting poses (although I've been told I possess a sick mind). Both legs are bent in front of you, but instead of criss-crossed the legs are stacked like logs. One leg rests on the floor, everything touching from knee to foot. The other leg rests on top of the first leg, skin to skin, right knee to left foot and left foot to right knee. It's not torture, really. Okay, for some it is.

Tree stance = A wonderful pose to utilize when washing dishes, browning hamburger, or making popcorn. One leg stands tall, while the opposite foot is held tucked up on the inside of the standing leg, knee held out to the side to stretch the respective hip. (Note the theme here?)

Warrior = A standing yoga pose with several variations, with legs set wide and arms either outstretched or held up above, depending on the variation. Strengthens legs and stretches the hips.

Intrigued? Or maybe just confused? I highly recommend Sage Rountree's book *The Athlete's Guide to Yoga*, Ekhart Online Yoga Classes, and Yoga with Adriene Online Yoga Classes

PLAYLIST

INSPIRED BY GUS'S LIFELONG LOVE OF MUSIC,
EACH CHAPTER TITLE COMES FROM A SONG:

1. HAPPY BIRTHDAY
2. WISH YOU WERE HERE by Pink Floyd
3. IT'S STILL ROCK AND ROLL TO ME by Billy Joel
4. ROAD TO NOWHERE by Talking Heads
5. STAY UP LATE by Talking Heads
6. GREAT BALLS OF FIRE by Jerry Lee Lewis
7. (PLEASE) DON'T LEAVE ME by Pink
8. THE STRANGER by Billy Joel
9. I WILL REMEMBER YOU by Sarah McLachlan
10. I WANT TO RIDE MY BICYCLE by Queen
11. HOT FOR TEACHER by Van Halen
12. (HE) BLINDED ME WITH SCIENCE by Thomas Dolby
13. STOP MAKING SENSE by Talking Heads
14. HURTS SO GOOD by John Mellencamp
15. WHO'S THAT GIRL by The Eurythmics

16. UNTIL I FALL AWAY by Gin Blossoms
17. (MY) LIPS ARE SEALED by The Go-Go's
18. DR. FEELGOOD by Motley Crue
19. UNDERGROUND by David Bowie
20. PRESSURE by Billy Joel
21. EVERY BREATH YOU TAKE by The Police
22. FIREWORK by Katy Perry
23. KILLER QUEEN by Queen
24. DANGEROUS by Michael Jackson
25. THE LADY IN RED by Chris de Burgh
26. WELCOME TO THE JUNGLE by Guns N' Roses
27. COLD AS ICE by Foreigner
28. LIKE A VIRGIN by Madonna
29. CLOSE MY EYES FOREVER by Lita Ford & Ozzy Osborne
30. TRY NOT TO BREATHE by R.E.M.
31. EVERYBODY HURTS by R.E.M.
32. LET'S GET PHYSICAL by Olivia Newton-John
33. STAND BY ME by Ben E. King
34. WE ARE THE CHAMPIONS by Queen
35. STAND BY YOUR MAN by Tammy Wynette
36. BITTERSWEET SYMPHONY by The Verve and The Rolling Stones
37. LOVE IS A BATTLEFIELD by Pat Benatar
38. DON'T FEAR THE REAPER by Blue Oyster Cult
39. LIGHT MY FIRE by The Doors

ACKNOWLEDGMENTS

Always a voracious reader, I owe a huge debt of gratitude to all the authors whose amazing minds allowed me to expand my own. *Dead Girl Running* is a cross between *The Giver*, *The Handmaiden's Tale*, Agenda 21, and everything I have learned from running both down the road and along the trails.

Holli Anderson from Immortal Works Press, thank you for encouraging me to finish this series after taking a long break from writing. Time marches on, but heartfelt gratitude remains towards those who helped guide my books: Tori Merkiel, Colleen Chmelik, Christa Worrell, Kristin D. Van Risseghem, Danielle Allen, Michael Kalmbach, Rachel Erickson, Matthew S. Cox, Emma Adams, Samantha Bryant, Yolanda Renee, Katie Hamstead, C.M. Spivey, and Josh Noser.

Silvia's dependence on running reminds me of my first coach, Mary Allen, who introduced me to the sport. Even though I called Cross Country "hell in a bucket" at the time, thank you for planting the seed that grew into such a lifelong love. My caring college Cross Country coach, Jen Arneson, always put her athletes first. Thank you for showing me life can lead you down any road you have the courage to follow. Eternal gratitude to all my "running peeps" from high school, college, and today. Extra kisses to my current canine running buddy, Stella, who is always so eager to join in our adventures.

ABOUT THE AUTHOR

Growing up an only child, I learned to entertain myself. During summer vacations, my greatest form of exercise consisted of turning the pages of a book. Now I'm all grown up, and full of stories half-written in my head. I write them down to find out what happens next.

This has been an
Immortal Production